# A KILLER WELCOME

*Haunting Avery Winters Book* 1

## DIONNE LISTER

 Created with Vellum

*For my awesome Twitch family. Thank you so much for sticking with me through the writing of this book. A special thanks to Vic who was there from the beginning. You've all helped me stay accountable, and for the first time in ages, I made my deadline. Yay, us!*

# CHAPTER 1

T he young woman at the real-estate office's reception desk looked up at me through her gold, angular designer glasses. She must've been about my age—twenty-six—but the disdain in her gaze was more like an adult looking at a child they were about to discipline. "I'm sorry, Miss Winters, but we don't have another key. Fiona, our agent, took it last night. She was going to meet you at the property, but she's been called out to another urgent appointment. The owner should be able to let you in. Just knock on her door."

I heavy sighed and tried not to let my frustration show. I'd gotten off a plane from Australia about twelve hours ago and hired a car for the long drive here. Apart from maybe two hours' sleep in cattle class and four hours' slumber in a hotel last night, I hadn't slept much for almost two days. Travelling from Australia to the UK was not for the faint of heart, or the weak of stomach. I'd thrown up in the airport in Dubai... much to the dismay of the other passengers in the waiting area. Yep, I hadn't made it to the bathroom in time. Vomit can sneak up on a person. "Do you know if she'll be home? Can you call her?"

She smiled an evil, I don't-really-care smile. "She leaves her phone off the hook. I can try, but I bet it won't ring."

I gritted out a smile through clenched teeth. Okay, so it was a grimace, not a smile, but I was trying... sort of. Or maybe not. Actually, I was. If I hadn't been trying, I'd be yelling by now. "Try. Please."

She rolled her eyes.

"Bit of a cow, that one. Like my ex-wife." The older man's voice came from next to me. I wanted to answer, to agree—about the receptionist, not his ex-wife—but since he was likely a figment of my imagination, and no one in the UK knew I was crazy yet, I kept my words to myself. My brain had concocted the seventy-something-year-old when I'd hopped off the plane. His thinning white hair was evenly dispersed on his head. It was light and floaty, like a muppet's. I didn't mind him—so far, he always said what I wished I could. I figured it was my subconscious keeping me company. Ever since I'd been struck by lightning, different people followed me around... people no one else could see.

It was why I'd left Sydney.

It was why my boyfriend had left me.

It was why I'd left my family behind. Okay, so I couldn't blame everything on my mental state—my parents, especially my father, were less than understanding. When I'd come clean about the fact I thought I could see ghosts, they'd laughed at me. Then things got serious—they'd called the psychiatrist and admitted me to hospital for a few days. I came out heavily medicated and stayed that way for months. Now I had to believe in myself. I still wasn't sure the apparitions were ghosts, but maybe, just maybe my gut was right. In any case, I didn't have time to think about that right now.

Cow lady with the designer glasses hung up the phone with a flourish and gave me a sarcastic smile. "See. Told you. Just turn up. She doesn't go out much, and she's likely to want to check you out anyway. I would imagine she's set aside her morning to wait for you."

I wasn't getting any more help from this one. Best to get on the road and hope the old woman was home. "Ah, what's her name?"

"Mrs Margaret Collins. Best call her Mrs Collins. She's not very friendly." She gave me a forced smile and looked back to her computer screen, obviously dismissing me. The British were known for their *good* manners. Shame no one had told her.

My heart raced—it knew what I was going to do. "Right, well, thanks for not helping." Did I really do that? Said what I wanted? Adrenaline shot through my stomach.

Her head snapped up. Her mouth half opened as if she wanted to say something, but the surprise at being called out must have blanked her brain. I hated when that happened… to me. It was satisfying for it to happen the other way around for once.

Old guy next to me laughed. "Nicely done."

Before the receptionist could figure out how to respond, I turned and left, my strides longer than normal as I hurried. I wasn't running away. Not. At. All. *Naughty, Avery, giving in and falling to her level.* But if it was so naughty, why was it so much fun?

I hopped into my diminutive red hire car, and the old guy appeared in the back seat. I turned to look at him. "You're a bad influence. I don't normally speak my mind."

He laughed, revealing a missing canine. "You should do it more. It's entertaining."

I shook my head but smiled. At least with my brain giving me people to talk to—I wasn't quite ready to trust my gut on the ghosts—I'd never get bored or be alone. The burn of tears took me by surprise. I wasn't even two days out of Sydney, and I missed my family, even if they weren't very nice to me. Damn. I was not going to cry. I sat up straighter, wiped my eye with the back of my hand, and turned on the ignition. *You got this.*

I pulled out into the street. According to my GPS, my destination was only a few kilometres away. Everyone spoke in miles here, but that would take time to adjust to.

At least the scenery was nice. I yawned.

"Don't fall asleep there, lassie."

"I won't. Especially with you there to keep me awake." I laughed at how crazy yet helpful that often-maligned state of being seemed to be. Even still, if I could take back being struck by lightning and get rid of these pretend people, I would—ghosts or not. My life, as it had been, wasn't perfect, but it had been good enough. A little voice—in my actual head this time—told me that maybe I deserved better than "good enough."

The car crested a hill, and as I drove down the other side, I wrinkled my forehead. Was that what I thought it was? These weren't more apparitions created just for me by my brain, were they?

Two women wearing revealing white dresses sprinted down the footpath. Their harried expressions were too severe to be because they didn't like running. Something was wrong. One of them waved at me to pull over. My day had already gone to hell, so why not stop and help? At least I'd feel like I'd done something good for the day.

I pulled to the side of the road, and a young woman with brown hair, and cleavage busting out of the top of her dress, hurried to my window. She was carrying a cat. Could this get any weirder? I wound the window down. "Are you okay?"

"Those men back there are after us. Can we please get in?"

"They look like trouble." Old guy—I hadn't asked his name because it was just me, only older and male—made me pause. I flicked my gaze to the rear-view mirror. He shook his head. I scrunched my face up, trying to tell him that he was wrong. He shrugged and gave me his gap-toothed grin. I could also see those men getting closer, and they didn't look like they wanted to give these women flowers. My eyes widened.

I jerked my head back to look at the stranger at my window. "Yes. Get in!"

Before the women got in, a crackle and sizzle came from behind us. Huh? A huge *boom*! I jerked my head around and screamed. The footpath exploded, dirt and rocks shooting into the air. Sweat broke out on my forehead. Oh God. Ever since being struck by lightning, anything that sounded like thunder freaked me out. Anything exploding wasn't good, even if it didn't come from the sky.

The woman at my window opened the back door and jumped in. The other one opened the front passenger door and practically fell in, her skimpy dress almost exposing everything. The woman in the back seat shouted, "Drive! Drive!"

Without thinking, I slammed my foot on the pedal, simultaneously looking for cars as I death-gripped the wheel. Thank God there weren't any other cars coming because those men had almost reached us.

The cat in the back meowed. "Sorry, kitty. I didn't mean to squeeze so hard."

The old guy frowned at my passenger and her cat. Hmm, not a cat person? I loved animals. Weird that my brain would create someone who didn't like them.

I accelerated, my small engine whining with the effort. It wasn't true—red cars didn't always go faster.

Terror radiated from the woman next to me, her gaze that of a shellshocked person. To be honest, I didn't feel much better. My hands shook on the steering wheel, and I did my best to breathe slower, more evenly. My first day in England really wasn't going very well. "W— What the hell of all hells was that?"

The woman in the back seat hesitated before answering. "I don't know. Maybe they have explosives?"

What kind of country had I moved to? "Right. Okay." Old guy shook his head at me again via the rear-vision mirror. "Don't say *I told you so*," I mumbled under my breath.

As we reached the next village, the girl in the front passenger seat looked my way. "We're so sorry, but thank you so much for picking us up. Can you just drive us to the next village?"

"Oh. Ah, okay. That's where I'm going anyway, I think." I met the woman in the back seat's gaze in the rear-view mirror. If I wasn't mistaken, she was a fellow Aussie.

The old guy next to her said, "Don't do it. Drop them off here. They're trouble. There's something about them I don't like."

I shook my head as if to shake his comment off. There was nothing awful I could detect from them. "Is that an Aussie accent?"

She smiled. "Yes. I'm from Sydney. What about you?"

I grinned. Finally, something familiar. "Me too! I'm from Narrabeen. What about you?"

"Cronulla."

"Ha, cool. I'm Avery, by the way."

"I'm Lily, and this is my best friend Liv."

"Hi." Liv gave a small wave and an even smaller smile.

I didn't really want to drop them off if they had no help, and unless they had a phone hidden in their underwear, they didn't appear to have any means of contacting friends. "Do you need to call someone? You can use my phone."

Lily answered. "Really? That's so nice of you. Thank you."

"It's in my bag, Liv. Just grab it out."

"Are you sure?" Liv asked, probably wary of going through someone else's personal belongings.

"Totes." I had nothing to hide, and I was pretty sure they'd seen everything I had in there before.

Liv bent and grabbed the bag from next to her feet, then pulled it onto her lap and rummaged through. "Passcode?"

"654321." I chuckled. "Yeah, it's stupid, I know, but I've never lost a phone, and I didn't want to make it too hard to remember."

Liv managed a small laugh. "I hear you." She punched the numbers in, turned, and handed the phone to Lily. "You do it. I'm not sure what to say."

Lily spoke to someone and explained what had happened. After a minute, she met my gaze in the mirror. "What's the next town called, the one we're going to?"

"Manesbury." The place I was going to start a new life, a better life, so I hoped.

"Okay, thank you." Lily hung up and handed the phone back through the gap in between the two front seats. We made small talk for the ten minutes it took to reach the village.

I pulled up in front of the post office, a two-storey free-standing stone building with a thatched roof and red front door. It was as quaintly English as it got. Maybe I was going to like my new home. "Are you two sure you'll be okay?"

Lily nodded. "Yes. Thank you so much. You literally saved our lives. That guy and his mate kidnapped us and dressed us in these stupid dresses." Wow, what in Hades?

I gave Liv the once over. There was no doubt about it—they weren't dresses the average woman would pick for a stroll down the road. "It looks like something a stripper might wear to her wedding."

Liv looked down at herself, maybe noticing for the first time. "Oh, my. You can almost see my underwear."

I chuckled. "Almost, but not quite. Your modesty in that area has been preserved. Your cleavage, however, is another story."

Liv's cheeks darkened, and she placed a hand over her boobs, which were almost fully exposed. "Oh, God."

"You can stay behind me, Liv. Come on." Lily hopped out and leaned in my window. I looked up at her. "Thank you so, so much. You really are a lifesaver. I owe you one. If you ever need a favour, just ring that number that's in your phone. That's my boyfriend, Will. He'll give you my number."

I smiled as Liv got out of the car. Even though this had been totally wild, I was actually happy I'd met them. I didn't feel quite so alone in this new country. "Will do. Feel free to call me and let me know if the police catch those guys. I'm not sure if I should've moved here now. I just flew in from Oz yesterday." Was the area around Manesbury more dangerous than I'd realised?

"This was personal. You should be fine. But I'll let you know when we catch them... um, when they're caught, rather. Good luck, Avery. I hope your move turns out to be awesome."

"Me too."

The old guy in my back seat said, "Doubt it will. You should've stayed in Australia."

Before I realised what I was doing, I turned and pulled a face at the old dude. *Oops.* I jerked my head back around to look at Lily. There was no point trying to explain, so I waved and drove away slowly.

Other than being hit by lightning, my life had been pretty quiet at home. It usually consisted of work and home, work and home, and repeat. Today had been way too exciting, in a bad way.

I took a deep breath and tried to take in the village I'd be calling home. Quaint stone buildings lined the narrow main street, pretty signs declaring Best Breads Bakery, Crafty Crafters Craft Supplies, and Heavenly Brew Café hung in a welcoming line in front of the row of shops.

The old guy in my back seat laughed. "You're not off to a

very good start, are ye, lassie?" Grrr. I looked in my rear-view mirror and scrunched my face. If only my brain wouldn't interrupt when I was with other people. It would be fine if my invisible friends showed up when I was by myself. I knew I was different, and I could live with it. It was only a problem when others were around.

I shrugged off my irritation—it was time to find my accommodation. Hopefully, getting the keys and settling in would be drama-free. Except, with the day I was having, the chances of that were slim to none.

# CHAPTER 2

L uckily I'd hired a small car because the roads around here were narrower than a bowling lane. Oh, cat's bum, the road actually stopped before it got to the flat I was renting. I parked the car and hopped out. According to my phone map, the building wasn't far at all, maybe another forty or fifty metres up the gradual incline.

Mature trees grew on both sides of the street, behind which stone cottages hid. Oh, wow, one of them had a thatched roof. Low stone walls bordered the properties as well. This was just like the pictures on the internet. It was a shame I couldn't afford anything as nice. From what I'd seen, the upstairs flat I was renting was last updated in the seventies, but at least it had looked clean and tidy. If it were any more luxurious, I wouldn't have been able to afford it.

"Where ye be going?"

I jumped and turned, my heart rate spiking. The old guy stood just behind me. "Damn it! Why did you follow me out of the car? And how can I even be surprised by my own imagination?" Why hadn't leaving my stress behind in Australia stopped these apparitions? My shoulders sagged. Was I going to have to see a psychiatrist and get some medication? Maybe my parents were right—I was crazy, and I needed to just ignore my invisible friends. If only they were invisible to me too.

But what if my parents were wrong? What if I could really see ghosts? The fact that some of them had accents other than Australian made me wonder. There was part of me, deep down, that insisted I wasn't unhinged, but that voice was still drowned out by my parents' and my ex-boyfriend's voices.

"What are ye waiting for?"

"You to leave. I can do this by myself, thanks."

"Right ye are, then." He gave a wave and disappeared. Well, if that's all it took to get rid of him, why hadn't I done that before? I shook my head at myself.

Time to grab my keys.

I wandered up the hill, walking on the grass. The footpath ended where the wide road did. There was a dirt road that a motorbike or wheelbarrow could fit down, but not a car. Grocery shopping was going to suck big time. Oh well, it was what I could afford. If I hadn't agreed to my ex's demands that we rent an expensive apartment in Kirribilli, I would've had a lot more savings. I'd always let other people sway me to what they wanted. But not any more. England was a new start. A place where I would do what I wanted when I wanted, and I was taking no crap.

The laneway dog-legged to the right, and a row of three two-storey terraces sat behind a low stone fence. Two of the terraces had pretty gardens. One did not. Guess which one I was renting?

I went through the gate and crossed my fingers that Mrs Collins would be home. Thanks for nothing, real-estate cow. I knocked on the green door, a loose paint flake stabbing my knuckle. "Ow."

I listened, but no one came. I knocked again, louder. And waited.

Finally, the knob on the other side of the door rattled, and it opened.

A woman, I assumed to be Mrs Collins, stood there, and true to her reputation, she didn't look particularly friendly. Her beak of a nose curled over frowning lips, and her brown eyes emanated a level of distrust even I couldn't achieve, and I'd been let down by a lot of people over the years. She narrowed those suspicion-laden eyes. "What do you want?"

*Wow, get right to it, why don't you.* Phew that I managed to keep that to myself. "Hi. I'm Avery Winters. Pleased to meet you, Mrs Collins." I could lie with the best of them. "I'm renting the flat from you. I was hoping you could let me in and give me the key."

"Where's your key?"

"I wasn't given one. The real-estate woman said the agent who was supposed to give me the key had another urgent appointment. She said you could help me." A dizzy spell hit me, and I swayed.

She leaned back, putting distance between us, as if I might have the plague. "What's wrong with you, then?"

"I've hardly slept in the last two days because of flying here. I'm exhausted. It'd be great if you could just show me up to the flat. Please?" I tamped down my frustration and gave her a tired smile. I was feeling all the tired and none of the smile.

She looked me up and down and huffed. "All right. Wait here." She shut the door. I blinked. Seriously? What did she think I was going to do? She was about to give me a key to the upstairs apartment, and surely a key to the front door too. Maybe she didn't want me following her into her home?

I turned and took in the surroundings past the front fence. A narrow dirt road separated us from two houses opposite. At the end of the dirt cul-de-sac, next to the terrace adjoining the one I was renting, a carpet of green began. Fields spread out beyond, a narrow path worn into the longish grass leading the way into nature. I breathed in the almost warm, fresh air. The knot in my shoulders from the never-ending flight, long drive, and subsequent stress loosened. "Ahhh."

I mustn't have heard the front door open again because I started when she yelled. "Well, don't just dilly-dally. I have other things to deal with. Young people these days—so selfish."

I turned and bit my tongue. Getting on the bad side of the landlady wasn't going to end well for me. The receptionist had said she wasn't very friendly, so maybe this was her normal way of interacting with people and I wasn't on her bad side just yet. One could hope. I steeled myself and went back to the door.

"Here." She held out the key. I reached to take it. She made sure to hand it to me without touching me. Germophobe maybe? Or maybe she was repulsed by human touch as well as humans themselves?

"Thank you."

"You can show yourself up there. The red key is for the front door. The silver one is for your apartment. I don't want to hear any noise after 8:00 p.m., and I like to keep to myself. If you have any questions, you can call the agent." Before I could thank her and try and be polite, she spun around—rather agilely for an old woman—hurried into her apartment, and shut the door hard enough to make me cringe, although it wasn't quite slammed.

Well, this was going to be fun.

I decided to check out the apartment before I grabbed my two large suitcases. As far as furniture went, this apartment came fully furnished, and I'd sold most of my stuff before I'd come. I didn't plan on returning to Sydney if I could help it. The only person in my family I wanted to see was my sister, and she was intending to fly here when she'd saved enough and could get time off work. My birth home held too many depressing memories.

Life was hard enough without struggling through the quicksand of other people's expectations every day.

I stepped through the front door and shut it behind me—I didn't think crabby Mrs Collins would appreciate me not being security conscious.

This terrace seemed to comprise of two apartments—the one on the ground floor that Mrs Crabby lived in, and the one on the top floor that would be my home for who knew how long. Wallpaper in an orange seventies flower motif assaulted my vision. Dizziness hit me again. I shut my eyes and waited it out. I really, really needed to get some sleep. When I opened them again and started up the steep staircase, I was careful to only look at the stairs themselves. At least the brown seventies carpet wasn't trying to make me feel worse, and it looked like it had recently been vacuumed. The place was old, but it appeared to be clean.

At the top of the stairs, a window cast light over a small landing that was just big enough for two people. My front door sat to the right. I put the silver key into it and tried to turn. Stuck. Typical. I hated trying to open unfamiliar doors—the keys never worked the first time. I grabbed the handle and pulled it towards me, then tried again. *Click.* Success! The first thing that had gone right today. I would've called out woohoo, but Mrs Crabby might take exception to the noise.

I pushed the door open. *Please, be okay.* I'd only been going by the pictures on the internet, and as a journalist, I knew how liberal the editing department could be with images. Real estate agents held themselves to even lesser standards if my last house hunt was anything to go by.

I smiled as I stepped inside.

My joy turned to horror.

There was nothing to do but scream. So I did.

Then I remembered Mrs Crabby and slammed my hand over my mouth. But it was too late. Her footsteps were clomping up the stairs. As I took in the dead woman lying on the floor, Mrs Crabby appeared behind me. "What's all this noise? I thought I told you to be quiet."

I didn't take my eyes off the dead body when I answered. "You said to be quiet after 8:00 p.m. It's still early. Besides, I had a legitimate reason." I stepped aside so she could get a good look at my welcoming party.

Her scream was louder than mine.

❧

Being the researcher I was—you couldn't not like researching if you were a journalist—I knew to dial nine, nine, nine. In Australia, we dialled triple zero in an emergency, but I wanted to be prepared for any situation when I went away. Not that I could've foreseen this. This was next level. It said something about the situation I'd left behind that I still didn't want to go back home.

I helped Mrs Crabby down the stairs and outside. Well, by helped, I walked in front of her down the narrow stairs in case she fell, so she'd have something soft to fall on. It was impossible to walk two abreast down those stairs. We waited outside for the police and paramedics to come. I'd swallowed my terror and the ickiness of touching a dead body and checked for a pulse. Maybe I just thought she was dead, but nope. Totally dead. The paramedics would confirm my unprofessional assessment, but other than that, there was nothing they could do.

The front fence was low enough that we could sit on it. So we did. It took them about ten minutes, but the police showed up first. Since they couldn't drive up to the house, the two male officers walked quickly. I supposed an already-dead body didn't require hurrying for. The older of the two policemen, whose beer belly and friendly face put me at ease because he looked like a regular dad, was the first to speak. "Good morning, ladies. So, who called in the deceased?"

Mrs Crabby looked at me. I put up my hand. "Me, sir." I didn't normally call men sir, but being questioned by a policeperson always put me on edge. The compulsion to scream that I'd done nothing wrong was strong. Whenever I'd been pulled over for a breath test, I felt guilty, even though I had never drunk and driven. It was like being guilty by association—if they were talking to you, you'd probably done something wrong; they just hadn't worked out what it was yet.

"And what's your name?"

"Avery Winters."

"And this is your address?"

"As of today, yes."

The other policeman had a notepad out and was writing everything down.

"Where is the deceased, and do you know her?"

I turned and pointed to the house. "Through the front door and up the stairs." I turned back to him. "I just moved here today from Australia, and Mrs Cra—" Oops. "Ah, Mrs Collins gave me the key. When I went inside, I found her. She's on the floor in the living room. I've never met her before."

The policeman looked from me to Mrs Crabby. His gaze stuck to her. "I'll have a few questions for you later. Please don't go anywhere, Mrs Collins." He turned to me. "You wait here too. We'll be back." He looked at his partner and jerked his head towards the house. They set off.

While they were gone, the paramedics arrived. I pointed the way to the body, and they went up. Then it hit me—where was I supposed to go now? There was no way I was sleeping in that flat tonight. And surely they needed to undertake an investigation. The headache that started earlier ramped up, and I couldn't help asking *why me?*

Mrs Crabby stood from the fence and went inside without a word, leaving me by myself. A visit from one of my imaginary friends would've been good about now. Instead, the older policeman came back. "Miss Winters, did you touch anything in the flat?"

"Just the body. I checked for a pulse. Am I a suspect?" Oh my God. If my DNA was on her, would they think I did it? Isn't that what always happened to the new girl in town in mystery stories when they found the body? They were unrealistically believed to be a suspect. Why would I move to a new country just to kill someone on my arrival? Despite my logic, today had been one of the weirdest days of my life, so maybe my first night here was going to continue that theme and be spent in jail.

"That's okay. I just needed to confirm. The body is cold, so it's been there for a while. When did you say you flew in?"

"Last night. I stayed in a hotel in London, and I drove here this morning. I just arrived. I can give you details of the hotel and hire-car place so you can confirm."

He nodded. "Okay, thank you." He frowned. "We'll be getting forensics in here, so I'm afraid you'll have to find somewhere else to stay for a few days. Do you have any friends or family you can call?"

"No." I could call my parents, but they were on the other side of the world, and they would only say "I told you so." They weren't much for helping or sympathy. In fact, they would've done all they could to make me feel worse. I knew he really meant here, but the only people I'd met so far were the cow from the real-estate agency and Mrs Crabby, oh, and those two nice women I'd saved, but there was no way I was calling any of them. I'd figure this out on my own... as usual. "Can you recommend anywhere around here that's cheap?"

"The pub at the edge of the village is nice enough—The

Frog and Trumpet. They do a great fish and chips too. I think their rates are reasonable."

"Okay, thanks."

"Can I grab your number and those other details before you go? We'll probably have some questions for you later."

"Yeah, sure." I pulled a piece of paper out of my pocket and recited my new number—I'd only gotten it today, and I hadn't had time to memorise it. Then I gave him the details of the hotel and hire-car place.

"Thank you, Miss Winters. You're free to go. For now." Why did "for now" have to sound so ominous?

"Thank you, Officer." I gave the house a little wave, then walked back down the hill to my car. At least it was only a short drive to the pub. It was the last commercial building in the long line of shops as you headed for my new street and sat on a corner block. There was a small parking area at the back of the quaint, white two-storey building. Hopefully the policeman's idea of cheap was the same as mine. And would I get a rent reduction from Mrs Crabby since I couldn't stay there? It wasn't my fault that someone had died or been killed in my apartment. Maybe the young woman had keeled over from a stroke or heart attack —although her age made that unlikely. I couldn't remember any blood. Even though I'd stared at the body, I hadn't taken every-thing in. Her face and immaculately straightened brown hair stuck in my mind, how pale her skin was, her blue-tinged lips. How *still* she was. I shuddered. *Stop thinking.*

I went through the back entry and into a hallway that seemed to run straight through to the pub's dining room and bar, if the scent of cooked food was anything to go by. My mouth watered, but a hint of nausea from my flight remained, not to mention seeing a dead body. That was a great appetite suppressant. All I really needed was sleep. If they didn't have a room, I was totally sleeping in the ladybug with wheels outside. It was small, but I didn't care if I had to sleep curled into a ball.

Rustic timber tables and comfortable-looking timber chairs were scattered throughout the room, with a couple of cosy booths next to one of the brick walls. There were a few patrons drinking or having a meal, the clinking of glasses and chatter a warm world away from the coldness of the apartment I'd just left. I went straight to the bar where a lanky guy about my age was pulling a beer for a customer. His long, sand-coloured fringe covered his eyes. When he looked up, though, his honey-brown eyes were revealed as they met my green ones. I sucked in a breath as my stomach somersaulted.

That wasn't what I needed. I frantically looked around. Thank God the sign for the bathroom was in view. I ran before disaster struck.

When I was done throwing up, I rinsed my face and mouth and went back to the bar. To the hot guy. I didn't usually throw up when I was physically attracted to someone, but on top of everything else today, that was one dollop of excitement too many. This time I was ready for his hotness, and I managed to swallow rather than embarrass myself again.

He looked at me. "What can I get you?"

A new life. A new apartment. Family I could rely on? "Do you have rooms for rent? I need one for a few days."

He smiled. "Yeah, sure. You from New Zealand?"

How could people get confused? Yes, both countries spoke English, but the accents were totally different. Oh well, he was handsome, so I could forgive him. "No. Australia. I flew in last night."

His brow wrinkled. "How come you didn't have anything booked?"

"I did, but it fell through. At least until next week."

"Oh, too bad."

Normally, I would've enjoyed chatting to an attractive member of the opposite sex, but I was ready to collapse. All I wanted was a bed. "So, about that room?"

"Oh, sorry. Hang on a sec. I'll just grab my sister. She deals with the accommodation side of things." He left but returned within two minutes to deal with another pub-goer. His sister, thank goodness, wasn't far behind.

She was just as lanky as her brother and a few inches taller than me, which wasn't hard because I was only five foot five. Not that *that* was super short. I was average—not tall, not short. Her auburn hair was styled in a pixie cut, which gave more emphasis to her large brown eyes and delicate features. She smiled. "I hear you're looking for a room."

"Yes, thanks. I flew in from Sydney last night, and my accommodation was, er, compromised. I just need a single room for a few nights till it's available again."

"We can definitely help you. I just need to grab your credit card." I handed it over. She handed me a guest card and pen. "Please fill in your details. I'll be back in a sec." She went to a small table in the corner behind the bar. When she'd done that, she returned and handed me a key and my credit card. "Room three. We do room service for lunch and dinner, but only until 9:00 p.m. Breakfast is in here from six thirty until ten. Your room price includes breakfast."

"Oh, cool. How much is it?"

"One hundred and five pounds per night."

Bloody hell. Our dollar was terrible compared to that. It was going to cost me two hundred Aussie dollars. My savings weren't going to last long if I got stuck here. "Ah, yeah, fine." I supposed it included breakfast, so that would save me some money, not that I was a huge breakfast eater.

"Just go out that door and up the stairs." She pointed to a

door to her left, which looked like it led to a hallway and the establishment's front entry.

"Thanks."

"My name's Meg. Pleased to meet you, Avery."

Oh, that's right—she would've gotten my name from the guest card. "Pleased to meet you, too, Meg." I smiled. "Now I'm off to have a shower and go to bed. I haven't slept much for two days."

Her eyes widened. "Yikes. Well, happy sleeping."

"Thanks." I hurried out to my car, grabbed both suitcases, and brought them around the side and into the front door. I didn't want all the diners staring at me trying to navigate around chairs and tables. One suitcase wasn't bad, but two were awkward. I carried one at a time up the creaky stairs. When I reached my room with the second case, I crossed my fingers before I opened the door. *Please don't be a dead body.* You knew life wasn't going great when that was something you had to say to yourself.

I used the key card—despite the pub being well over one hundred years old, they'd modernised things somewhat. Thankfully, I stepped into a clean, cosy room. The dark blue carpet appeared to be fairly new. White linen decorated the double bed, a kettle and toaster sat on a bench next to a bar fridge, and clean white towels rested on the foot of the mattress. The curtains were closed, and I couldn't be bothered to check out the view. I was at the back of the building, so the room probably overlooked the car park and hills beyond.

There would be time for sightseeing tomorrow as I didn't have to check into my new job until after lunch. Because my mum had dual British/Australian citizenship, and I had a job sponsor, I was allowed to come here and work without too much drama. For once, my parentage paid off.

Now it was shower time. Then I could sleep. While I

wondered what tomorrow would bring, it was probably safer to not think at all.

"Welcome to The Frog and Trumpet."

My head snapped around. A middle-aged woman in a sixties-era sleeveless shirt and knee-length flary skirt smiled. Wow, my imaginary friends were really mixing it up with their clothing, and her accent sounded similar to Meg's. "Thank you."

She smiled and faded away. Maybe that was all my brain could manage to conjure since it was exhausted... unless she really was a ghost. This building was old, after all. I cringed at the memory of my father's angry face when I insisted I could see ghosts, my mother standing behind him crying about how crazy her daughter was. I shook my head. My brain didn't have enough energy to fully explore this right now.

I put one of my bags on the bed, opened it, and grabbed my pyjamas and bathroom stuff. I eyed the bed. Almost there. Sleep would soon be mine, as long as I could block out today's events.

One thing was for sure—my first full day in England had been more nerve-wracking than I wanted. All I could do was hope things would settle down.

But, as I turned the shower on, somehow I knew they wouldn't.

# CHAPTER 3

I slept until just after ten in the morning, local time. And, of course, I missed breakfast. Bummer. Didn't pubs know that people slept in on holiday? Not that I was on holiday, but whatever. I dressed and went downstairs. My stomach grumbled as I walked out the pub's front door. Meg was coming the other way. "Hey, Avery. Did you have a good sleep?"

"Actually, yes, thanks. It was nice and quiet, and the bed's comfortable."

"Excellent. What are you up to today? Sightseeing?"

"Kind of. I need to grab breakfast. Idiot me slept through it. And after lunch, I'm going in to meet my new boss. I start work tomorrow."

She shook her head. "No, no, no." She grabbed my hand and pulled me back inside. "What do you want? I'll have the cook make it."

My cheeks heated. "No, it's okay. I don't want to put anyone out."

"Don't be silly. I heard you had a terrible day yesterday. Let me help Manesbury make it up to you." She dragged me into the dining-cum-pub area and plonked me into a chair by one of the two multi-paned bay windows. "Now sit. What would you like?"

I scrunched my forehead at the reminder of yesterday. "What did you hear?"

"Just that you found a dead body at Mrs Collins's rental flat. That must've been such a shock."

"Yes." There wasn't much else to say, really, and I didn't want to elaborate, talk about the details. Not that there had been much to see, except for her pale skin and blue lips. I shuddered.

"Sorry, Avery. I guess it's not great conversation at the breakfast table. So, what can I get you?"

If it would get her away from talking about yesterday, I'd order. "Can I please have a cappuccino and two pieces of wholemeal toast?"

She smiled. "Coming right up."

I turned and stared out the window. A small hedge grew just outside the bay but was low enough for me to see it but not for it to impede my view. Beyond that was the main village street, which was one slim lane each way. At least the weather was sunny again today. I'd heard so many bad things about English weather, but so far, it'd been nice to me. At least something here had.

"Can I get you anything, love?" I spun my head around at the woman's voice. How many people worked here? Oh, it was the figment of my imagination from last night. I didn't bother answering her lest someone see. Meg could come back at any moment, and getting kicked out of here and into a mental ward wasn't a high priority on my list right now. It didn't stop the woman hovering, so I ignored her.

Eventually, Meg returned with my breakfast and set it on the table in front of me. "There you go, Avery." Then, she sat. Oh. I wasn't really in the mood for company, especially if she was going to question me about yesterday.

"Thanks." I forced a smile. The other reason I didn't want to sit with anyone was that I wanted peace and quiet. I had this uncanny knack for seeming interested in people. It was part of my job, and it was awesome when people just answered everything I wanted when I was in journalist mode, but when I was in not-at-work mode, I needed a break. That didn't apply to my friends, of course—I always had time for them. I frowned. My friends from school had drifted away since I started dating Brad because we'd tended to spend our free time with all of his friends. Hmm, now that I thought about it, he usually decided where we would go and what we would do on our weekends. I couldn't remember the last time we'd done something I wanted.

"Are you okay, Avery?"

I gave a minute shake of my head and looked at her. "Oh, sorry. Probably still tired from yesterday." I smiled. "I'm fine." I buttered my toast and put some strawberry jam on it.

"Oh, good. When do you think you'll get to go back to the flat?"

I shrugged and swallowed. "I'm hoping within three or four days. They have to examine the flat and whatever else they do. With a bit of luck, it'll be sooner rather than later."

"For sure. So, can I ask your opinion?" Here we went.

"Ah, yeah, sure."

"I broke up with my boyfriend recently... well, not super recently, but recently enough. Do you think I should do online dating? Have you done it? I never go out anywhere because I'm always at work, and the guys who come in here are the boys I grew up with. Most of them are married, and the ones who aren't, well, there's a reason they're not married." She laughed. And here we went—people oversharing because I gave off a tell-me-everything vibe that I didn't know how to turn off.

"I've never done online dating." I hadn't needed to. I'd met Brad at work. He was four years older than me, an editor for the publication I worked at. We'd lived together for three years, and before that, I'd been hanging out with my girlfriends having a good time. I hadn't cared about meeting anyone, and I was pretty sure I was back in that frame of mind. "But from what I've read, it's pretty hit and miss."

"Oh. Do you think I shouldn't do it? I've heard some horror stories."

I looked at her. "I suppose you could try it, and if it doesn't work out, stop. Maybe take some precautions before you agree to any dates—like let a friend know where you're going and when. Don't go to his place, that kind of thing."

A thoughtful expression settled onto her face. "Hmm, that sounds reasonable." She sat up straighter and smiled. "Thanks, Avery. You give great advice."

I smiled, her happiness contagious. As much as I'd wanted to eat alone, her friendliness came as a relief. At least not all the people in this place were ornery. "My pleasure. And thanks for this." I nodded at the plate.

"My pleasure." She stood. "I have to get back to work, but you have a lovely day."

"Thanks, you too."

So, today had almost started off in below-average territory—missing breakfast—but it had improved with Meg's kindness. Maybe I could dare hope the good-day trend would continue.

❦

The new media company I was working for had offices in a charming two-storey stone-and-glass building in a laneway off the high street. MacPherson Media, in thick gold lettering, decorated the large glass window looking into the reception area. A brass bell hung on the wall next to the black front door. Next to that was a modern intercom. I pressed the button. A woman's voice answered. "Hello?"

"Hi. I'm here to meet with Mr MacPherson."

"Which one?"

*Huh?* "The one who works here? I didn't know there was more than one."

"That would be Julian. Come in." The buzzer sounded, and the door clicked. I pushed it open. I still wasn't sure what that was all about. Obviously, there was another Mr MacPherson, but they didn't work here. Did people mix up the addresses of the two that often? Maybe it was a father-and-son team who worked in different offices. From my research of the company, they had five offices around England, four located in towns or small villages, and their head office in Exeter. They tended to specialise in the places the large news agencies didn't care about. Their audiences were the people who lived locally, and some of the stories were just light and fun, or updates on what was happening in the area, like village markets.

I pushed the door open and entered a brightly lit room. Honey-coloured timber floors and eggshell-blue walls gave it a modern feel. The receptionist sat behind a semi-circular black counter/desk combo. Her scarlet lipstick matched her short-sleeved wrap dress. She moved the mic of her headset away from her lips and smiled at me. "Your name?"

"Avery Winters."

She typed something on her computer, then moved her mic back. "Avery Winters to see you, Mr MacPherson." She looked up at me. "You can go in. Just straight down the hallway"—she pointed to her left—"up the stairs, and it's the door at the end of the hall."

"Okay. Thanks." I took a few deep breaths as I made my way to his office. I'd gotten this job online, through an agency, so I'd never met anyone in person. Would the boss dislike me on sight and decide to rescind the job offer? What if he was horrible and gave me the job but made life hell? I couldn't afford not to work here. Yes, I could take a waitressing job—I'd had those before, when I was studying at uni—but I'd need two or three jobs to make ends meet if I lost this one. The pay was actually quite good. Not to mention that it would likely affect my visa and ability to stay here long-term.

I reached his door, crossed the fingers of one hand, and knocked with the other.

"Come in."

The heavy timber door opened silently. The blood whooshing past my ears was way too loud. Could Mr MacPherson hear it? I'd laugh at myself, but he really would hear that, and my chances of getting fired on the first day would increase. And this wasn't even the first day. It was the pre-first day. Would that be a record, to get fired the day before you started a new job? *Argh, Avery, stop with the negative self-talk. You can do this.*

Mr MacPherson sat forward on his large cream-coloured office chair behind his desk and drummed his fingers on the table in a regular beat. His lips moved as if he were singing something. Maybe he was?

I held in a nervous laugh and concentrated on walking. Why was it when one did that, it felt weird? It was as if I'd forgotten how to walk, and every step was an adventure in trying to do it properly. Did I look funny?

No matter what I looked like getting there, I made it to the black, stainless-steel-framed chair in front of his desk without tripping or saying anything stupid. Yay me. When I sat, a young girl appeared in the chair next to me. She wore a long white dress and bonnet. Her short legs swung back and forth. She smiled at me. I smiled back. Oops.

"Hello, Miss Winters." His expression was unsure, and his fingers stopped drumming. Probably because I'd just smiled at the empty chair next to me. Gah, if my invisible friends could just stay away for this interview, I'd be able to get through it.

"Hello, Mr MacPherson. Lovely to meet you."

"Likewise." I tuned out the little girl and resisted the urge to fold my arms. *Don't appear nervous or defensive.* Stupid body language. Folding your arms was also comfortable. Did they ever think of that? No.

Mr MacPherson had a shaved head, a five-o-clock shadow of hair ringing the bald part in the middle. He wore a Hawaiian shirt, the bright red-and-orange pattern distracting and at odds with the contemporary, rich vibe of his office. Three thick wooden shelves, the same colour as the floor, hung on the stone wall behind him, covered with odds and ends, including two small, black, swirly sculptures that could be awards... or book-ends. I wasn't sure which. His refined accent was also at odds with his shirt. "I trust you found our offices okay?"

"I did, thank you."

"I also heard about that incident yesterday. How's the pub?"

I blinked. How the hell did he know about everything? "Um, the pub is quite okay, thanks."

He chuckled. "Don't be so surprised. It's my job to know the news. Also, small town, news travels fast. It's not a cliché for no reason." He winked.

I hoped he wasn't a serial winker. That could get creepy. "I'll have to get used to it."

"Indeed. So, are you ready to work?"

"Definitely. Am I still starting tomorrow?"

"Yes. I'll get you to go out with one of my top journalists—Finnegan Walsh. He can show you the village, tell you about the people, let you know what I want."

"Ah, okay. Great." I was sitting right here. Why didn't he just tell me what he wanted? Surely the job couldn't be that different to what I'd done before?

"I expect five small, community-based stories a week, and one serious one. Do you have a good phone? We don't have a photographer, so you'll need to take your own photos for the articles. I expect at least one for each article, but if you can take a few, then we can pick which one we run with. Our photo editor is at our Exeter office. She can fix almost anything, and at a pinch, we can use Shutterstock images, but we prefer not to, especially if it's about our locals."

"Okay. My phone's fine, I suppose." I had a two-year-old iPhone. If that wasn't good enough, bad luck because I couldn't afford a brand-new one.

"Good." He wiggled his backside in his chair, as if it was hard for him to sit still. "You'll be on a base wage, as explained in our offer letter, and any bonuses will come from those serious articles, which can include health or science-type pieces as well as investigative journalism. I pick my favourite one each week, and the journalist gets a fifty-pound bonus in their pay packet."

"So, I'm competing against other journalists?"

"Yes. I sometimes go with a piece from one of other offices, especially if it's political, but generally it will be out of you, Walsh, and Carina Kelly. Although Kelly usually does her own thing and doesn't compete. She tends to cover our arts scene, so maybe leave those articles to her. Anything about baking or knitting, that kind of thing. She can get a bit stroppy if you cross into her lane."

"Oh, right. Thanks for the heads-up. Um, why did the other journalist leave?" I knew they were replacing someone—the recruitment lady had mentioned something—but I didn't know if it was pregnancy leave or not. Would I still have a job in nine months? And surely if that was the case, they should've mentioned something.

He cleared his throat. "Issues with the other staff. He wasn't a team player." Phew, not pregnancy, then.

"Oh, so I have to be competitive but a team player?" Oh, cat's bum. Why did I say that aloud?

"Yes, definitely. You catch on quick." He pew pewed me with both hands. "If you have questions, fire them at me. I'm ready." He made a come-on motion with his hands. Ooookay. He was... energetic.

"I don't like him much." The little girl next to me frowned and folded her arms. I wasn't going to judge her for doing that— she wasn't the one in the interview. "He always tells me to get out of his office." Could he see her too? He'd looked at me funny before, when I'd smiled at her, unless he wondered if I could see what he could see? Hmm, maybe not. It didn't appear that he could see her at the time. Maybe he sensed her? What I wouldn't give for ghosts to be the real deal—not that that wouldn't scare me a bit, but it would definitely make me feel saner, and it would mean I was right and my parents wrong. And if they were wrong about that, what other horrible opinions of theirs were wrong?

*Focus, Avery.* "What time do I start?"

"The early bird catches the worm. Get in here at eight and bring an Earl Grey tea, an English breakfast, short black, and cappuccino, and whatever it is you're having." He leaped out of his chair and slapped a twenty-pound note on the table. I jumped at the noise and unexpected movement. My heart raced. Being in this office was scarier than covering a story. At least in a small village like this one, there shouldn't be too many violent crimes.

Maybe the dead woman in my apartment had a heart attack? Ooh, that could've been my first story. It was too late now, or was it? "Would I be able to cover the dead-woman story?"

He sat back down. "I don't see why not, but just a heads-up —Walsh is already covering it. I'll only publish one article on it, so be prepared to lose—he's good."

I put on my best fake smile. It was going to be like that, was it? "Not a problem." If I didn't get many bonuses to start with, it was fine. As long as my rent didn't go up, my budget could handle it. I just had to hope I wasn't stuck in the pub much longer. There would come a point, though, where I wanted to save money. Once I'd warmed up to the job and gotten to know the people here, it would be game on. Walsh better watch out.

"Well, if you don't have any more questions, take that money and skedaddle. See you bright and early tomorrow."

The girl beside me rolled her eyes and disappeared. I stood and leaned in to shake his hand. He waved it away. "We're not formal here. The only rule you have to obey, other than the ones regarding the other journalists, is do whatever I say. If you do that, we'll get along just fine." He gave a satisfied smile and opened his laptop. "Ciao, Winters. Enjoy the rest of your afternoon."

And with that, I was dismissed. I wasn't sure if I liked him or not. At this stage, I was firmly in the middle. Only time would tell which way I'd swing.

Then a thought hit me—what if the other journalists were terrible to work with? Would they try and get me fired? The last person had left under a cloud, after all. Maybe they'd pushed him until he broke? "Wasn't a team player" could mean so many things.

Gah, too many questions and not enough answers, and that killed the journalist in me. I needed to know. Maybe this Walsh guy would fill me in tomorrow. Or maybe he wouldn't. Either way, I'd have to learn to fit in.

Hopefully, that would be the hardest thing about this job. Whatever happened, I was going to find out tomorrow. I just had to make sure I was ready for anything.

# CHAPTER 4

For a small village, the café was rather busy. Huddled on the ground floor of another quaint, two-storey stone building, the Heavenly Brew Café was warm and filled with the mouth-watering aromas of hot breakfasts—even in early summer—coffee, and tea. I checked the time on my phone. Argh, ten minutes of standing here. This certainly wasn't the city. I shifted from foot to foot. Only five minutes until I had to be at work. Being late on the first day was not the impression I wanted to make. I was always punctual. Adjustments were going to be in order if I was going to survive here.

*Just breathe.*

"Can I help you?" Oh, I'd reached the front of the line. Relief stopped my feet from shuffling.

"Can I please have an Earl Grey, English breakfast, two cappuccinos, and a..." Oh, cat's bum—was I supposed to order a long or a short black? Doh! Maybe I'd just get a long because if they got more coffee rather than less, they'd be happier than getting less rather than more. "Long black, please."

"That'll be twenty-two pounds." The young, blonde woman

behind the register smiled, but there was an edge to it. Had I done something wrong? Was my British etiquette off? Were my shuffling feet and impatience offensive?

Of course Mr MacPherson had only given me twenty pounds, so this little duck would be paying for her own coffee. Looked like I'd have to earn my place there, and my free morning beverages. I gave her the money and stood aside to wait.

When they were all ready, she lined them up on the counter. "There you go."

Trying to carry five drinks and my laptop bag required the skill and dexterity of a seasoned waiter. Even though I was sporty —I'd done gymnastics as a kid, and I was a brown belt in Hapkido—I didn't think I was capable of balancing those without experiencing a disaster. "Do you have a tray or something?"

She cocked her head to the side, maybe considering whether she had any today. Then another woman came along, this one older. Her brown hair was pulled into a tight ponytail, and even though she was probably in her fifties, when she looked at me and smiled, it took ten years off her. "Of course we do. Here." She reached under the counter and brought one out. She put four of the hot drinks in there and handed the tray to me, then the single drink. "You the new girl from Australia?"

I smiled and looped the handle of my laptop bag over my hand so it hung off my wrist, then picked up the drinks. "I am."

"Welcome to Manesbury. I'm Anna." She gave a nod at the younger woman who was busy making more coffees. "This is Joy." So far, she hadn't lived up to her name.

"Lovely to meet you, Anna." I gave her a big smile. Then I turned to "Joy" and my smile retracted somewhat. "You too. See you again soon."

Anna gave me a small wave; then I turned and left. It was a

two-minute walk to the office. I buzzed the intercom. The same voice from yesterday answered. "Hello, can I help you?"

"It's Avery Winters."

"Who?" Seriously?

I looked up to the sky, then sighed quietly. It wouldn't do to make an enemy out of anyone I had to work with. "The new journalist. I have everyone's beverages."

"Oh, that Avery." Huh? How many other Averys were there in this place? I was betting none.

"Yes, that Avery." The buzzer buzzed, and the door clicked. I pushed it open and entered.

I considered going straight up to the boss's office and handing out his drink, and everyone else's, before coming back down to give this woman hers, but that would be asking for trouble. I'd play it cool and see how things went. Maybe she just took a few days to be nice to a new person. I stood in front of her desk. "Which one is yours?"

"The short black." Of course it was. The one I couldn't remember.

I put all the drinks on her table and grabbed hers out of the cardboard tray. "Sorry. I couldn't remember if I was supposed to get a long or short black, so I got the long. I figured more coffee, just in case."

She didn't smile. Her expression was bland—not quite annoyed but not making any effort to be friendly. "Okay, thank you. I suppose it's better than nothing."

"Ah, yeah. I suppose it is." My stomach tightened. I was going to ask her a question, but I didn't want to get shot down. Still, I had to know what to call her. "What's your name? I'm thinking I should know it if we'll be working together."

"I'm Bethany."

"Cool. Hi, Bethany. Enjoy your long black." I smiled—this

time it was genuine. Kill them with kindness, they said. Until I knew for sure she was picking on me specifically, I'd do just that.

I stuck the extra cup in the holder and made my way up the stairs to Mr MacPherson's office. The door was open. MacPherson sat behind his desk—this time wearing a different coloured Hawaiian shirt to yesterday. This one was green and blue. Two people occupied the only other two chairs in the office. A short, blue-haired woman who looked to be in her thirties, and a rotund man in his sixties. They must be Carina Kelly and Finnegan Walsh. I smiled and placed the drinks on the table.

"Good morning, Winters." MacPherson smiled—at least someone was happy to see me today. "I'll have the English breakfast, please." I pulled it out of the tray and handed it to him. "Where's my change?"

"Change?"

He raised his brows. "You're not holding out on me, are you, Winters?"

"How much change were you after?"

"About seven pounds."

Bloody Joy had stiffed me good. I gritted my teeth together and blew an angry breath out of my nose. "Just a sec." I grabbed my purse out of the small bag hanging at my hip. I counted out seven pounds and put them on the table. "There you are." So, my morning cappuccino had cost me nine pounds. Bargain.

His face showed concern. "You don't seem very pleased about giving me my change."

Should I fess up to what an idiot I was? It had seemed expensive, but what did I know about what things cost here? Although, I should've twigged since the pound was almost twice the Aussie dollar. I'd just spent eighteen dollars on a coffee. Nausea swished in my stomach. I wasn't going to cop that. Stuff it. I'd go get my money back at lunchtime. But what if the owner didn't believe me? She hadn't been standing anywhere near Joy when she'd taken my order or asked for the money. She would totally believe her employee before me. Crap on a stick. I was going to have suck it up. My hope that today was going to be better than yesterday was sinking faster than the Titanic. At this rate, I'd be penniless by the end of the week.

He put his change in his desk drawer and smiled again. "Please sit."

Huh? I looked at the two chairs. They were both obviously occupied. My gaze took in the whole room. Well, sitting on the floor would just be consistent with how everything had been since I'd gotten here. I grabbed my cappuccino out of the tray and sat on the floor next to Carina's chair.

Carina stared down at me, her expression clearly indicating that she thought I was mad. MacPherson's voice came from behind his desk, but I couldn't see him from down here. "Are you all right, Winters?"

"Yes, Mr MacPherson. Just sitting down."

He must have stood because his face appeared over the table. "But why are you sitting on the floor?"

I was about to answer when footsteps sounded behind me. Mr MacPherson shook his head and looked up at the new person. "Ah, Walsh. Good of you to join us. Running a bit late today?"

"Sorry, Julian. I slept in." He was on a first-name basis with the boss? What hope did I have of ever getting my article chosen for the weekly bonus?

I turned and peered up at the newcomer. His vibrant blue eyes—which stood out way too much against his raven hair—crinkled at the corners, and he chuckled—likely at the fact I was sitting on the floor. Oh, no. He was altogether too good-looking. My stomach did a little flip. Noooo. Attractive men were bad news, and there were too many in this village. They knew how to get their way with everyone. No wonder Mr MacPherson loved him. I'd have to tread carefully. Hopefully he was gay so I knew I had absolutely no chance with him. The last thing I needed was to lose my common sense over a man. Because my last relationship had gone *so well*. If I'd stayed in Sydney, I would've had to quit my job. Seeing Brad every day at work would've killed me. And imagine seeing him date someone else? Argh. No thanks.

Finnegan Walsh bent and held out his hand. "I'm Finnegan. You must be Avery."

I grabbed his hand and shook, ignoring the prick of electricity that stung my palm. "I am."

He released my hand and straightened. "It would probably be more polite of me not to ask, but why aren't you sitting on that perfectly good chair?" He gave a nod to the chair in question. I looked at it.

Squished brown bananas. It was empty. My stupid brain was doing its best to derail me. Life in this place had so far been difficult enough without me sabotaging myself. If only I hadn't been hit by lightning. I blinked back the tears threatening. There was no use thinking like that. It had, and I had to make the best of what I was now.

"I figured being the new person here, I should take the floor. I knew another person was going to show up." I smiled.

He blinked. "Oh, that's very polite, but you didn't have to do that."

I shrugged. "It's done now. Go ahead. Sit. I like sitting on the floor. It's good for my core muscles." Carina's brow wrinkled—she obviously thought I was weird. I couldn't argue with that, though. I totally was. "If you sit in a chair and lean back, you don't use your stomach muscles much, if at all, but if I sit here with my back straight, I'm basically getting a workout. You should try it." I grinned.

Carina tilted her head to the side, her long blue hair fanning out to the side. "Fair enough. Each to d'eir own, I always say." If my accent radar was correct, she was Irish.

Finnegan sat, then leaned across to grab his cappuccino, and Carina grabbed the Earl Grey, which reminded me of my own coffee. *Please don't be bitter.* I took my first sip. Ahhhhhh. At least the coffee was good. *Hallelujah!*

Mr MacPherson slapped the table with both hands. I jumped. I never used to be like this, but ever since being hit by lightning, any loud noises freaked me out, especially ones out of the blue. "Kelly, Walsh, I've had a chat to our new recruit." His gaze moved to Carina. "She knows not to cover your stories."

"T'ank you." Her Irish accent was awesome. So were all the English ones. That was one thing I'd enjoyed since arriving—thank Zeus there'd been something to enjoy. She looked at me. "We'll get along just fine." Her lips tilted up into a ghost of a smile.

"Great. Looking forward to it." I returned her smile.

MacPherson looked at Finnegan. "You can show her the ropes. I've explained our system."

Finnegan gave me the side-eye. I had no idea if it was because he was annoyed at getting stuck with the newbie or if he wanted to keep whatever he was working on today a secret. "Sure thing, Julian."

Mr MacPherson was sitting again, so he couldn't see me. "Can you please stand up, Winters?" I stood, careful not to drop my coffee. It was the only thing I had left to be happy about. "Right. I don't expect anything from you for a couple of days. Familiarise yourself with the town, introduce yourself to everyone—they'll be more likely to talk to you and answer your questions." He didn't need to tell me that. But, also, he didn't know about my secret—people loved to tell me their life stories. Hopefully, it was still true here. Unless they didn't trust someone with an Aussie accent because that meant they were an outsider.

If that was the case, I was going to struggle more than a jelly blubber trying to climb a tree.

"Will do, Mr MacPherson."

"Good. You're all dismissed."

Carina and Finnegan stood and went to the door. I followed. Carina gave us a wave. "Check you bot' later."

"Bye." I gave her a wave as well. Didn't want to offend her by giving a lesser goodbye than what she'd given. Sheesh, I was becoming paranoid.

Finnegan looked at me. "This way, Lightning."

I stopped. "What did you call me?"

He grinned. "I did some research on you. You're one of the 90 per cent who survive lightning strikes." Of course he'd researched—he was a journalist. It's what we did.

"Yep. I'm just that special." I gave him a sarcastic smile.

"Well, you managed to land this job, so you couldn't be that bad."

Was that compliment to butter me up, or was he being genuine? Since I wasn't going to ask, I'd never know. A little voice came from next to me. I flicked my gaze there and back. The little girl from yesterday. "He's nice." She sighed. "He has such white teeth." Um, okay. She was right, but that was a weird thing to say. She was dressed in clothes that looked to be from maybe a hundred or more years ago. She might have been comparing him to people she knew. *Okay, crazy lady. Your brain didn't know lots of people with yellow, crooked teeth. Ignore her.* I was, in essence, asking me to ignore me... maybe. If only there was a way to tell whether she was a ghost or not. I shook my head. Now would be a good time for a drink... of the alcoholic kind.

Finnegan gave me a strange look. Oh, that's right, I hadn't answered him. Oh, well, the opportunity had passed. "Our office is this way."

"*Our* office?"

"Yes. You'll be sharing with Carina and me."

Oh dear. He was going to be such a distraction. Hopefully my desk wouldn't face his. If it did, maybe I'd have to get blinkers, like a horse.

He led me past one door. "That's the stationery room."

"You need a whole room for stationery? This is the era of the internet, memory stick, and computers. Surely you don't have to print everything out?"

He chuckled. "No. We also store spare chairs in there, a whiteboard, and an extra table. This office used to have three other journalists, but a couple of years ago, we downsized by two people because of our competition."

"Who are they? The competition, not the journalists."

"Ares Media. We've shut down three of our other offices because of them. They're always coming in and taking our work." Ares was a Greek god of war. They must take their name seriously if they were out to conquer and destroy. "They spend a lot on internet advertising, so they get the readers and the advertising dollars. We tend to do okay in places where the residents still want the physical paper. We have a website, of course, and it's popular enough, but we make more money from the newspaper. Locals rely on us for all their neighbourhood news."

It was getting harder to earn a living from news and journalism. Some sites paid well for articles, but some didn't. And there was so much competition. I took the reality check and appreciated that I'd landed this job. "Doesn't MacPherson Media run a local news station too?"

He nodded. "Yep. But it's run out of a studio at Exeter."

"Interesting." It wasn't super interesting, but I had to say something.

He kept walking and went through the next door on the right. "This is it. Your home away from home."

It was a decent-sized room—twice as large as Mr MacPherson's office. Four desks were in here—one held a printer and desktop computer. The two others—each next to one of the two tall windows in the room—held personal effects as well as random office paraphernalia—staplers, pen holders, notepads.

"This is your desk." My desk was across the room from his, against the wall, and it looked to the front of the room. If I wanted to ogle my co-worker, I'd have to turn my head. That was a good thing. I wasn't going to embarrass myself by staring at him. He was hard not to look at, but I felt I was doing a good job staring everywhere else but at him.

I went around to the chair side of the desk and put my coffee and laptop down. I opened the top drawer on the right-hand side. Empty.

"You can grab whatever you need from the storage room. Just fill in what you take from the book in there."

"Okay, thanks."

"You probably won't need anything this morning, so you can leave your computer here. We'll have a wander around, and if you have any questions, just ask."

"Thanks."

He went to his desk and grabbed a notepad and pen. I grabbed my coffee again, and then we were good to go. When we passed the reception, Bethany called out, "Bye, Fin!"

"Bye, Beth."

Kill them with kindness. I ignored the lack of a mention. "Bye, Beth." I made sure to shorten her name like Finnegan had. There was probably nothing that would annoy her more than someone she didn't like acting familiar. I smiled at her silence as I let the front door close behind me.

On our walk around the village, Finnegan tried to drag me into Heavenly Brew. "I've already been in there." I wasn't ready to face Joy yet. She would know she'd won, and she'd probably try to charge me again for the coffee in my hand.

"Oh, okay." He then took me past the post office, the butcher, and the pet-supply shop. Further up the road were the small supermarket, deli, and bakery.

When we'd reached the end of the high street on one side— in front of the pub—he was about to cross the road to the other when I stopped. "Don't worry about it. If I wanted a silent walking tour, I could take myself. You haven't introduced me to anyone."

He grinned, as if that would soothe my anger. I had news for him—it wouldn't. "You'll meet them all soon enough anyway, Lightning."

"Do you have to call me that?"

"You don't like it?"

"Not particularly, no. I prefer Avery, if it's not too much trouble."

"A very what?"

"What?"

"A very what? A very angry woman? A very annoyed journalist?"

I wrinkled my forehead. Why had I picked this village out of all the villages in England? Because there was cheap accommodation and a journalism job, neither of which were panning out very well so far. More bad choices to add to my list. "You're not funny. If it's all the same to you, I don't need you to show me around, Vinegar."

He waved a finger at me. "Ooh, good one, Lightning."

"See you around." We were near the pub, so I figured I'd go there and have a glass of water and calm down, then go and introduce myself to the different shop owners and staff in the village. I walked off.

He ran and caught up to me. "Hey, don't go. It's my job to show you around, so I will." I raised my brow, so not convinced. "I promise I won't be a git."

I blew out a breath. I'd give him one chance. "Fine. I have nothing better planned."

"Such a complimentor. Come on, then." He walked off, past the pub.

"There's no shops up here."

"I know. We're going to your new digs."

"I'm staying at the pub."

"Not forever. I happen to know that you're the one that found the body. Care to give me any info?"

"No. I thought I might do a story on it." What would he make of that? I'd had a front-row seat to the whole thing, which, I figured, put me in the lead for best article.

"You're kidding, right? This is your first day. You don't know anything about this place."

"I know what I saw when I opened my front door."

He pressed his lips together. "Fine. I'll just ask Mrs Collins—she'll tell me. She likes me, you know."

Oh my God, what a child. "Lucky you. You're one in a million."

His lips twitched. "You're not the only one who thinks so." He turned his head and winked. I rolled my eyes. All the time, he kept walking towards the laneway that led to the flat. "As it so happens, I live up here."

My eyes widened. "You what?"

He smiled. "I'm your next-door neighbour."

"What are the odds?" I mumbled.

"What?"

"Nothing."

We turned into the laneway. Parked further up, at the dead-end, was a police car. Finnegan rubbed his hands together. "Ooh, information." He stopped and looked at me. "You might want to wait here. Just in case there's anything confidential they want to tell me."

"You're serious?"

"Deadly."

"Okay, fine. I'll just sit over here on this fence." I wandered over to a knee-height stone wall. As if the police would tell him anything. And as if I'd let him just steamroll me. Once he was satisfied I was staying put, he turned and kept going up the hill. I stood and quietly followed him. His confidence was such that I was betting he wouldn't turn around. Imagine that. I was right.

He'd only just started his conversation with the policeman who'd questioned me about finding the body when I settled in behind him. Both men had their backs to me as they watched Mrs Collins's place.

"Anything you can tell me, Sid?"

"You know I can't say much, Fin."

"What about off the record?" That old chestnut. A lead was a lead.

Sid lowered his voice. "Fiona Daniels, local estate agent. Looks like she was murdered. But that's all I'm willing to say. And if you tell anyone your source, you'll get nothing more from me. Ever." Oh, wow. It was the woman who was supposed to give me the key.

Finnegan lifted his hands up. "You can trust me, Sid. When have I ever exposed a source?"

"Never. And it better stay that way. I may be your father's best friend, but I don't want to lose my job helping his son."

"Understood." He patted Sid on the back, then noticed me. His mouth dropped open. "How long have you been standing there?"

47

I shrugged. "You tell me."

Sid turned. He did well to hide his surprise by morphing it into an imposing frown. "Miss Winters. What are you doing here?"

"Finnegan's showing me around. I started work at the paper today." I didn't want to get him offside, so maybe changing the subject was in order. "Do you know when I can have my flat back?"

"In a couple of days. We're making sure we have everything, and then Mrs Collins wanted us to clean the living area."

I hadn't seen any blood, but there could've been some underneath her, or even other bodily fluids. I wasn't going to argue. "Sounds good to me." The raised eyebrows that Sid threw Finnegan's way didn't escape my notice. "Don't worry. I didn't hear any of your conversation. If the English TV shows I watched back home are anything to go by, you lads were probably talking about football. Not my thing." Lying wasn't my default setting, but when the situation required it, I could fool the best of them. "Can I call you Sid, or would you prefer officer?"

"Sergeant Bellamy would be fine."

"Great." I gave him my most innocent smile. Even though his was small, he did smile back. I'd been told I was pretty, on more than one occasion, and I knew from experience that people thought I was innocent and sweet upon first meeting me, so I ran with that and hoped both men underestimated me. I'd play the clueless card as long as I could.

"I'll make sure someone from the station lets you know as soon as it's safe to move back in."

"Thank you so much. That's very considerate."

"Right, well, if you don't have any information, I s'pose I should keep showing Avery around."

"Right you are, then." Sergeant Bellamy gave us both a nod and walked towards the house.

Finnegan spoke without taking his gaze off Bellamy's retreating form. "Fancy a cup of coffee, Lightning?"

"I still have one, thanks, Vinegar." I held up my takeaway cup, which still contained a mouthful of coffee. Finnegan was definitely souring my view of this place, stymying me getting to know people and, therefore, being able to do my job. And now that I knew that estate agent had been murdered, I had questions to ask, research to do.

Finnegan looked at me, confusion on his face. "I'm inviting you into my place for a coffee, and you turned me down?" His gorgeous blue eyes stared into mine, maybe trying to sway me, but for what? He just wanted to manipulate me into not writing the article. He was a conman, and this little possum wasn't going to fall for it. Maybe the lightning had knocked some sense into me as well. The Avery who'd existed before that fateful day probably would've been eating out of his hand.

"Yes, I'm turning you down. I have work to do, people to meet, etcetera, etcetera." I smiled, then turned my attention from his too-handsome face and stared at the house I was soon to live in… if nothing else went wrong. My forehead wrinkled as another one of those figments of my imagination walked out of the closed front door. Hmm, what was this all about?

I walked towards the house.

"Hey, where are you going?"

"Just having a look. I was freaking out last time I left here, and I didn't get a good look at where I'm going to live." I kept walking. When I neared the front fence, my possibly imaginary friend reached the gate. She stopped and looked at me, sadness on her face.

She looked familiar. Oh my God, she was wearing the same navy-blue pant suit and white shirt the dead real-estate agent had been wearing. Her hair was the same, and her face seemed the same, although it was a bit difficult to tell since her eyes had been closed when I'd seen her. Why did my imagination have to put a dead person's image on things? It couldn't be her ghost, could it?

"You have to find my killer. I think I knew him… or her, but I can't remember."

I frowned. Should I just go with the ghost theory? But what if I was wrong? Maybe I'd just pretend she was a ghost and see what happened. If it turned out it was my nutty brain fooling me, I'd figure that out later. For now, I'd see where this led.

Finnegan reached me and stood at my side. He hugged himself and rubbed his arms. "Brrrr. It's chilly here." He squinted into the sun. "Weird for such a nice day."

Come to think of it, it *was* cold. Goosebumps peppered my arms. I'd been too focussed on thinking through my craziness to notice. "Yeah, it is."

"I heard those police talking in there. You're the girl who found me."

I nodded. With Finnegan here, I wasn't about to talk to myself. Although, maybe it would get rid of him, and if he said anything to anyone, I'd tell them I was trying to make him leave. Hmm, that could work.

The woman stared at me. "Did you see anything?"
"No."

Finnegan's forehead wrinkled. "What do you mean no? You just said you agreed with me."

I turned my head to look at him. "I wasn't talking to you."

He gave me a "you're nuts" look. "Are you feeling all right?"

"I'm fine. Look, this thing where you're showing me around, it's not working out. You might as well go and do your own thing, get that article written."

His face relaxed into a "ha ha, you can't fool me" look. He pointed at me and waggled his finger. "You can't get rid of me that easily. I bet you were going to go in there and ask the police some questions. Sorry, but you're stuck with me for the day."

I shrugged. "Have it your way, then." I turned back to the woman. "Did you see anything?"

She shook her head. "I don't remember. The only thing I do remember is pain around my neck, and I couldn't breathe. I'm dead, aren't I?"

I blinked. I wasn't sure what it would accomplish, but I had to see her reaction. "No. You're a figment of my imagination."

She shook her head. "I don't think so. That can't be right. I have memories of people in my life." Tears glistened in her eyes. "I am dead. I'm sure of it. I feel... nothing. No heat, no cold." She stood facing the stone fence and hinged at the waist, moving quickly, slamming her head on the top of it. I cringed at the impact, even though nothing could happen since she didn't really exist. "There, that proves it. It didn't hurt." She reached a hand up and touched her forehead. "There isn't even any blood."

I might as well go for broke and prove the ghost thing to myself once and for all. "If you're not one of my imaginary friends, tell me something I can check out later."

Finnegan gave a nervous chuckle. "Okay, Avery, joke's over. I won't even call you lightning any more if you'll just be normal."

I looked at him and grinned. "This *is* my normal, Vinegar. You might as well get used to it." Other than annoying him, it was good to just be me, even if that me was crazy. I wasn't hurting anyone, so why should it be anyone's problem if I talked to myself? Other people did it—they just didn't have the visuals to go along with it.

"Seriously, you're going to keep pretending?" He shook his head, maybe deciding whether I was worth bothering with or not. He held up his hands in surrender. "Fine. You win. I'll leave you to your own devices. If you have any questions about anything, you can call the boss. I've got work to do."

"See ya." I gave him a wave.

"Yeah, bye." He turned and started back down the hill.

I looked back at the woman—I might as well call her Fiona, after the woman I'd potentially fashioned her from. "Fiona, what can you tell me about your life? Something I wouldn't know." When I'd confessed I'd seen ghosts, my parents had repeatedly said "Avery, you're crazy. They're not ghosts. You're seeing imaginary people, which is not normal." Everyone had asked what had happened when I died—because who wasn't curious about death. I'd admitted I'd experienced nothing but blackness. I'd never seen ghosts before or heard unexplainable noises. The one time I freaked out because I thought the Devil was wheezing and summoning demons outside my window, it turned out to be a possum. My parents had used my experience to back their hypothesis that I was crazy. This was my chance to prove to myself that I wasn't always wrong. Besides, I didn't have much else to do today, except hop on the internet and carry out some research on Fiona Daniels.

She cocked her head to the side and absently stroked her fingers over her jacket lapel. "I have a husband, Simon." She dropped her hand, and her shoulders slumped. "I can't even check on him. I think I'm stuck here until I feel better. There is one other place I can go, but I didn't recognise it. I think I knew it... before."

"Where is that other place?"

"A field." She shrugged. "Like I said, I don't know where it is." Her eyes widened. "Oh." She disappeared.

"Fiona?" I turned three hundred and sixty degrees and scanned my surroundings. She'd gone. Damn brain. Probably cutting me off because I was being stupid, but still, I had potential information to follow up. If Fiona's husband's name was Simon, it would either be a freaky coincidence, or I'd be onto something. At least I had a purpose to my day now.

I smiled and started off down the hill, excitement bubbling away inside me. I wasn't willing to think further than checking out the information. If ghosts existed, I could rejoice at being sane, although, the flip side to that coin was that ghosts existed. I thought about the movies *The Exorcist* and *Poltergeist* and shuddered. Hmm, now I wasn't so sure I wanted that information to check out.

Nevertheless, I kept walking towards the office. A journalist always had to know; consequences be damned.

# CHAPTER 5

Compared to Australia, it was crazily easy to find personal information, like an address, in England since all electoral-roll information was available online. When I'd seen that Simon was really Fiona's husband's name, it had given me goosebumps. It was looking more and more like I really had conversed with Fiona's ghost, and other than the story I wanted to write, it made me want to know who killed her. Was it personal, or was the killer looking for more victims? The best place to start was interviewing those closest to Fiona; so here I was, standing on her front porch.

I knocked on Simon Daniels's door and crossed my fingers that Finnegan hadn't thought to interview the husband yet. I'd called Sergeant Bellamy to get more information, but he refused to tell me anything, so I didn't even know if Mr Daniels was a suspect, but they always were, the husbands. Questioning him, if he would even speak to me, would be a precarious balance between getting relevant information and not offending him.

Hmm, was he even home?

I knocked again and put my ear close to the door. Footsteps

approached from inside, so I stood back, lest I be caught looking like an idiot with her ear to the door. When the door opened, the man standing there was drawn and tired, bags under his eyes, short red hair sticking up this way and that, as if he'd just gotten out of bed. He was dressed in shorts and T-shirt. "Can I help you?" His exhausted and monotone voice gave the impression that he was the one who needed help.

"Hi, Mr Daniels. My name is Avery Winters. I'm sorry for your loss."

Recognition of something—probably pain—flickered in his gaze. He swallowed, his Adam's apple bobbing. "Thank you. Do you… did you know my wife?"

My mouth went dry. Cat's bum. Why hadn't I thought of this? I was such a crap human. "Sort of. I was renting a flat through her." I took a deep breath. "I'm the one who found her."

He hadn't looked well to start with, but his face paled, and he grabbed the door jamb to steady himself.

"I'm sorry. I can come back later if you need some time." Guilt soured my insides that I had ulterior motives for being here, but the journalist in me was too much of a bulldog and wanted to get the job done, as did the sympathetic and maybe a little bit scared part of me who wanted to find her killer. I ignored the little voice inside me that also said I wanted to beat stupid Finnegan and impress Mr MacPherson.

He looked at the ground for a bit, then back up at me. "No, no, it's okay. Please come in." He moved aside. Even though I hated myself for doing this, I went in and down the long hallway. Several pretty watercolours hung from the timber picture rails on both walls. Spring flowers and children playing at the beach gave off a cheery atmosphere. It seemed as if Fiona had lived in a happy home.

I walked through the door at the end of the hallway, which opened to a cosy living room. Cream lounges sat on a crimson rug over timber floors. The couches were spotless—they obviously didn't have small children, and I couldn't see any pets.

"Please, sit down. Can I get you a tea?"

I gave him an apologetic smile. "No, thanks. I'm sorry to take up your time. If you want to grab one, feel free."

"No." I sat on the two-seater lounge, and he sat in one of the two armchairs.

A marble mantle surrounded the fireplace in the middle of one wall, pictures of Fiona and her husband lining the cold surface. They looked like an outdoorsy couple—kayaking, horse riding, and windsurfing. And they did it all together. I returned my gaze to the grieving man. Surely he hadn't done it. Which made what I was about to say all the meaner of me. "I haven't had a chance to mention that I'm also with the local newspaper. I wanted to do a piece on Fiona... on the person she was and what she meant to the community. Finding her had a huge impact on me."

His sad gaze met mine. "I bet it did. The police won't say much, but how was she? Was it...?" He ran a hand through his messy hair. "Was she...?"

"She looked peaceful. I couldn't see anything wrong... no injuries. She was just lying there, like she was asleep." I wasn't going to mention the blue lips—he could likely do without that. "I thought maybe she had a heart attack. Did they tell you how she died?"

"No. They said they're still looking into it, and they have to complete the autopsy." He picked at a thread on his shorts. "I don't think it was a heart attack. I would think they would've said something by now if it was? And she was healthy. We did so much outdoors. She loved keeping fit, getting out into nature. She had no health problems."

I slid my notebook and pen out of my bag. "Do you mind if I write this down? For my article. I won't talk about the police stuff, of course, just that she loved sports and being outside. Do you have any pets?"

"No. I'm allergic to dogs and cats. She wasn't really an animal lover."

"Okay. How long had she worked in real estate? Did she enjoy her job?"

His brow furrowed. "Ten years, and she loved her job. She loved that she got to go out and about, not be stuck in the office all day. She also enjoyed dealing with people. She mostly did sales, but some of the landlords asked specifically to deal with her for their rentals because she was so good at her job. She cared about her clients."

"I'm sorry I didn't get to meet her. She sounds like a wonderful woman."

"She is." His head fell forward into his hands, and his voice came out muffled. "Was." His shoulders shook. Damn. He was crying. Should I comfort him or ignore it? My hand hovered, ready to pat his back as I decided whether to stand or not.

He pulled a hanky out of his shorts pocket and drew it across his eyes. Sitting it was. He sniffled. "I'm sorry."

"Oh my God. Don't be. You've just lost your wife. You're allowed to cry. Just take it one day at a time, and don't place any expectations on yourself. You'll need time."

He nodded. "Thank you, Avery."

"I'm just sorry there isn't more I can do. Um… is there anything else you want to tell me about her that I should include in the article? Are her parents still alive? Does she have any siblings?"

His forehead wrinkled, and his lips pressed together. Had my questions annoyed him? "Her father died a couple of years ago, and her mother lives in Canterbury, so they hardly saw each other. They don't really get along. She has a younger brother and an older sister." He shrugged. "They had an okay relationship with her, but they both had kids, and we didn't. We couldn't. They do a lot of stuff together because of the kids. We're sometimes invited, sometimes not."

"Oh, I'm sorry."

"Don't be. We came to terms with it."

I wanted to know what he did for work—which I could probably find out if I checked his social media—but I had to be subtle. "Are you having time off work?"

"Yes. My boss has given me two weeks." He twisted his wedding ring around his finger. One rotation, two rotations, three.

I had my lead-in. Now it wouldn't be suspicious. "What do you do?"

He looked at me. "I'm an accountant. I work for a firm nearby. The work would be a good distraction, but I can't concentrate, so I'd probably stuff it all up."

"Have you got anyone to support you while you go through this?"

He nodded. "I have a couple of mates, and my parents. They live a few miles away. I'm thinking of going to stay with them." His gaze slowly moved around the room. "But I feel closer to Fe here. I don't want to leave."

My natural instinct was to reach out and hold his hand, comfort him, but I held back. That would be way too weird, and I didn't want him to think I was coming onto him. "Did you and Fiona have any favourite places you liked to visit... out in nature?"

His gaze strayed to the mantlepiece, and he almost smiled. There was a subtle lifting of his grief for a moment. "She particularly loved our hikes at Dartmoor."

"Nice." I smiled and made a note in my notebook. I had no idea where it was. Stupid Finnegan would have the upper hand until I got my bearings.

His pained eyes landed on me. "Do you have enough for your article? I think I need to lie down. I'm not feeling the best."

My heart went out to him. There was no way he was faking it, and why bother with me? I wasn't the police. "I'm sorry. I've kept you too long." I stood. "I'm sure I have a lot. Can I just ask one more favour? Do you have the phone numbers for her brother or sister? I'd like to get their take on Fiona too. And I'm sure they'd like to be mentioned when it comes to their sister."

He shrugged. "Sure." He stood and went to the next room, then returned with his phone. "What's your number, and I'll text you the details."

I told him my number, and soon my phone dinged with a message. "Thanks. I appreciate it. And again, I'm so sorry. She did look peaceful when I found her. I hope that helps."

He didn't nod or shake his head. He just looked at me, then wiped his eyes with his hanky. Not wanting to make this any harder on him, I turned and went to the front door, his slow footsteps behind me. I let myself out, shutting the door. That poor man, facing a horrible few months trying to find his place in the world again. But at least I had some leads.

Now to chase them up.

# CHAPTER 6

As soon as I hopped back in the car—which I was going to have to return tomorrow because I couldn't afford a rental for an extended period—I tried calling Fiona's brother and sister. Neither of them answered, so I left messages. To be fair, I tended not to answer the phone if I didn't know the number. It was pot luck whether you got a real person or scam robotic call telling you you'd broken some tax law, and now you had to pay a fine or be arrested. Ha ha. Like I'm going to believe you. Unfortunately, some people did, otherwise they wouldn't keep trying it on. With any luck, one or both of Fiona's siblings would call me back today—then I could potentially meet with them in person because I still had my wheels.

It wasn't what I really wanted to do, but I was going to swing by the estate agent's office. Maybe someone other than the cow at the front desk would help me. It didn't take long to get there, and I found parking easily, which was a bonus. Hopefully my luck would continue inside.

I took a deep breath and opened the door—as tough as I talked inside my brain, I wasn't quite that tough on the outside.

Seeing that receptionist again was nerve-wracking. I walked in—an alarm-beep thing announcing my arrival—and straight to her. She didn't look up from what she was typing until I actually spoke. Right, so she was still as rude as yesterday. "Ah, excuse me."

She looked up. When she realised who it was, her lips pressed together. I was going to guess that she definitely wasn't overjoyed to see me. "Oh, it's you. Come to complain about what happened the other day?"

"No, of course not. I'm sorry for your loss." Okay, that's not why I came, but I might as well start with the niceties. And as much as I had no friendly feelings towards this woman, she might be grieving, and I could respect that.

Her expression softened. Not enough that she was looking kind or anything, but at least she didn't appear to want to throw me out. "Thank you."

"I know everyone here is probably rather upset, so if this doesn't suit, it's okay. I'm doing an article on Mrs Daniels and how she was an asset to the community, and I was wondering if you or anyone here would like to give me some insight into who she was."

"I'm sorry, but I don't have time. The boss might be able to help—Mr Schmidt. He's in. I'll just call and see if he has time." Well, that was more than I expected.

"Thank you. I appreciate it."

While she made the call, I wandered to the floor-to-ceiling glass office front. There were a lot of properties for sale, each one displayed on its own large square. Terraces, large houses, a couple of flats, and a development site. There was even a farm. I sighed at some of them—so pretty, yet so unaffordable.

"Miss Winters."

I went back to the desk. "Did you have any luck?"

She gave me an almost smile. "Yes. He'll see you now, but he only has five minutes."

Relief washed through me, and I smiled. "I'll take it. Thank you so much."

She pointed me to a door in the middle of the wall that separated the private offices from the reception area. "Just go through there, and it's the last office on your right."

"Great, thanks." I went through and quickly found his office. I took a moment to appreciate that I was back into the swing of work—after the problems I'd had so far, this was almost too easy. Touch wood.

I knocked.

"Come in." I opened the door and stepped inside. Mr Schmidt stood from his black high-backed office chair and offered me his large hand. His smile was sad. "Pleased to meet you. I understand you're doing a story on our Fe. Please have a seat." He gestured to the three grey chairs in front of his desk.

"Thank you. And sorry for your loss." I sat and pulled my notebook and pen out of my bag. I sometimes recorded stuff on my phone, but this was going to be a short interview, and some people didn't like to be recorded. "I know you don't have much time, so I'll get straight to it."

"Thank you."

"I hear she loved her job. What was she like as an employee?"

He smiled. "She was our top salesperson. Consistent, hardworking, the clients loved her—she always went above and beyond. She'd been working long hours lately. I don't know how I'm going to cover her workload with only a few staff who are already run off their feet. She really did do the work of two people." He shook his head. "It's just so sad. She had a light inside her. Always smiling, always enthusiastic, and nothing was too much trouble. We're really going to miss her. I can't imagine what her husband is going through." He swallowed and ran a hand over his balding pate.

"Yes. It's very sad. She sounds like an incredible woman."

He looked at me and smiled. "She really was." He cleared his throat. "I'm sorry, but that's all the time I can spare. I have an appointment with prospective vendors in fifteen minutes at their place. I'll show you out."

I could take a hint. Hiding my disappointment, I stood—I'd hardly gotten any information. I was no closer to finding out who murdered her than I was last night, which was to say, not at all. "Thank you for your time. I appreciate it. And I'm sure Mr Daniels will appreciate your kind words when he reads the article."

He gave a nod. "Of course." He moved, which was more of a hint. I made my way out, said goodbye to the receptionist who was back to ignoring me, and left. Time to head back to the office and hope stupid Finnegan wasn't there.

⚜

Bethany buzzed me in, but true to form, she ignored me after that. Just to annoy her, I said, "Hello, Beth," as I walked past. When I stepped into the office, Finnegan and Carina stopped their little conversation and jerked their heads towards me. Nothing like being talked about when you weren't there. I smiled and went to my desk. "Hi. How's it going?"

They both smiled. Carina answered first, "Good, t'anks. Where have you been? Getting some leads on your first day?"

"Yes, actually it's been good so far. I came up with some decent ideas when I was talking to myself earlier." I tried not to snort. This being-myself thing was fun.

Finnegan's eyes widened, and Carina spurted out a surprised

laugh. She twirled a few strands of her blue hair around her finger and nodded. "I t'ink I'm going to like you."

I grinned. "Thanks, but don't sound so surprised."

"Well, you never know what d'e new hire is going to be like, and we've had some real nitwits in the past. When Fin told me you'd given him a hard time, I'll admit you earned some respect right dere."

Fin gave her a dirty look. "Whose side are you on?"

"The side of a gorgeous woman who doesn't fall for your cow manure."

I sat and pulled my laptop out of the bag. "Thanks, Carina. I appreciate your support. Us sensible ladies need to stick together."

"We do need to stick toged'er. For sure."

Finnegan rolled his stupidly mesmerising blue eyes. "I know where I'm not wanted. I'm going to grab a coffee. Anyone want anything?"

"The usual."

Finnegan looked at me. "Lightning?"

My eyes shot invisible lasers at him, but I didn't react verbally. I wasn't going to encourage him. "I could use a cappuccino, no sugar, thanks." I reached into my bag for my wallet.

"No, I've got this. You can shout another time."

"Are you sure?"

"Positive, Lightning."

"Vinegar." I wished I had something more insulting, but I wasn't that creative, despite being a journalist. Given enough time, maybe I could think of something better, but for now, tart and sour it would have to be. Hmm, that actually suited him just fine. I was sure the ladies in this village and beyond could attest to him being both.

"Ooh, look at you two getting along so well." Carina's laugh was like a little magical bell that cascaded unannoyingly. It was more infectious than anything. I grinned. She'd looked so serious and scary earlier this morning, but turned out, she wasn't so bad. Maybe I would actually come to enjoy working here.

"See you soon, ladies." Finnegan waggled his brows at me as he left.

Or, maybe not.

# CHAPTER 7

Noisy chatter floated around the dimly lit room, intertwining with the enticing fragrance of roasted meat and garlic bread. I cut into my steak and mushroom pie, saliva bursting in my mouth. Mmm, the best thing about living at the pub was dinner. Not cooking was awesome.

As I savoured a delicious mouthful, I let my shoulders relax, and my back sank into the chair. I was well on my way to writing my first story—not that it was the bonus-grabbing story, but I figured I could make the piece on Fiona one of the smaller ones. Once I'd spoken to her siblings, I'd have enough sources to quote and a better idea of who she was.

Unfortunately, though, I had more questions than answers when it came to her murder.

I'd jumped online this afternoon and checked out her Facebook and Instagram accounts. She shared a lot about work on both. If she'd shared anything about her private life on Facebook, I couldn't see it. Her Instagram showed lots of happy snaps of her and her husband doing their weekend sporty stuff. But, funnily enough, there were no photos from the last three months.

Maybe she'd gotten bored with Instagram, or maybe she'd been working too hard to take time out?

I drained the last of my beer and frowned. Bummer. All gone. Should I have another one? It was Friday night, and I could sleep in tomorrow. I didn't have to go into the office on the weekends, but because I had stories to write, I was likely really going to be working seven days a week until I got settled and built relationships with the people here. I had no reliable sources, and no insight into what people even did here for fun. Tomorrow would be for strolling around and checking things out. Who knew, if I was lucky, maybe they'd let me move back in this week-end? It was kind of creepy that there'd been a dead body in my flat, but once the body was gone, it was gone. There were so many old houses here that it would be likely someone had died in many of them, and no one was the wiser fifty years later.

"Hey, Avery. My brother thought you might be thirsty." Meg stood next to my table and smiled, then placed another beer in front of me.

I smiled up at her, then looked towards the bar. Her brother was staring at me, but as soon as our eyes met, he turned quickly to serve someone. He was cute… not that I needed a man in my life right now. I should just keep reminding myself. It was a shame there were too many tempting men around this place. It was going to be hard to keep my promise to myself of no dating and no relationships.

My gaze found Meg. "Thanks. Is this on the house?" I wasn't trying to be rude, but I couldn't afford to splurge too much, and if they were going to give me drinks I had to pay for just because I looked thirsty, I'd have to set them straight.

"It sure is. Our best guest gets special perks." I totally didn't deserve such consideration. Here I was worried I'd have to pay for it when they were only being sweet.

"Aw, thanks. Are you bribing me to stay longer?"

She laughed. "Maybe…. How's it going, anyway? Do you have a move-in date yet?"

"Sergeant Bellamy said two to maybe four days, I think. I'm hoping tomorrow, but that's wishful thinking."

"Well, good luck. We'll miss you, which brings me to what I wanted to say. Mind if I sit?"

I shrugged. "Go ahead. It's your pub." I chuckled.

She grinned and sat. "I know you don't know anyone, and this is kind of awkward, but I think you're nice. I'd be happy to befriend you and show you around… properly. I heard about the mess Finny made of it."

"Finny?"

"Bailey and I went to school with him—he and Bailey are still close. That's what all the kids used to call him when we were little. I like being a pain, so that's what I still call him." She smirked.

"Ha! Serves him right. He is a pain. I'm sensing that he's Mr Competitive."

"That he is. I'm having a day off tomorrow. My dad's coming in to look after things—it used to be his pub, but after Mum died, he decided he wanted to enjoy life more. He has a motorhome and travels Europe. He's home for a couple of weeks, so I'm taking my opportunity for a few days off."

Warmth settled into my stomach—and it wasn't from the food. I wasn't great at making new friends, and what little skill I'd had, disappeared when I was dating Brad. I was way out of practice, so it was nice Meg was initiating this because I didn't know if I ever could be that brave. Rejection sucked, and opening myself up to people was terrifying. My relationship with my parents had taught me to be careful. Whenever I let my guard down with them, I paid the price. I shook my head and blocked them out—there was no point ruining my night lamenting about something I couldn't change.

"That would be great. I do have to take my rental back tomorrow. Maybe after that?"

"Where do you have to leave it?"

"Exeter."

"I'll come with you and give you a lift back. Maybe we could have a coffee there. I'll show you some of the sights."

I smiled. "That would be lovely. Thanks, Meg."

"I'll knock on your door at ten. I'll be working late tonight, by the time we clean up and I balance the till. I don't want to be half-asleep for our day tomorrow."

"Sounds great. See you at ten."

Meg got back to work, turning to say hello to the people on the table next to me, then taking their dirty plates away when she left. There was another waitress rushing about, and another guy behind the bar with Bailey, but it looked like they kept it small. How in Hades did they keep up with everything? It seemed pretty stressful. The amount of time I had to research and write my articles seemed like a holiday in comparison. Which brought me back to what I was working on. Hmm. An idea formed.

I finished my dinner and my beer and took my dirty stuff up to the bar. Bailey's forehead wrinkled. "You didn't have to do that."

I shrugged. "It's fine. You guys are busy. Thought I'd make it easier."

He gave me a shy smile. "Thanks, Avery." He stared into my eyes for a beat too long, sending butterflies flitting in my stomach. *Down flutterbyes. I don't need you in my life.*

The imaginary woman or ghost who'd been following me around the pub since I'd arrived stood next to me. "He's a lovely man. You could do worse."

I turned to her and gave a "thank you, but can you mind your own business" smile. Why did these interruptions have to happen in front of other people? It really was bad timing.

Whether it was me or a ghost saying that I could do worse, getting involved with anyone at this stage of my life, when I was trying to find myself and start again without the expectations and bullying of my parents and ex, was a terrible idea. How would I ever know who Avery was if everyone else's voice was louder than my own?

I turned back to Bailey. "Have a good night."

"Yeah, same, Avery. Same." He gave me another smile, spun, and hurried to the other end of the bar, where a gorgeous young woman needed service. Relief settled amongst the disappointment, the butterflies dissolving into nothing. *Well, you don't want this. Stop being such a crazy person.* I turned my back on the woman I'd conjured and went out to the hall. Instead of going left towards my room, I turned right and walked outside.

After being in a room full of people, the cool twilight air nipped at my face. I shivered. *You'll warm up once you start walking.* I headed along the footpath in the direction of the flat, passing a group of teens hanging outside the supermarket, which closed at nine. They were eating chips—which I'd discovered the British called crisps—and laughing, mucking around. Ah, to be a teen again. Although, I wouldn't want to go through all the crap I'd been through again. Meh, maybe being twenty-six was okay.

An older couple, maybe in their seventies, walked holding hands. The man gave me a nod, and the woman smiled. "Hello."

"Hi." I returned her smile, and we all continued on our way. That was nice. Aside from the receptionist at the estate agent, oh, and the one at work, and the chick at the coffee shop, and Mrs Crabby—I chuckled to myself because they were adding up—everyone had been fairly friendly. Finnegan hadn't been unfriendly per se—he'd been more a thorn in my side.

I was questioning my decision to move less tonight than I had yesterday. With a bit of luck, as the days passed, I'd stop questioning it altogether.

Before long, I was rounding the corner and striding up the hill. There was nothing like an evening walk to help banish the fullness from a hearty dinner. Lights were on in the houses I passed, welcoming beacons, reassuring me that people were around, and they were happy living their cosy lives. Logically, I knew that they couldn't all be happy, and I might never be invited in to share that warmth, but it was still comforting. Could one absorb that sense of wellbeing by osmosis?

As I stepped into the narrowest part of the street leading directly to the little copse of dwellings that contained my future home, shadows darkened the ground, as if the night were more advanced. Heated from my vigorous walk, I shouldn't have shivered, but I did. I glanced around, confirming that no one was following me. Nope. All alone. I shook off the feeling of being watched and quietly approached Mrs Crabby's fence. The last thing I needed was her coming out to chastise me for stalking.

Would my brain invoke Fiona, or would she turn up? I was hoping my subconscious might have picked up on something while speaking to her husband and that it would reveal a new piece of information I thought I'd missed. I licked my bottom lip and looked around. I was more willing to believe she was a ghost, but I couldn't ignore that coincidences existed—maybe I'd fluked her husband's name? I really needed to decide where I stood. *Come on, Avery; it's not that hard.* Unfortunately, it wasn't easy to shake off my mistrust in my own opinions after being gaslit my whole life.

Still alone.

My heartbeat kicked up a notch. I was going to risk Mrs Crabby hearing me, just in case it helped get Fiona here. I hiss-whispered, "Fiona. Hello?" Man, was I courting a new level of craziness. That was me—embracing it and jumping in belly and face first, arms and legs spread wide, ready for the sting of impact. "Fiona Daniels, if you're here, please let me know." Oh God, now I sounded like I was leading a séance.

She appeared on the other side of the low stone wall dressed in what she was wearing when I first saw her in real life. "Avery." Her forehead furrowed. "Have you got news for me?" She rubbed her throat.

I swallowed, well aware of what this would look like if anyone saw me. I kept my voice low. "No. I spoke to your husband. He seemed really nice, and he misses you."

"Really?"

Huh? "You sound surprised." The more I carried on this conversation, the more invested I was in the fact that Fiona could be a ghost. It certainly felt like I was talking to someone else.

"I didn't remember this before, but it came to me after I spoke to you last time. He hasn't been too happy with me lately. I've been working so hard, and we weren't spending quality time together. We'd had a few arguments." Cat's bum. If only I'd brought my notebook and pen. I had my phone, but I didn't want the screen light to give me away. I'd just have to remember it all.

"But you don't think he killed you, do you?"

"I don't think so." She stared past me, as if thinking about it.

The hair on my nape stood. I glanced around. No one else was out here, and no one was watching from the windows of the terrace next to Mrs Crabby's. Finnegan lived there, but whether he had the whole place, or it was split into apartments like this building, I didn't know. In any case, it seemed the coast was clear. The last thing I wanted was for Finnegan to see me here. He'd want to know why. There was no way I was letting that competitive smooth-talker find out any of my information.

I looked back at Fiona. "Can you tell me anything else about your life that I wouldn't be able to find out via the internet? Something so I know that I'm really talking to Fiona the ghost, and not just making up this whole thing?" I was leaning more in the "yes there are ghosts" camp than before, but if I could get one more piece of information, it would make it undeniable rather than a coincidence.

Fiona touched the skin at her décolletage. "Oh, I know. I have a locket—I don't wear it because I'm not really a jewellery person—it just gets in the way when I'm doing things, and I don't want to lose it. But it's at home in the top drawer of my bedside table. It has a picture of me with my brother and sister when we were little. I'm on one side, my sister is on the other, and my brother is in the middle."

"Okay, great." How could I confirm this without going back to her husband? I didn't want to upset him by asking, and if it wasn't true, he was going to wonder why I asked. If it was true, he'd probably wonder how I knew. Maybe I could ask one of her siblings, if they ever returned my calls, and say her husband showed it to me. Hmm….

Her brow wrinkled. "I have to go now. Will you come and see me again? Will you let me know if they find my killer?"

"Yes, I will. Is there anything else you can remember?"

She frowned and rubbed her throat again. "No. That's it."

Before I could say goodbye, she disappeared. I tilted my head back and stared at the sky. Clouds had moved in, and twilight was fading. At least I had another direction to travel in the hunt for clues. I still wanted to find her killer because I didn't feel safe; plus finding her body made me feel close to her. No, I hadn't known her in life, but being there in death forged a link between us I couldn't quite articulate. Whether I'd been talking to her ghost or not, I'd developed—at least in my mind—a relationship with her, and I needed to find answers to what happened to her. And maybe this was also for all the women and girls I'd reported on in the past, victims of violence, not all of whom saw justice. This was me trying to do my little bit.

As for the article, if this turned out to be nothing but me

being, well… me… I could drop the article about her murder investigation and just write a piece about how nice she was and what a loss to the community that she'd died.

But I had to admit—I didn't want to let Finnegan win.

Except, if this all turned to nothing, that's exactly what would happen.

# CHAPTER 8

My trip to see "Fiona" had set my brain into overdrive. As a result, it had taken ages to fall asleep, so I was more than happy that Meg had wanted a late start. I drove my rental into Exeter, Meg following in her slightly beat-up army-grey-green Land Rover. I handed the keys back at the rental office and hopped into Meg's car, which was surprisingly comfortable on the inside. I'd expected it to be tattier, but the leather seats were immaculate, as was the rest of the interior.

She smiled. "Let's do this."

I returned her smile. This was what I'd come here for—soaking up the atmosphere of a new place, a place with the depth of European history that Australia lacked—the old buildings, cobbled streets, the aesthetic. The only thing I wasn't sold on was the weather. I didn't mind a bit of cold, but we were in early summer, and today was only going to be fifteen degrees Celsius. Oh well, nothing was perfect. At least it hadn't rained since I'd arrived, which, from everything I'd researched, was a win. I'd take it.

We started at Exeter Cathedral, a gothic Anglican church with an imposing façade. Rows of statues carved out of stone and inset into the front of building looked like chess pieces. A massive archway fanned out above them, inset with colourful stained glass. Inside, crowds of people milled about, more than I would've expected, although it was Saturday. Maybe people were looking for things to do. As we wandered around, more than the intricate, expansive ceiling caught my interest. I whispered to Meg, "Why are they dressed in period costume?"

"Ah... dressed in period costume? Who?"

Oops. My crazy was showing. "Um, no one. I made a mistake. That woman over there looked like she was wearing an old dress." I gazed at a middle-aged woman with long brown hair in a plait down her back. Her purple dress was kind of flowy. It could be an *honest* mistake.... Probably not, but it was all I had. Why did these apparitions look exactly the same as real people? Maybe there was a tell I was missing? If there was one, I hoped I would find it before I made a mistake so obvious that I wouldn't be able to explain it away. I wasn't going to mention the woman in an olive-green corseted dress that covered everything except her face and hands. I was pretty sure she wasn't visible to normal people since no one was looking at her, which they would've been doing because of her out-there dress.

Meg cocked her head to the side. "Kind of. They do some-times have re-enactments for special festivities, but not today."

"Cool." Argh, how lame of me. I was going to scare off my new friend before she truly became one. I didn't care about scaring off Finnegan, but this was different. My ex and I spent most of our time with his friends, not mine, and at times, I felt isolated. I didn't come halfway around the world to feel that again. As much as I wanted to embrace who I was—whether that was a person who could see ghosts or a person who had halluci-nations—I didn't want to end up friendless and lonely. If they really were ghosts, I'd figure it out, but if my parents were right, and they were a figment of my imagination, I'd seek professional help. I shuddered. Last time they'd made me visit a psychiatrist, it had done nothing but seen me drugged up to my eyeballs and depressed, yet the apparitions hadn't disappeared. *Please be ghosts.*

I shook off my misgivings—because this was a day to enjoy—and we visited a park, then grabbed lunch at a café. On our way home, my phone rang. I pulled it out of my bag. Ooh, it was Fiona's sister. I glanced at Meg. "Sorry, I have to take this. Been waiting for this call… for work."

"Go right ahead, lovely."

"Thanks." I answered it. "Hello, Avery Winters speaking."

"Hi, Avery. I'm Alice, Fiona's sister. Just returning your call."

"Hi, Alice. Thanks so much for getting back to me. I'm sorry about Fiona." I slid my notebook and pen out of my bag.

There was a pause before she spoke. "Thank you. I appreciate it. We're all a bit stunned at the moment."

"I can't imagine how shocking and difficult this is for you, out of the blue like that."

"Yeah. She was the healthy outdoors type. Didn't smoke, had the occasional glass of wine." So, the police hadn't told them yet. Had Sergeant Bellamy made an assumption before he had the facts? He was an experienced policeman, so he could probably deduce certain things from observing the scene, but, still, that's what forensics was for—proving beyond a reasonable doubt. He wouldn't have said anything to Finnegan if he wasn't sure, would he? And if he was sure, why hadn't they made that clear to the family yet?

I jammed my phone between my chin and clavicle so I could write. "As I explained in my message, I'm doing an article on Fiona and what an asset to the community she was. What kind of sister was she?"

Sadness and fondness thickened her voice. "She was always

there when I needed her, except when she was working. She loved her job, and don't get me wrong, if there was an emergency, she put her family first. When we were growing up, she was always so much fun. We hung out a lot together until we both got married, and she got into her career."

The moment of truth. Nerves pitter-pattered in my stomach. "Her husband showed me a locket she treasured. The photo of you both with your brother was just adorable." I held my breath.

"I have one too. We bought them on the same day. But she didn't wear hers much—she was scared to lose it. I never take mine off. That picture was taken when I was six and she was four. Our little brother was only two. Mum had to lie on the ground behind him and hold him in place so they could get the shot." She sighed. "Those were the days when things weren't so complicated."

My stomach somersaulted. I breathed out and grinned—this was the proof I needed! My heart beat faster. I really had been talking to ghosts. This changed everything. My stupid parents were wrong, and I was right. And, yes, that felt as satisfying as it should, but also frustrating. So, what did it mean for me? What was I supposed to do with this ability? Did I have it for a reason, or was it a fluke and something to ignore? Not that I could. I mean... ghosts existed! I shook my head slowly, then realised no one had spoken for a while. I banished my smile so it wouldn't sound in my voice. "Thanks for sharing that. Was she close to your children?"

"She used to be. The last year, we haven't seen her much because we've both been busy, but she's my oldest daughter's godmother. My kids love her. They're going to miss her, as will we all." Her voice faded to an almost whisper at the end.

I had no more questions—anything else would be too intrusive, especially since the police hadn't confirmed she was murdered. And really, at this point, I didn't know for sure either

—although it was pretty safe to assume since young, healthy women didn't often drop dead out of the blue, and Bellamy had told Finnegan she was killed. "Well, thank you for your time, Alice. I really appreciate it."

"That's okay. When will the story run? I'd love to grab a copy of the article when it's out."

"I'll text you with that when I know. It should be on the internet as well as in print."

"Great, thanks." A child called out, "Muuuuuum," in the background. "I have to go. Cheers."

"Bye." I hung up and put my phone back in my bag, then finished writing the notes and placed my notebook and pen in the bag too.

Meg put her blinker on and turned the corner. "Is that about that estate agent, Fiona Daniels?"

"Yep. I'm doing an article on her. Did you know her?"

"Not well. My dad sold his house through her. She seemed nice enough, and she got him a good price. Not much else to tell, really."

"Cool." So if she was so nice, why would a random stranger or an acquaintance kill her? It must be someone she knew well, and whilst I'd initially ruled out her husband, I put him back on the list. He was the most obvious choice at this stage. Maybe he thought she was spending too much time with others or at work and not enough with him?

The Land Rover lurched, rocking me side to side, as Meg drove into a pothole in front of the pub driveway before turning into the car park and sliding into the spot reserved for management near the back door.

My phone rang again. The mobile number wasn't one I recognised, so I let it go to voicemail. If it was legit, they'd leave a message. Meg looked at me, eyebrows raised. "Trying to avoid someone?"

"No. I didn't recognise it." My phone dinged with a message. "There you go. They left a message. I'll listen to it." I called my voicemail.

"This is Julian here. I have a story I want you to cover today. Get back to me." He hung up without saying goodbye. Man, I hated that. How hard was it to complete the conversation properly?

"It's the boss. Have to call him back."

"I'll see you inside when you're done." Meg smiled and hopped out of the car. I got out, too, so she could lock it.

"Sounds good." I pressed the red number on my missed-calls list as she went inside. "Hi, Mr MacPherson. You said you had a story for me?"

"Hello, Winters. Call me Julian. And yes. Billy O'Connor's mouse had pups—the mouse kind."

I laughed. "I figured. That would be a story and a half if it were the dog or seal kind."

"Indeed. I'll text you the address. If you could get there in the next fifteen minutes, I'd appreciate it. Mrs O'Connor has to go out shortly."

"How far away is it?"

"Walking distance from the pub. Should take you about seven minutes on foot."

"I'd better get to it, then."

"I'll call her and let her know you're on your way. Good luck."

"Ah, yeah, thanks." He hung up before either of us could say goodbye. Jebus, this guy was a premature hanger upper. I wondered if it spilled over to any other areas of his life.

I hurried into the pub and found Meg in the bar area. She tried to hand me a beer, but I put my hand up to stop her. "I'm so sorry. I have to interview Billy O'Connor about his new mice babies. I'll be back in about half an hour. Is that okay?"

"Of course. I'll drink this one. I'll get you a new one later." She winked. "See you soon."

"Bye." I walked out the front door. At least I had everything I'd need—phone for recording the conversation and taking photos, and the backup notepad and pen. When it was nothing stories like this, people didn't care if you recorded them—I'd still ask, of course, but it wasn't like they were giving me information that was going to make them a target of the mafia or anything.

With the help of my map app, I found the O'Connor house easily, and it only took six minutes. When I knocked on the door, a short, skinny woman answered. She wore a sleeveless blue dress with huge pockets at the hips. "You must be Avery." She smiled.

"I am. Lovely to meet you, Mrs O'Connor."

She waved as if swatting a fly from in front of her face. "Don't be so formal. You can call me Rose."

"Okay, Rose. Thanks."

"Come in." She stood aside to let me pass. "Billy's in his room—the second door on the left. Go straight through."

The first thing that hit me when I opened the door was the stench. I gagged, several times. Today had been warmish, so I didn't even have a jacket to cover my nose. I used my bicep instead.

Billy jumped up from his bed. "Are you the reporter come to do the story on me?"

I smiled, then remembered he couldn't see that through my arm. Reluctantly, I moved my arm away from my face. "I sure am, Billy. I'm Avery. So, what have you got for me?"

"Nuffin. But I can show you my mice."

I looked at the ground for a second to compose myself before looking up again. "Great. Let's see them."

He swept his arm towards his bed like an excited game-show model. I scanned the covers, then squinted and leaned forward. "Is that them there, those little pink things on that tissue?"

He nodded vigorously. "Yep."

I moved to the bed. "Wow, seven. Is that a lot?"

He shrugged. "I dunno, but it's the same as my age."

I took out my paper and pen. This wasn't going to be that complicated—notetaking would suffice. I wrote what I knew so far. "Well, that's cool. Is this the first time your mouse has had babies?"

"Yep. And you shoulda seen her before. She was so fat, like old Miss Perkins next door. I got in trouble from Mum when I asked Miss Perkins if she were having seven babies too."

I licked my bottom lip and jammed my lips together to keep from laughing. I bet that had gone down well. "What's the mum mouse's name?"

"Pebbles."

"Have you named the babies yet?"

"Nup. They all look the same. Mum said we should wait till they're a bit bigger."

"How long have you had Pebbles?"

He put a finger up to his cheek, thinking. "Um.... About a month, or maybe two." His face scrunched up, as if he were straining on the toilet. "It might be three. I don't really know."

I held in my sigh. So helpful. I'd just make it up. "Where's the daddy mouse?"

"The cat ate him." He was awfully matter-of-fact about it.

"Oh. That's sad." I wrote some notes. *Kid might be a future serial killer.* Was I being too harsh, or would I be back here reporting on his killing spree in ten years?

He shrugged. "We all die. Nothing to get upset about. When Gran died, Dad said it was about time. He was really happy when he bought the new car."

Oh, jeeze. What the frick was I meant to say to that? I slid my phone from my bag. "Why don't I get a photo of the mice and then one of you with them?"

He grinned. "Yeah!"

I got close to the mice and clicked off a couple of photos, then stood back. "Why don't you sit next to them, put your face close, and look up at me and smile." He did as I asked, and I took two shots. I checked them to make sure his eyes were open and everything looked okay. He had that forced grimace that kids tended to get when trying to smile for the camera, but it was kinda cute. "Looks like I'm done."

"Do you want to see the cat that ate the dad?"

I slammed my hand on my mouth to keep from spluttering a laugh. "Yeah, sure, Billy."

Billy took me to the living area, where a black-and-white cat with a fluffy tail sat on an armchair. "This is Pie."

"Hi, Pie. Let's get a picture of you." Mouse killer. I wondered how long it would be until the cat finished off Dad's offspring. I took two pictures of the cat.

Mrs O'Connor, who'd been following me but keeping a bit of a distance, clapped her hands once. "Right. Time to get going, Billy. We're going to Great Aunty Sonia's."

He looked at his mum. "But she smells funny. Do we have to?"

She gave him a "shut up or else" smile. "Yes, darling, we do." She looked at me. "Lovely to meet you. I'll show you out." As we walked to the door, she asked, "When will it be in the paper?"

"I have no idea. I'll let you know. Hopefully early next week, or maybe tomorrow? Who can say?"

"Oh." Her expression blanked for a moment. "Right. Bye."

"By—" The door shut in my face. What the hell was it with these people and their atrocious goodbye etiquette? I shook my head and stepped off the porch.

As I walked back to the pub, my phone rang again. Another number I didn't recognise. This time, I answered it. "Hello, Avery speaking."

"Hi, Lightning. Thought I'd let you know I've got the scoop."

Argh, Finnegan. "What flavour did you get?"

"What?"

"Chocolate is my favourite, but I don't mind a bit of choc chip and spearmint."

"Ha ha, very funny. So, aren't you curious?"

"Not really, but if you're desperate to tell me, go ahead. I bet you can't beat the story I just did."

"I bet I can. Julian is running with my article on Fiona Daniels."

"And?" I knew he would. I was the new girl on the block, and I hadn't even submitted anything yet. It was hard to win when you hadn't entered the race. I had time though. Once I settled into this town and workplace, Finnegan wouldn't know what hit him.

"She was murdered—strangled."

"Oh, that poor woman. Was it in my place?"

"They think so. They're still investigating, but at least we can print the article that says she was murdered. It's coming out on the net this afternoon and will be in tomorrow's paper."

"Well, congrats on the bonus. You'll be living in a mansion before you know it." Silence. "Hello, are you still there?"

"Yes. Anyway, just wanted to let you know you can lay off your article. I won. Bye."

"Ah, yeah, sure, Vinegar. Bye." The call ended. At least he'd said goodbye, even if he was being a jerk before that. I supposed no one was all bad. Saying goodbye was his good point. One was better than none.

Funnily enough, I didn't feel disappointed, and I still wanted to research what had happened to Fiona. If I could find out who killed her before the police did, maybe I'd still get that article. I also wanted to submit the piece on what she meant to her family and work colleagues, and the community. Her family deserved that. *She* deserved that. If MacPherson wanted that to be one of my small pieces, so be it. It didn't make it any less important.

Back at the pub, I met up with Meg, had afternoon tea, then headed up to my room, excitement building within me. It was time to write an article—something I hadn't done for a few months. After being hit by lightning and going crazy, I'd lost my job. Those first few weeks of learning to live with my invisible friends had been hell. To avoid them, I'd stayed in bed with my eyes closed, and even then, they'd found me—they'd stand in my room, chatting away. But now that I'd come to terms with who I was, and that ghosts existed, I could handle work.

At least I thought I could.

It was time to find out.

# CHAPTER 9

I spent Saturday night writing my article on mouse boy and researching more into Fiona. I delved deeper into the agency website. Five agents worked there, not including the boss—one woman and four men, one of whom had a particularly smarmy grin in his headshot. Had one of them killed her? But why would they? Jealousy at how good she was?

Scrolling further led me to a recent article on their site. Fiona had won best sales agent for the month... and it seemed, every month in the last twelve. I would imagine that peed off her colleagues. I made some notes in a larger notebook I used when I was on the net. My smaller one was good for when I was out and about, but this was more practical for swathes of information. When I'd discovered all I could, I called it a night. I'd have plenty of time to research more in the coming days.

After a good night's sleep, the best I'd had in ages, I emailed my mouse-boy story to Mr MacPherson. My instincts told me it was a good enough story—considering the subject matter—but who knew how picky this guy was. It sometimes took a while to figure out what the editor wanted from you. Some loved stuff I hated, and some hated the stuff I was sure was good. Go figure.

I went downstairs for breakfast. Meg wasn't around—she was probably making the most of her time off—but an older man with salt-and-pepper shoulder-length hair pulled into a ponytail was clearing off one of the breakfast tables. His white short-sleeve collared shirt was open to the second button, a smattering of grey chest hair peeking out. That must be her father.

Not wanting to be rude, I went and said hello before I raided the buffet table. "You must be Mr Fisher."

He smiled, his brown eyes lighting up, multiple lines fanning out from their corners. I didn't know the man, but I would bet he was cheeky. "Hello. You must be Avery, our esteemed guest, misplaced by a dead body." He chuckled.

What could I do but laugh? So I did. "I am, and you would be right."

"Are you worried your flat will be haunted when you go back?"

I smiled and shrugged. "No. Ghosts don't bother me, except maybe in the way of past mistakes."

He nodded sagely. "Like ghosts of boyfriends past, you mean?"

"Exactly."

"I wish my wife would haunt me. It was the worst day of my life when she died." He frowned. "I think I travel everywhere because I miss her and I'm trying to distract myself. Although, I do enjoy the travelling, I suppose. But I'm lonely. It hasn't been the same since she left this world." His eyes watered; then he looked at me and blinked, his eyes widening as if he hadn't meant to share all that.

"Oh, that's sad. I'm sure she's hovering around somewhere nearby, or maybe waiting in another place for you. Not that you should hurry to see her." Oh, God, what if he took that to mean he should off himself. Yikes. I needed to watch my mouth. Why did people have to overshare with me?

"Maybe. Well, love, I'd best get back to this, or Meg will kill me." He turned and carried the dirty plates out of the room.

"And I'd best have breakfast before my stomach eats itself."

When I sat to eat, the ghost I'd met earlier sat opposite me. "Morning, Avery. Are you enjoying your stay here?"

I glanced around. Mr Fisher hadn't returned yet, so I could risk whispering, but I tried mental telepathy first. Maybe ghosts could pick up on thoughts. *I am, thank you.*

Her forehead wrinkled. "Did you hear me, child?"

Apparently they couldn't. Oh well. I whispered, "Yes, thank you. What's your name?"

"Mary Fisher. I'm Meg's grandmother."

If only I could tell Meg. I'd bet she would love to talk to her via me, but, of course, I'd never tell her. I had a clean start here that I did not want to ruin. "Why are you still here?"

She turned her head, looking around, then back at me. "I love to see how they're all going, and I have no interest in finding out what's on the other side. My daughter stops by once in a while too." Did she mean Meg's mother?

I had to remind myself to whisper. "Did you die in your fifties? You don't look very old."

She looked at her hands, then moved her fingertips over her face. "I can't remember, but that rings a bell. The last memories I have from my first life are burning up with fever, delirious. It matters not anymore. I'm here now."

"Yes, you are." And I wished you weren't because someone was going to notice me talking to you and think I was nuts. "I can't talk to you anymore. Sorry."

Her smile radiated amusement, and she disappeared. I breathed out my relief. I was going to have to learn to ignore my otherworldly visitors because eventually I'd make a mistake I couldn't explain.

After breakfast, I went for a walk, more for exercise than anything. Usually towards the end of the high street, I turned left to head towards Mrs Crabby's, but today, I decided to keep going. The road out of the village rambled up a gradual incline. On the way down, the vista opened to my left—rolling hills, a scattering of trees, and in the distance, squares of fields delineated by lines of fencing and dotted with sheep.

Ah, the gorgeous English countryside. Heaven.

To my right, a six-foot stone wall followed the road. The line of a green hedge was just visible over the top of it. There must be something grand hidden behind there. As I passed the ornate black gates affixed to stone pylons, I glimpsed a huge two-storey home at the end of a meandering driveway. Trees blocked most of my view of the structure.

I considered who might live there. Chances were, I hadn't met them yet, but if I had, I would think it was Mr MacPherson. He was likely the richest person out of my new acquaintances. Lucky him. Money, as far as I was concerned, was a means to an end, not an end in itself. I'd love to have money, but just so I didn't have to worry about paying the bills and being on top of where every cent went. It'd also be nice to help other people. If I were ever rich, I'd be a philanthropist. Ha, a grand goal for someone who would be lucky to ever just buy her own flat. Oh well, I had my health… and my life. If that nurse hadn't been nearby when the lightning hit, I wouldn't be walking along this road right now.

My stroll took me another fifteen minutes up the road. Such gorgeous countryside. I was in love.

"Why are you smiling?" A guy, aged maybe eighteen or nineteen, stood next to a large tree, his expression curious. He wore black jeans and blue shirt, the jeans those low-crotch ones that made guys look like they had ridiculously short legs and long bodies. I never could get onboard with that look.

"Just enjoying the day."

I would've kept walking past him, but his expression changed. His forehead wrinkled, and he rubbed the back of his neck. "I'm Patrick. I've been here for a long time, and I can't seem to leave. I was hoping you could help me."

Huh? Maybe I should be running away? I pulled out my phone, in case I needed to simultaneously run and call the police. "What do you mean, you can't leave?"

"Every time I walk away, I get about half a mile in any direction; then I'm stuck."

I raised my brows. I looked around. We were alone. Maybe I should just turn around? If I tried to make a run for it, it might aggravate him. He could be mucking around, but I didn't think so. But then again, I didn't know this guy from a bar of soap.

"I can tell you don't trust me. I won't hurt you. I promise. I'm just... stuck. Can I just walk with you and see?"

I sighed. It wasn't like I could stop him walking with me. At least he'd asked. I shrugged. "I s'pose so. I'm heading back to the village."

His smile reeked of relief. "Thanks. Maybe if I'm with someone, I'll get through."

I turned and started the journey back. "Do you live in the village?" Was he maybe a ghost? He was certainly acting strangely enough.

"Nah, the next one—Cramptonbury. I live there with my parents and sister... or used to."

"What's your last name?"

"Smith." A popular name. Something my brain could easily come up with. Yes, I now believed in ghosts, but it wouldn't hurt to ask. Old habits and all that—not that the habits were that old. It was taking time for me to adjust to this different reality.

"Are you a figment of my imagination?" Although now the question was out of my mouth, I realised how stupid it was. It wasn't like you couldn't lie to yourself. I gave a small self-deprecating laugh.

He laughed too, but more the amused kind. "No. Although, things have been strange lately. My brain feels fuzzy. I have trouble remembering things, and like I said, I've been stuck here for ages."

"How long?"

"I have no idea."

"Are we talking hours, days, weeks?"

He shrugged.

"Well, if you're not a figment of my imagination, and you've been here for days or weeks, you would've died of thirst by now and be emaciated. I mean, you're slim but not skeletal."

He looked down at himself. "True. Maybe I just feel like I've been here for ages?"

We walked for a bit without speaking. Patrick stared into the distance. "We're getting close."

"To where you can't keep going?"

"Yeah."

I was careful to watch him as we went. Sure enough, between one step and the next, he disappeared. I walked a few more paces, stopped, and looked back. He was gone. I gazed around, turning full circle. Gone. Might as well see if he reappeared if I headed back into his zone.

When I reached the point he'd disappeared, he reappeared. "See. I can't go further. And then I couldn't see you. And it looks weird. Everything here is clear, but beyond that line, I can't see people, and everything is faded, washed out."

I scratched my forehead. This was new. I mean, that old guy —who I now could assume was a ghost—had travelled with me from the airport to the hotel and to the estate agents. That had been a fair distance—a few hours of driving. Maybe it was just random and different for each spirit?

I met his gaze. "I'm sorry, but I don't have any answers. When I crossed that line, I couldn't see you either."

His eyes shone. Was he about to cry? "Please don't leave me."

Oh, cat's bum. I swallowed a gelatinous blob of guilt. *Come on, Avery. Even if he's not alive, he deserves some help.* But how would standing here with him for eternity help him? Sadness lodged in my chest. "I'm sorry, but I can't stay here."

"Will you come back soon? Please? I'm scared."

Crap on a stick.

"Okay. I'll come back tomorrow."

"Promise?"

"Promise."

"What's your name?"

I smiled. "Avery."

"Thanks, Avery. I'll see you tomorrow."

I gave Patrick a sad smile. "Yeah, see you tomorrow."

I turned and headed back to the pub, my smile a distant memory. If only the gorgeous English countryside was enough to heal me. Unfortunately, it appeared as though it wasn't. Was I destined to run into ghosts every five minutes? And what was I supposed to do about their problems when I could barely keep my own life in check?

I sighed. Whatever complaints I made to myself, I would still research Patrick Smith and see what I could do, out of curiosity and duty. It was hard to say no to a person in need, even if they were already dead. If I added that to the research on Fiona's case, I probably didn't have a lot of time to waste strolling about the countryside. I really had no idea what I was doing, but I'd jump in anyway.

My parents had always said I was good for nothing. Now it was time to prove them wrong.

# CHAPTER 10

Monday morning, and I was at my desk at 8:00 a.m. I'd had my coffee at the pub because after the highly emotional meeting with Patrick yesterday, stopping to get takeaway from that harpy was just too much. Not to mention the stress of everything that had happened since I'd arrived, plus the move itself. I really could do without the added antagonisation.

Finnegan and Carina arrived shortly after me. They both said good morning when they walked in. Carina's smile was friendly, and Finnegan's was bright—whether it was because he was genuinely happy to see me or he was gloating about the article, I couldn't tell. I'd have to assume the latter. It was an unfortunate reality that I often thought the worst of people. A side effect of being surrounded by people who often let me down or worse. I sighed.

Carina sat at her cluttered desk and looked over at me. "What's wrong, Avery?"

I smiled, hoping to deflect the scrutiny. "Oh, nothing. Just taking a moment. It's been pretty full-on since I arrived. Hoping things settle down soon."

Carina opened her mouth to say something when Mr MacPherson strode through the door carrying a newspaper. He stopped in the middle of the front of the room and held up the paper. "'Mysterious Murder in Manesbury.' Congratulations on the article, Walsh."

Finnegan grinned. "Thanks."

"And, Kelly, nice coverage of the Manesbury Needles get-together yesterday. Those old biddies just keep keeping on."

"Yes, they do." She smiled and pulled a yellow lump of knitted wool out of her bag and held it up. On closer inspection, it had little brown bobbles on it. "D'ey gave me dis tea cosy. Isn't it lovely!"

I smiled. "It's… nice."

MacPherson laughed. "It's ugly, Kelly. Chuck it."

She shook her head. "I won't chuck it. You don't t'row gifts away."

Finnegan and MacPherson shared a look that said they would both chuck it. *Argh, men.* MacPherson swivelled around and pointed at me. "And, you!" I started. Sheesh, a bit of warning would've been nice. "Your article on that snot-nosed kid with the mice was entertaining. 'Billy O'Connor Saves the Day after a *Cat*astrophic Mousacre.' Great first article. Looking forward to your next one."

I grinned. Getting that feedback warmed my heart. It was as if my shoulders had become lighter—part of the stress I'd been carrying evaporated. "Thanks, sir."

He waved his hand around. "Let's not be too formal. I know we're known for our stuffiness in England, but in this office, we call each other by our names. I know I've told you before, but I'll say it again: call me Julian."

I gave a tentative smile. I'd much prefer the clear delineation between boss and worker. "Ah... okay... Julian." It felt weird calling him that. We weren't best buddies, and I doubted we ever would be.

"That's better. Okay, team, time to get back to work. I need more articles." He cast an eye over Finnegan and Carina. "You both owe me two more each today." I blinked. Yikes. If they had to write a few a day, that would soon be in my future.

I put my hand up. "Excuse me."

MacPherson turned to me. "Yes, Winters?"

"Do you also get articles from out of office?"

"We do. I have journalists who do contract work, but we don't always need them. Just depends. It's also good for our residents to hear about things happening out of area. They all like to keep in touch. We also get a few articles from our other offices, and our front-page articles make it to their papers too."

"Okay, cool." That took some of the pressure off. I didn't see how three journalists could write a paper's-worth of articles every single day.

He clapped loudly, causing me to jump again. Cat's bum. I rubbed my sweaty palms on my skirt. After being hit by lightning, loud noises were not my friend. Even when I knew I wasn't in a dangerous situation, my body reacted. Stupid amygdala. That was everyone's lizard brain, the bit that made you react in a primal way. It was where one's fight or flight originated. I'd been trying to retrain it since the incident, but so far, I hadn't managed to fix it. "Have a fab day."

And then he was gone. Thank God.

Finnegan strolled over to my desk, sat on the edge of it, and looked down at me. I ignored the urge to lean closer to him and rolled my chair back instead and folded my arms. He raised a brow. "Scared of me, are you?"

I lifted my chin. "No. I don't like the way you smell." *Liar, liar, pants on fire.*

His brow furrowed, and he shook his head. "So, what are you working on today?"

"I'd prefer not to say."

"Why?"

"At my last job, some people tended to steal other people's ideas."

He held a hand over his heart. "Oh, how you wound me, distrustful maiden." He smirked. "I don't need to steal ideas—I have plenty of my own. I was actually going to offer you help." He stood. "But if you don't want it, fine."

"Thanks, but no thanks. I don't need it, and nor do I want it." Guilt kicked me in the shin—I wasn't trying to be difficult, but for all I knew, he was out to sabotage me. The last journalist who worked with them was encouraged to leave—I still wasn't sure if he quit or was actually fired—because he apparently "wasn't a team player." Maybe he was just sucked in by Finnegan's nice-guy act? Hmm, I wasn't really getting on with him right now either. There had to be a balance where I kept to myself but didn't annoy everyone. "Look, sorry. I just want to stand on my own two feet here. I appreciate your offer, but I'm fine." I crossed my fingers that he would accept that and back off —I wasn't about to spew my life story to these strangers.

"Give her a break, Fin." Carina smiled at me. "I get it, hon."

"Thanks."

Finnegan shuffled back to his own desk. "Okay, but if you need any help, just shout out."

"I will. Thanks." I gave him my most genuine fake smile, the one I used to get people off my back, the one I pulled out when I had to agree with my parents when I didn't agree. It was easier to pull out this smile and pretend everything was fine than it was to go against them. He cocked his head to the side, shook it, then turned away and sat.

Time to get to work. Thank God.

I checked my emails—there was one from MacPherson sending me two leads for small stories. I'd start on them later. Right now, I wanted to look up details on my friend from yesterday—Patrick Smith from Cramptonbury. My mouth dried, and adrenaline warmed my stomach as I put the details into the search bar.

The moment of truth.

I held my breath.

An article from two years ago popped up, a picture of a grinning Patrick filling the top half of my screen. I sucked in a breath and put a hand over my mouth. The caption said "Local teen, Patrick Smith, tragically killed in horror car crash just outside Manesbury."

Prickling heat needled my skin. I shook my head back and forth, back and forth. *No. Freaking. Way.* Yes, there were ghosts, but niggling fear that I'd jumped the gun on my no-longer-crazy self-assessment prodded me constantly. I read the article. Apparently Patrick—whose family in Cramptonbury was devastated—was driving with his mate to see another mate when the car lost control and hit a tree. Patrick's best friend, Colin, was driving and swerved to miss a fox. The road was wet, there was a tree, and, well, that was that. His friend swore he'd never forgive himself. Putting my shock aside, I let sadness seep in. So many lives destroyed by a fraction-of-a-second bad decision. Life could be so cruel.

Tears burnt my eyes at this third confirmation. *You can believe in yourself, Avery. You've totally got this.* I gave myself a mental hug at what my parents had put me through. *You didn't deserve it.*

Carina called out from her desk. "Are you okay, hon?" Both she and Finnegan stared at me.

I gave the wall at my left the side-eye before looking back at them. Cat's bum. I'd been too caught up in the situation to keep the reactions in check. Now what? "Um… I'm fine. Just read an article that resonated with me. That's all. Some teenager called Patrick who died in a car crash near here a couple of years ago." Here came the lies. I'd prided myself on being an honest person before, but hiding hallucinations, or ghost sightings as I now knew they were, so that people didn't think I was nuts all the time had required a level of dishonesty I was now finding easy. "A good friend of mine died in a car accident a few years ago too. It just took me back."

Carina's eyes held sympathy. "I'm so sorry, Avery. Do you need a hug?" She pushed her chair back, ready to rush over.

"Thanks, but it's fine. I'm fine." I gave her another of my fake smiles. There was no way I was opening up to these two. I needed this job if I didn't want to end up back in Sydney, knocking on my parents' door. What a nightmare that would be.

"Are you sure?" Carina was a persistent little peach.

I smiled, for real this time. It was nice that she genuinely seemed to care. "Yes. I'm fine. Definitely."

Finnegan, who'd been sitting forward, relaxed back into his seat. He gave a small nod and turned back to his computer. Carina gave me one final looking over, then smiled. "Okay, but if you ever need anyone to talk to, I'm here. I know you don't know anyone yet. My door is always open." She gestured to the lack of a door next to her desk.

I laughed. "Thanks."

Thankfully, everyone went back to work, the clatter of their keyboards a comforting drone in the background.

So, now what? Could I use information from ghosts to solve crimes and write insightful, hard-hitting articles?

With the possibilities and fear bubbling away inside me, I stood.

Was I about to get some real answers as to who killed Fiona Daniels, or would she still say she couldn't remember?

There was only one way to discover the truth. I flung my bag over my shoulder. "Just going out to do some research. See you both later."

"Good luck," they called out.

"Thanks."

I was going to need it.

# CHAPTER 11

I stood at Mrs Crabby's fence. The curtains at the front of her flat shifted. Busted. Would she come out and ask what I was doing? The front door opened. Yep. She limped down the two stairs from her small front porch. I waved. "Hi, Mrs Cr— Collins." Oops. That would've been fan-bloomin'-tastic if I'd called her Mrs Crabby. I wasn't sure where I could get new accommodation again on such short notice.

She made it to the fence. Was that deep divot in between her eyebrows always there? "What are you doing here? The flat's not ready yet."

I smiled, hoping to disarm her crankiness. "It's a lovely day for a walk, and I wanted to pass by, see if anything's changed."

She squinted and looked at the sky, then back at me. "It's not a nice day. It's cloudy, and it's going to rain." She rubbed her hip. "I have it on good authority. My arthritis always lets me know."

"Um, okay, well, it's not raining right now. Do you need anything?" Maybe she was cranky because her hip was sore. The least I could do was ask if she needed anything.

She scowled. "No. I wouldn't trust you young ones to do

anything properly. You're so irresponsible."

*Oh, wow, tell me what you really think.* "Oookay then."

"Now shoo."

I bit my lip and tried not to smile. What a funny old duck.

"Are you laughing at me? I don't take kindly to people making fun."

I cleared my throat and schooled my expression. "Certainly not. This is no laughing matter." Maybe a bit of truth would get rid of her? Might as well. What did I have to lose? *Only your accommodation,* the tiny bit of sanity remaining in my head answered. "I'm here to talk to Fiona's ghost, try and find out who killed her."

"Pfft. Stop taking the mickey. I'm not in the mood. Now move along. I don't want to see you back here until you actually live here." She waved me away with a shooing motion.

I sighed. If I stood here—because, really, she couldn't force me off public land—I was only going to antagonise her. Bummer. Looked like I wouldn't get any information from Fiona today.

"Hey, Marge, you being your usual stick in the mud, then?" I turned. A woman, roughly the same age as Mrs Crabby, exited from the front gate of one of the two houses across the dirt cul-de-sac. Her cute sandstone cottage had a thatched roof and dormer windows, and flowers crowded her front garden. So pretty.

"Get away with you, Josie. I don't have time for your nonsense."

Josie approached us, a huge grin taking up half her face. She looked like a troublemaker—my kind of person. Not that I was a troublemaker, but I could definitely appreciate that quality in others. A smile hijacked my lips, coaxed by her infectious joy. "Hi, Josie. I'm Avery. I'll be moving in here soon." I couldn't help encouraging her, knowing it would irritate the bejebus out of Mrs Crabby.

"Hello, love. I'm Josie Pringle, your neighbour from across the way. You moving in with this wet blanket?" For a short person, she had a loud voice.

I pressed my lips together to stop from laughing. "I'm moving upstairs, yes."

"You won't be moving anywhere if you encourage this nosey gasbag." I turned. Mrs Crabby's arms were tightly folded, and her expression was that of someone who'd just eaten a lemon.

Josie's laugh swirled around us. "Get over yourself, Marge. We could do with more young people around here. Some of us enjoy energetic company."

"Well, you can take your energetic company and go to your place. I've had enough." She huffed, turned, and hobbled back to her house. My mirth sank into the ground. Her arthritis was giving her hell. No wonder she was cranky.

When she shut the door, I looked at Josie. "Maybe we shouldn't be so mean. Her arthritis is playing up."

She waved a hand. "Pfft. It's always something. That woman would be cranky about winning the lotto; trust me. I used to offer to help her, but a person can only take so many rejections." She waved her hand. "Leave her to her crankiness, I say. You know, you remind me of my granddaughter. She's a solicitor in London and a genius on the guitar. She comes to visit every now and then, but she's so busy, so it's not nearly as much as I'd like. I do miss her. What about your family, Avery? You're from Australia, no? Do you have any brothers or sisters?"

I couldn't tell if she was a chronic oversharer or it was my influence, but I wasn't going to reciprocate. "Yes, I am. I flew here the other day. My family is back there." Thank God. "I have a younger sister."

"Oh, well, if you're missing them, pop by, and I'll make you a cuppa."

"That's so sweet of you. Thank you." Hmm, if that was the

only time she wanted me to pop by, she'd likely never see me.

She smiled. "I'm the neighbour who's willing to help if you need it." She winked.

I grinned at her Mrs Crabby dig. "Thanks. I will. I guess I better be going. I don't want to lose my flat before I even get to live there."

"Okay, love. See you soon."

I waved and wandered back down the hill. Okay, not a total waste of time—Josie seemed nice. In any case, I'd have to come back tonight.

My phone rang. What did Finnegan want? After his call the other day, I'd put him into my phone under Vinegar PITB (pain in the bum). "Hello." I kept my tone as uninterested as possible.

"What are you doing hanging around Mrs Collins's, or are you stalking my place hoping to get a glimpse of me?"

"You're an idiot. You're not even home. If I want to ogle you —which I don't—I could just sit in the office." I wanted to know how he knew I was here, but I didn't want to give him the satisfaction of me asking.

"That's what they all say. So, why are you there?"

"None of your business. Bye." I hung up. He was the last person I'd confide in. I definitely couldn't trust him. He was probably trying to steal information on the murder. It was flattering that he probably thought I knew more than he did. Hmm, maybe I should go chat to the police, see if they had any new information. There was always next week's bonus to shoot for, and I hated to admit that I wasn't getting very far with my own hunt for the murderer. Hmm, I didn't have a car anymore. Another thing to add to my list, not that I could afford one right now.

Time for Plan B. I hurried to the pub. I had intended to ask Meg's brother or dad where she was, but she was behind the bar. "Hey, Meg. Back at work already?"

She smiled. "Hey, you. Yes. Dad's still here, and I was going to catch up with a friend, but she's sick, and I was bored, so…" She looked around the room. "Here I am."

"I was wondering if I could ask a favour."

"You can ask, but I don't know if I'll do it." She chuckled.

"Very funny. I hate asking, but I was wondering if you could give me a lift to Cramptonbury police station."

Her smile fell. "What happened? Is everything okay?"

"Yes, yes, fine. I'm just working on a story. I wanted to ask Sergeant Bellamy a couple of questions."

"Of course I can give you a lift. I'd love a reason to get out of here." She called out, "Bailey, I'm off. Bye."

Within a few seconds, he appeared at the door to the rear hallway. As soon as he saw me, he smiled. "Hey, Avery."

I returned the smile. "Hey."

Meg looked at both of us and grinned. "Look at you two, getting to know each other." She waggled her brows.

I rolled my eyes. "Ha ha, very funny."

"Shut up, Meg." Bailey looked less than impressed.

Her grin had me shaking my head. I had no idea what she was implying, but I wasn't going there. Nope. Solo all the way. Thankfully, she hurried out from behind the bar. "Come on, then."

As we made our way past Bailey to the car park behind the pub, Bailey gave me an apologetic look. I smiled. Okay, so he was cute, but still. Men were a problem I could do without. My life was a kiddie pool full of wee as it was.

Meg chatted the whole way to the station. I put it down to her being excited to see someone who wasn't related to work. She pulled up outside a two-storey, cream-painted brick building. The Police Station sign out the front was a dead giveaway. I hopped out.

"I'll park just up the road. Come find me when you're done."

"Thanks. You're the best." When I finally got into my apartment, I'd bake her something yummy, like my lemon-drizzle cake, as a thank you.

Hopefully, Bellamy would give me some kind of information. At this point, I had almost nothing to go on. Fiona had practically begged me to find out who killed her. The least I could do was pass on the information if the police had figured it out. And if they hadn't, well, maybe I could discover who it was with her help.

I went straight to the unmanned front desk and rang the silver bell. Oh, look at that. It was attached to the countertop with a chain. A policewoman appeared on the other side of the protective glass. "Can I help you?"

"I was wondering if I could see Sergeant Bellamy."

"And who might you be?"

"Avery Winters. I wanted to see if he had any information on when I could move into my flat."

Understanding pinged on her face. "Oh, you're the one who found Mrs Daniels."

"Yep, that's me."

"Hang on a jiff." She picked up a phone on the counter and turned her back to me, muffling her words. *Dah de dah de dah. Waiting, waiting.* I crossed my fingers that he'd see me. He might just relay the message via this lady. She turned back around and hung up the phone. "He said he'll see you, but he doesn't have long." Story of my life.

"Yep, that's fine. Thanks."

She buzzed me into a door just to the side of the front desk. I followed her down the hallway to an open area of four partitioned desks. She took me to one of two half-timber- and half-glass-fronted offices at the far end of the room. The doors were dark timber grain. It was like being transported back to the seventies or eighties, not that I'd been alive then, but I'd seen the pictures.

The policewoman opened the door. "Here's Miss Avery for you, sir."

He gave her a nod. "Thank you, Constable." Bellamy sat behind a large, super-organised desk. A closed diary sat in front of him. A container of pens to his right, a three-tiered filing tray behind them, and a stapler to his left were the only things on the tabletop. Two four-drawer grey filing cabinets huddled in the corner behind him, and two framed certificates hung on his wall. He gestured to one of the two brown vinyl chairs in front of his desk. "Please sit, Miss Winters." I was sensing a theme here. *The ants go marching two by two, hurrah, hurrah.*

I sat, regretting that I didn't have baked goods to give him. I so needed to get into that flat ASAP, or how was I going to bribe people into giving me information? "Thanks for seeing me, Sergeant."

"I understand you're keen to get into your flat."

"Yes. Any news?"

"We're finished with it as of this afternoon. The cleaners will be in tomorrow morning. I would check with Mrs Collins before you go round there, but you should be right to move in tomorrow afternoon."

I smiled. "Thank you so much!" Living in limbo in the pub wasn't the end of the world, but it wasn't great. I still hadn't unpacked all my stuff because I couldn't be bothered packing it all back up again, so I'd worn the same clothes to work today as I had on Friday, and I'd slummed around all weekend in the same T-shirt and jeans. I tilted my head to the side and tried to appear as harmless and cute as possible. "You've been so kind, keeping me up to date. When I get in there, I'd love to bake you something. What's your favourite cake?"

He picked his stapler up and clicked it several times. "There's no need to do that. Just doing my job."

"Oh, no. I want to." I smiled.

"Well, if you insist. I love a good tart…. Apple is my favourite." He laughed at his own terrible joke.

I laughed, too, because I wanted to get in his good books. Pretending was all part of the job. "Excellent. When you least expect it, I'll turn up with one." I conjured a surprised expression, as if I'd just remembered something. "Oh, before I forget. I'm doing an article on Mrs Daniels—a celebration of her life kind of thing—and I was wondering if there was anything you could add about what happened to her. Just so I could put something sympathetic at the end." Was that even believable? I was so out of practice. Maybe I'd get lucky, and he'd give me a morsel. The excuse he'd given Finnegan for spilling info might have been legit, or he might just like to feel more important and was willing to give anyone information in exchange for the kudos.

He clicked the stapler a few times and leaned back in his chair, his expression serious. "I'm afraid we don't just give information out willy-nilly."

"Oh, sorry. I didn't know whether you had anything unclassified to give out. You know, even just something like you know where she was killed. She wasn't killed in my apartment, was she? Oh my God. If she was, I don't know if I could go back there. Do you think she'd haunt it?" I furrowed my brow and bit my bottom lip. "I'm going to have to find somewhere else to live, aren't I?" I thought about my long-dead dog, Bristles—so named because his short fur was, well, bristly. He'd been my constant companion until I was thirteen. He died because my father left the gate open, and he ran into traffic. I heard him telling Mum that he did it on purpose because he didn't want to pay the vet bills for a surgery he needed. Tears burned in my eyes and the back of my throat. He'd been such a beautiful dog. My dad sucked big time.

Bellamy's eyes widened, and he leaned forward. "Don't cry.

Don't worry. We think the murder was personal. Whoever killed her probably isn't going to come back. Don't quote me on that though—I'll deny I said anything. I just want you to not be worried about moving in."

I sniffled. "You're just saying that to make me feel better." I shook my head. "I don't know if I should believe you. Do you know if there's anywhere else I can rent that's cheap; otherwise I'm going to be homeless."

He frenziedly clicked the stapler, squished staples raining onto the tabletop.

I sucked in a breath. "What if the killer comes after me? Is it a serial killer?" I widened my eyes for full effect. It probably wasn't a serial killer, but it didn't hurt to ask. Maybe I'd pry some information loose.

His expression turned fatherly, but not friendly fatherly, more like "now listen here." "You have nothing to worry about, Miss Winters. One murder does not a serial killer make. I can't comment any further, except to tell you not to worry."

"But how do you know?"

*Click, click, click.* Staples fell. I bit the inside of my cheek to keep from smiling. Was he about to crack? A middle-aged man appeared, standing behind Bellamy's chair. He placed a hand on his shoulder and looked at me. "Stop giving my lad a hard time. He can't tell you anything. They don't know." The man's hair was slicked back on the top, the sides short, and his sideburns were epic. His police uniform was similar to what Bellamy wore, except he wore a blue shirt rather than a white one.

So, this must be another ghost—who knew there were so many?! Should I be scared? He didn't look evil, and I wasn't getting any bad vibes. Bellamy shivered, and he looked around. "Do you feel that?"

The temperature had dropped slightly, maybe? I couldn't tell. Maybe I didn't feel it because I was busy seeing the ghosts and not paying proper attention? Although, I had felt it the day I visited Fiona with Finnegan in tow. "Not really. Are you okay?"

The ghost took his hand off Bellamy's shoulder. "Oh, that's better. It's gone." He shuddered. "As I was saying, Miss Winters, I can't pass on any information at this time." A knock sounded at his door. He looked past me. "Come in."

The policewoman who'd let me in stood in the doorway, her hand resting on the knob. "Mr Schmidt is here, sir."

"Good o, I'm just finishing up." He looked at me. "Miss Winters, good luck with your move." He stood. The ghost behind him gave a nod, as if to say, that's right. Off you go.

I pushed my seat back and rose. "Thank you for your time, Sergeant Bellamy. Good luck finding Fiona's killer."

He lowered his chin and kept his gaze on me in maybe a gesture of thanks, but he didn't say anything. I gave the police-woman a smile—you never knew when you'd need someone on your side, so I wanted to be as friendly as possible.

On the way out, I passed Fiona's boss. Was he here because he was offering information, or had they called him in? He gazed at me, recognition dawning. "Hello, Miss Winters."

"Hello, Mr Schmidt. How's everything going at work? How are you all coping?"

He rubbed the large bald patch on the top of his head. "We're okay. Business is still good. It's a scramble to cover Fiona's work, but we're getting there. Good day." Someone didn't want to chat. I took the hint.

Mr Schmidt waited for me to step out of the security door before walking through. The door clicked closed behind him, locking me out. I would've loved to have been a fly on the wall for that conversation, or maybe even a ghost. Scrap that. I didn't want to die. My life had only just begun.

# CHAPTER 12

That afternoon, my phone rang. Fiona's sister. I was in the office alone, so it was safe to take the call—Finnegan wasn't listening in, trying to steal my scoop. The less he knew about what I was up to, the better. "Hi, Alice. What can I do for you?"

"Hello, Miss Winters. Sorry to bother you. I hope you're not busy."

"Not really. If you have any news on Fiona, I'd be happy to listen. I went by the police station earlier, but they said they didn't have anything new to tell me."

"Well, that's sort of why I was calling. After they informed us it was a murder, they asked about Fiona's marriage. Fiona liked to think it was all going well, but she and Simon were having problems."

"Oh, I'm sorry to hear that." And even though I'd suspected as much from what Fiona said, Simon hadn't said anything when I'd visited, but then again, as if he was going to tell the journalist writing about his dead wife. It was private, and maybe relevant to her murder. "What kind of problems? Fi—" I coughed to hide my mistake. Yeah, Fiona told me that they hadn't been spending much time together lately. I shook my head at myself. *Idiot.* At least knowing I'd seen Fiona's ghost made things easier to understand. Although I didn't know what was worse—telling someone I was psychic or that I could see ghosts. I was going with ghosts.

"I... I'm not sure I should be telling you this, but I did tell the police, and they looked into it but said there was nothing to go on. Both people in this scenario have alibis, apparently."

I sat up straighter. This was getting interesting. "I promise to keep it to myself, but I will look into it."

"That would be good, thank you. I'd hate for this to be splashed across the newspapers. Do I really have your promise on that?"

"Yes. I won't put any of this in print... or on the internet." I wasn't about to break her confidence. "I'm happy to sign something if you like."

"No, no, that's fine. Right, well, I feel like I have nowhere to turn, and I can't afford a private investigator. I just want someone to take this seriously." I figured the police had taken her seriously, but I wasn't going to argue with her. "Fiona had proof that Simon was having an affair."

"Oh, wow. That's not good."

"No. She was upset and threw herself into work. She sent me a few emails she found between him and his mistress, Emily. Fiona confronted him about it, and he admitted it. He supposedly broke it off with the tramp. Fiona said he went to a couple of their counselling sessions but then decided he'd had enough. He promised not to do it again, but Fiona wasn't over it."

I frowned. How devastating for Fiona. Had she forgotten all this when she spoke to me, or did she not want me to blame Simon? She wouldn't be the first woman to protect an abusive or badly behaving husband. "So, you gave this to the police, and they said that Emily and Simon both had alibis for roughly the time Fiona was killed."

"Yes. They said that as far as they can tell, she was killed early the morning you found her."

"Oh." How had none of this come up before? Even Finnegan hadn't addressed this in his article. Looked like he either thought it was irrelevant or Bellamy hadn't told him. *Hmm.* Chances were good, then, that she was killed in my apartment. It would've been hard to carry a body into my flat in daylight with no one noticing, especially Mrs Crabby. This was a useful piece of information, considering Bellamy hadn't confirmed it when I'd visited him. Had the murderer gone there with her, or had they been waiting for her? I had to assume that the police had questioned all the neighbours and Mrs Crabby about whether they'd seen anyone coming or going. Did they have a lead, or had the person snuck into my flat before sunrise, knowing Fiona would show up for a walk-through before I arrived?

"So, will you help me? I want to find who killed my beautiful sister."

This probably wasn't a nice question, but I had to ask. "Why the hurry? The police will probably find who did this, even if it takes them a while. Forensics, technology, they're all helpful these days." Who knew, they might just find her leaving a premises with someone on security camera.

"Simon's booked to go on holiday next week after the funeral. They're releasing her body this Friday. We'll have the funeral on Wednesday next week. He flies out to America that Friday. I didn't know who else to turn to. My brother thinks I'm being stupid." She sighed, a bone-weary whoosh of air that blew away any hesitancy I might have had.

"So, we have just under two weeks to figure this out. I'll do my best. Do you still have a copy of those emails? Can you forward them to me and maybe let me know anything else Fiona told you in the email as well?"

"Yes. I can definitely do that. Thank you so much, Avery. I don't know why, but you seemed like the right person to ask, and you're so easy to talk to. I hope you don't mind me saying, but your voice is very calming."

"Um, thanks." Is that why people opened up to me? It was probably only part of it. Some people had resting B face; I had resting tell-me-all-your-problems face. "I'm just glad you felt you could talk to me."

She cleared her throat. "There was another reason I felt I should talk to you, but it might sound crazy."

I barked out a laugh. "I'm all about crazy. Trust me—whatever you have to say probably won't surprise me. My life has been all kind of weird lately."

"Fiona came to me in a dream. She told me to tell you. Said you could help."

"Right. It doesn't sound crazy at all. It might be Fiona, or it might be your subconscious. Whatever it was, here we are, and I'll do what I can. I'll call you if I find anything. If you don't hear from me for a few days, I'll call you on Friday and let you know how I'm going anyway."

"Okay. Thank you. I'll send you that stuff now."

I gave her my private email address. I didn't want it to get mixed up with work stuff and accidentally forward it to someone, not to mention that some workplaces monitored emails. This was my potential scoop if I managed to crack the case. I rolled my eyes. *Who do you think you are, Avery Winters? Sherlock Holmes?* "Chat soon, Alice. And thanks for trusting me."

"Bye, Avery." And that was that.

I gazed across the room to the windows. Daylight, and it would be for hours and hours yet. If only I could get into my unit now. The sooner I could speak to Fiona, the better, but I'd have to wait till it was dark. Stupid Mrs Crabby.

To fill in my afternoon, I'd work on my next small-article subject. I couldn't forget my other work, or I'd find myself without a job before the week was finished.

I pulled up my emails and opened the one from Mr Macpherson. He had two suggestions. *Eeny, meeny, miny, moe.* Okay, I'd go with the old lady whose blueberry pie looked like the Queen. This should be fun. As luck would have it, she was home when I called.

The ten-minute walk to her house was pleasant enough. The grey sky had been kind enough to keep its water to itself, despite Mrs Crabby's prediction. Note to self—buy an umbrella. I hadn't brought one with me from Sydney because I'd had enough to pack.

Ms Elders lived on a small acreage just outside the village in a single-level brick cottage that looked to have just been painted. Neat garden beds bordered the path from the street to the house, and fields spread out behind her abode.

When Ms Elders answered the door, she was not at all what I expected. About my height, she was rather rotund, and was maybe ten years older than me. Her ample bosoms looked like a pig had dived down her orange top, and its rear end was sticking out. Dimpled legs were on show beneath her thigh-length skirt. At least her orange stilettos were kind of cool…. She gave me a huge grin. "Are you here about me pie, then?" She practically hopped from foot to foot. People weren't usually this excited to see me.

I smiled. "I am. Lovely to meet you. I'm Avery."

"Please come in, Avery. I'm just so excited to 'ave you 'ere." She shut the door after me. "Come this way." She squeezed past me in the narrow hallway and glanced back as she walked. "Oh, you 'ave no idea 'ow surprised I was when I took the pie out the oven. I said to myself, it looks just like our dear Queen Elizabeth, it does. I knew I 'ad to tell someone. Things like this just don't 'appen to me, I tell you. They just don't."

We'd reached her homely country kitchen. I breathed in the heady aroma of freshly baked Queen Elizabeth pie. My mouth watered, reminding me I'd forgotten to have lunch. The white timber cabinets, dark bench tops, and a farmhouse sink gave the kitchen a real cosy ambiance.

Her stilettos clicked on the tile floor as she made her way to the island bench. "The pie's under 'ere." An orange tea towel with a lump under it sat in the middle of the island.

"I'm betting your favourite colour is orange."

Her mouth fell open. "'ow could you tell?"

"I'm psychic."

"Really?"

"No."

"Oh." Her hand hovered next to the tea towel. Her smile returned. "Ooh, I'm so excited. Are you ready for the big reveal?"

"Actually, I'll take a photo of the historic moment. Hang on a sec." I grabbed my phone from my handbag and brought up the photo app. "Okay. Drumroll…. One, two, three!"

"Ta da!" She whipped the towel off as if she were revealing a brand-new car. The pig's bottom wiggled, and I tried not to stare. It was oddly mesmerising.

Oh, I'd almost forgotten. *Click, click.* Photos taken, I lowered the phone and gazed at the blueberry pie. "Oh, wow, that really does look like the Queen." My brow tightened. "Um, did you do that on purpose?" The pie was in the shape of Queen Elizabeth's profile—there was even an eye. *Random my backside.*

"Well, yeah."

I blinked and held in my sigh. "I thought it was accidental."

"Well, it kinda was. I've tried before, maybe twenty times, and it didn't turn out. So, yeah, I wasn't expecting it."

*Jeeze Louise.* I took out my notepad and pen and wrote down the details. "How long did this take to make?"

"The shape took me forty minutes, but usually, it sags in the oven and looks more like a cow when it comes out. Honestly, this is a miracle. It *never* turns out."

"A miracle... yeah." Another dodgy article to add to my collection. So that made two stupid articles to zero good ones. *Yay, me.*

I asked her a couple more questions; then she offered me pie, which I declined. My appetite had disappeared, whether it was because of the pig's bottom bursting out of her top or the feeling I'd been had, I wasn't sure.

"When will you be featuring me?"

"I have no idea. Maybe tomorrow or the next day, probably."

She hopped from stiletto to stiletto and clapped. As annoying as this whole thing was, I couldn't help but smile—I'd made her happy. I'd look at it as my good deed for the day. "Thank you so much, Avery. And welcome to Manesbury. I 'eard you've recently arrived from Australia, the land of the long white cloud."

I rubbed my forehead. "Ah, thanks. That's actually New Zealand."

"Oh! Sorry. Well, in any case, welcome."

I smiled. "Thank you." Before she could start another conversation, I turned. "Best be going to my next appointment."

Her shoes clicked on the floorboards in the hall as she followed me to the front door. "'ave a nice day."

"You too. Enjoy eating the Queen."

She giggled. "Oh, I will."

I returned to the office, said hello to the receptionist without getting more than a grunt back, and sat at my desk. Finnegan was in. "Hello, Lightning. How's it going?"

"Not bad. I just met the Queen."

He cocked his head to one side. "*The* Queen or *a* queen?"

I chuckled. "A pie that claimed to be the Queen, or, rather, Ms Elders claimed that her pie looked like her."

"Did it?"

"Yes, it did, but it wasn't accidental."

He laughed. "Welcome to the exciting land that is Manesbury. People will say all sorts of things to get in the paper."

"I suppose it adds excitement to their lives. I shouldn't complain, really. Many of the stories I covered back in Sydney weren't nice. I reported on court results, domestic violence, the occasional lotto win, but it was usually serious stuff. This is... different."

He grinned. "Yes, it is. I used to work in London. Same kind of thing—violent crime, naughty politicians, all sorts of sordid and depressing things. For all its quirkiness, this job isn't that bad."

"I guess I'll get used to it, as long as no one decides they don't want me here and makes me leave." I narrowed my eyes at him. Might as well have this conversation now, considering what happened to the journalist I replaced.

He brought his hand to his chest and put on a shocked face. "I can't believe you think I'd do that."

"Am I wrong?"

He smirked. "Okay, got me. But the last guy was bad at his job, and he was rude to Carina. A real misogynist."

I didn't hide my surprise. "Right, well, maybe you're not so bad after all."

He smiled. "I'm sure I'm not... well, most of the time. Anyway, you're safe... for now." The grin he finished with exposed a dimple on one side of his face. I bit my tongue. *Stop enjoying how bloody attractive he is.*

"Great." I opened my laptop and got to work. After I'd

finished the article, I glanced at Finnegan. Good, he was working, paying no attention to me. Not that he could read minds, but I didn't want him even getting a hint that I had information on the murder that he didn't have.

I opened the email Alice sent.

*Hi Avery,*

*I've attached all the emails Fiona sent me. Maybe you can find some clues in there. I'm not sure if Simon killed her, and, honestly, I don't know if he's capable, but he certainly has motive—getting my sister out of the way. I think they each had a policy on the other. Not huge money, mind you, but maybe a hundred thousand pounds. And now that he's going away, it looks more than suspicious. I know Fiona never would agree to a divorce because she loved him. She hadn't forgiven him when she died, but she was working on it. If you think of any questions, let me know. Anyway, thank you for looking into it. I hope to hear from you soon.*

*Alice*

I read through the other emails she'd attached. My mouth fell open. Fiona had to have been gutted when she'd read these. Simon and Emily had been pretty graphic about what they wanted to do to each other. Simon's feelings towards this woman had been strong. Were they strong enough to entice him to kill his wife?

But how to figure it out for sure. I'd have to talk to Fiona, but I couldn't until tonight. Maybe I should go say hi to my other ghost friend—Patrick. Was there a reason I could see ghosts? And I didn't mean the hit-by-lightning thing. More, what was the purpose? Normally on TV shows, there was a bigger reason, like helping the ghosts somehow. Patrick did say that he couldn't leave where he was, and he certainly wanted to. Maybe I should try and help for no other reason than he was suffering.

Okay, I was officially crazy. Helping ghosts. This was so far out of my normal that I wasn't sure where to start.

I was a journalist. Maybe I should start there, ask him some questions, treat him as if he were alive. But he wasn't.

I shut down my computer and put it in my laptop bag. I'd drop all this at home on my way. I stood. "I'm off. See you later."

Finnegan mumbled something—he was intent on his work. *Whatever.*

I dropped my computer at the pub and speed walked to where I'd seen Patrick last time. He wasn't there, at least that I could tell. "Patrick, hello? Patrick, it's Avery."

After a minute, he materialised. "Ho, Avery. You came back! I didn't think you would."

I smiled. "Now that I'm comfortable with the fact that I can see ghosts, I decided I should try and help. Might as well go all in."

"Lucky for me. If I wasn't stuck here, in God knows where, I wouldn't believe in ghosts. But I think I am one. It's weird."

"What does it feel like?"

He stared up at the sky, likely thinking. Then he looked back at me. "Boring. Time doesn't move how it used to, though. And I don't feel hot or cold or hungry. I still feel happy or sad or scared, not that there's anything scary here, but sometimes it feels as if something bad is out there waiting for me. Everything looks like it used to look, except the bit past where I can't go. I don't sleep. I just exist in this little corner of Devon. And there's a heavy sense of... waiting."

"Hmm, interesting." It was... kind of. I'd never wondered what it was like to be a ghost since I hadn't believed in them prior to the whole lightning thing. Did this happen to everyone? Did you get stuck in one place forever, or was there something I could do for him to set him free? And then where did he go? Did it mean he could roam where he wanted like the old man who'd come with me from the airport to the estate agents? Or would he go to that old cliché—the light?

There was no way I was getting answers to any of that today, so best ask him some questions that could hopefully help. I made my way up the small hill behind the tree and sat. If I stood next to the road long enough, I'd end up like poor old Patrick. He came and sat next to me. "It's nice to have company though."

I smiled. "I'm glad. So, why do you think I can see you, and how can I help you? Those are the two questions I'd like answered today."

His eyes widened. "Do you think you can help me get out of here?"

I shrugged. "Who knows, but I'm hoping yes, or why else would I be able to see you?"

"Well, there's lots of things that exist for no apparent reason, so maybe you won't be able to help."

"Yes, jelly blubbers serve no purpose I can see, or marzipan, or horrible people. Let's not worry about that now. Is there something you need to tell someone? That's usually the way it works on TV."

He laughed. "So, you have no idea?"

My mouth quirked up on one side. "None. We still need to try though. Right?"

"Yes. To answer your question, I can see quite a few people when they pass by here, but they can never see me. It's like yelling at someone from underwater and behind glass. I know they don't know I'm there, and they look and sound kind of fuzzy, but you're clear to me. I thought you were dead when we first met, but then you kept going, past the barrier."

"I did die for a minute or two... I mean, not yesterday, but about seven months ago. I was hit by lightning, and a nurse brought me back. Since then, well...."

"You can see ghosts."

"Apparently. But I don't know what to do about them. Is there anything you wanted to say to someone? That seems like the simplest reason you're still here." Hopefully, falling back on clichéd TV show plots would work. If it didn't, we were both in trouble.

He picked at the grass, but nothing happened to it. Maybe the grass in his version of reality was tearing into pieces. His tone was subdued when he answered, "My best mate, Craig Archer. He was driving when we crashed. He's been back a few times, and he always cries. I know he feels bad for what happened, and while I was angry at first, I'm okay now. It was an accident. He wasn't even driving stupid or anything, maybe a bit fast, but not ridiculous." He shrugged. "I guess I want him to know it's okay..., that I've forgiven him. He was here last about three weeks ago, and I couldn't make him hear me." He clenched his fists, and a tear tracked down his cheek. "It's just so frustrating."

I swallowed the lump in my throat. So many people heart-broken by one split-second decision. Was there a way I could dampen their pain just a little? "Okay. I think I should go and talk to him. What would you like me to say?" I slid my notebook and pen out of my bag.

His hopeful gaze met mine, and I gave him an encouraging nod. He opened his mouth to speak.

I wrote every last word.

# CHAPTER 13

I waited until after 11:00 p.m. to visit Fiona. I snuck up the hill, walking in a crouch. Okay, so I felt like an idiot, but I really didn't want anyone to see me. Everyone's lights were off, except for one window in the house across the way, the cottage next door to Josie. I hadn't met that person yet, or maybe it was a family. Who knew? In any case, Mrs Crabby's lights were off, and so were Finnegan's. They were the two I was most worried about.

The hairs on my nape stood on end, and my heart raced as I crossed the open area from where the street narrowed into the laneway. It was about thirty metres to Mrs Crabby's fence. It was difficult to sprint and crouch at the same time. I probably looked like a gorilla.

When I reached the low stone fence, I knelt and peeked over the top of it. I didn't dare speak louder than a whisper. "Fiona. Fiona, it's Avery." Would she show up? Going on my experience so far, she would. My glance pinged from window to window, and I craned my head around to make sure no one from across the street had heard me. I tried again. "Fiona. Fiona?"

"Avery, I'm so glad you came back. Do you have news?" She stood on the other side of the fence and looked down at me. "Are you hiding?"

"Yes. I don't want anyone to see me because I'm not supposed to be here. I do have news, sort of. Your sister, Alice, called me."

She brought both hands to her mouth. "Is she okay? She must be upset that I'm gone."

"She is upset, but she's coping. She wanted my help because she thinks the police aren't taking her seriously. I thought I'd ask you some questions."

"But I don't remember anything new about that morning."

I swallowed. According to Patrick, he still felt emotions, so I had to assume Fiona could too. This wasn't going to be a pleasant conversation. "I wanted to ask about Simon's infidelity."

"Oh." She shut her eyes for a moment, and her head dropped to her chest. "What about it?"

"Did he want to put it behind you, or did he ask for a divorce?"

She raised her head and bit her lip. "He asked if I wanted one, but he said he didn't, that he wanted to make it up to me. I said no divorce."

"Did he stop seeing her straight away?"

"Yes, as far as I know. I did check up on him after he promised, and I didn't find any new correspondence between them. Do you know something? Is he with her?"

"Ah, no, not as far as I'm aware. And when I went to see him the other day, he was by himself, and he didn't look happy, but then again, if he killed you, he'd be acting up a storm anyway."

Her brow furrowed. "I don't think he's capable. He can't even cut raw meat—he has to have his steak well done. I cut my finger once when I was cooking. There was blood everywhere, and he fainted."

"Okay, that's good, but your body wasn't cut up as far as I could tell. I didn't see any blood. I think the consensus is that you were strangled. Do you think he could do that?"

"Maybe." She shook her head. "I really don't know. He's never been violent. I wouldn't be surprised if his girlfriend could though."

"Ex-girlfriend?"

"Whatever."

I took some notes, not that she'd given me anything new. "Was there anyone else you were having trouble with?"

"I'm sorry. I find it so hard to remember things from before, especially recent things."

"Can you at least try?"

"Okay." She pondered for a few minutes. "Hmm, there was something I remember from work."

I sat up straighter and checked our surroundings for any signs of people. Thankfully, we were still alone. "Go ahead."

"My boss, Mr Schmidt, he asked me out a couple of times when he found out that Simon and I were having problems. I said no, of course, but he never did like it."

"Did he threaten you?"

"I can't remember. I don't know."

"Would there be any evidence of him wanting to date you?"

"I don't think so. He's too clever for that. He didn't message me or anything. He asked me face to face. Oh, and there was another of the agents at work who really hated that I'd gotten that big land deal. It was for a huge development site." She blinked and stared at nothing. "Hang on. There was something about that. We had an argument." Her brow furrowed; then her eyes widened. "I wanted out of that deal, but I didn't want to give it to Crowley... the other agent. But I can't remember why. If I could've negotiated a sale on that property, it would've been the biggest deal I'd ever pulled off.

Looked like the point is moot, though, since I died before it sold."

"Interesting." I wrote it all down. Two more suspects, as far as I was concerned. So, we were up to four. But was her turning down Schmidt for a date a motive for murder? People had killed for far less, so I was putting that in the "there's a chance" pile.

"Can you remember anything else about the people at work or that deal?"

"Nope. Nothing. I'm sorry."

"Don't be sorry. You're doing the best you can. Just another question. Did your husband know you had a change of plans that morning to come here super early?"

She bit her bottom lip. "Um… yes. Work called me before I left home, and I complained to Simon about the change. It was going to throw my whole day out, and I told him I wouldn't be home until seven thirty. He wasn't happy."

"Okay, great." Well, it wasn't so great. That meant he had time to race here and hide in my apartment before she got here because she had to stop in at the office first. He supposedly had an alibi, but I didn't see how I was going to find it out. Hmm. His office was in the opposite direction. Maybe he turned up there at a time that proved he couldn't have done it? I sighed. I'd prob- ably never know—it wasn't like I could call his office, Bellamy, or Simon and get any of them to answer that question. This was not as easy as those Sherlock shows made it look. Maybe that was because Sherlock was a genius, and I was just, well, me.

"Can you come see me tomorrow? I might've remembered something else by then."

"I hope so. If I've moved back into my flat, we can talk as much as you want."

Her expression was apologetic. "I am sorry about that, not being there to meet you… alive, at least. That must've been quite a shock."

I smiled. "It was, but I'm okay. It was hardly your fault. I'm pretty sure you got the raw end of that deal."

She chuckled. "I guess you're right. I shouldn't laugh, but if I don't laugh, I'll cry." I frowned and resisted the urge to stand and give her a hug. There would be nothing to hug anyway.

My phone buzzed with a message—I'd had the forethought to put it on silent when I left the pub. I looked at it while it was still in my bag because I didn't want the light revealing I was there. "Oh, I have to go. Anyway, you've given me everything you can think of, so we'll reconvene tomorrow night."

"Thanks, Avery."

I looked up to say goodbye, but she was already gone.

# CHAPTER 14

The next morning, I went into work early, got the details for my next article, and hurried out again. I was covering a story on the new bus timetables. Riveting stuff, but essential for the community, and probably useful for me since I didn't have a car. At least I didn't have to deal with any strange people this morning and pretend their story was exciting —it was too early for that, and I'd only had one coffee. Okay, that was mean of me, but I hadn't gotten into journalism for the crazy articles. I wanted to write serious, investigative stories, something meaningful, but I needed a job, so I'd do what was asked and find some way to enjoy it.

When I returned to the office, I wrote up that story—because it was urgent—and emailed it to Mr MacPherson. Carina came in when I was finishing up. She stopped in front of my desk. "Hey, Avery. How's it going?"

I smiled. "Good thanks."

"How are you enjoying t'ings here?" Her relaxed demeanour told me that she wasn't asking for any ulterior motive except just being generally interested. Unless that was her journalist face.

"It's okay so far. And thanks for being so welcoming. I appreciate it."

She smiled. "Not a problem. Okay, well, I have a lot of stuff to get done, but I'm glad to hear t'ings are going okay." Her lilting Irish accent was sweet. I had an urge to try it out, but, of course, I didn't. I didn't want to look like an idiot or offend her. She settled in at her desk, and I turned back to my laptop.

Patrick had given me his best friend's address, as far as he knew. I was going to check whether his friend had moved since the accident. Mr MacPherson had sent me a welcome pack via email. Hopefully that would have details of where I could access the info. I pulled up the welcome pack. After a couple of minutes of flicking through, I found it—a link to see details of people on the electoral roll. Considering Patrick's friend had been driving, and it had been a couple of years since the accident, he would definitely be over eighteen, the legal voting age here.

I put his name and the town Patrick had given me into the search bar. A listing came up. Bingo. He lived with James and Ellen Archer—most likely his parents. Right, I had the address. I took a deep breath to quiet the flutters in my chest. How was I going to go about this? They were going to think I was nuts, and that was the best-case scenario as far as I could see. What if I upset them as well because they saw me as some sicko preying on their tragedy?

This wasn't as easy as I'd thought. I tapped my index finger on the table. Possum poo.

"Avery, are you okay, lovey?"

I blinked and looked at Carina. I also jumped back and slammed my hand on my heart. My chair rolled back with the force, and Finnegan laughed. "I have such a strong effect on you. I knew it!"

"Oh my God, not funny. I didn't know you were standing there."

"Sure, sure, tell someone who'll believe it." Finnegan's stupid smirk made me want to outer axe him—that was a hapkido hand strike, and no actual axes were involved. I wasn't normally violent, but apparently he had that effect on me.

Carina laughed. "You should've seen your face, Avery." She pulled her expression into something a little less mirthful. "Sorry, but it was funny. But, seriously, is everyt'ing okay? You were totally in a world of your own."

There's no way I was telling them. "Yeah, I'm fine. Just wondering how my sister's going. She messaged me last night. She was going on a job interview, when I was asleep. I'm hoping she did okay." Well, I wasn't lying. My sister had texted when I was finishing up with Fiona's ghost. Oh, God, did I sound crazy or what?

Finnegan finally had enough of looming over my desk and sat at his own. Carina gave me a sympathetic look. "She'll be fine. Don't you worry about it."

"Thanks." After that little bit of excitement, everyone went back to work. I still hadn't solved my problem though. My phone rang. I wouldn't lie—it was a welcome distraction. "Hello, Avery speaking."

"Hello, Avery. This is Jessica from Schmidt Estate Agents. I'm calling to let you know that the apartment is ready for you now."

*Yay!* "Thank you so much, Jessica. I appreciate it." I couldn't help grinning.

"Mrs Collins has agreed that your rental date will begin today, rather than when you were originally supposed to move in." Yeah, the day I found a dead body. Surely there should be a discount for that, and what about a discount to cover the money I'd spent living at the pub? I blew out a breath and shoved my wishful thinking out the window. I was such a dreamer.

"Okay, thanks."

"Bye."

"Bye." As annoying as the money thing was, I was still happy. I could finally settle in properly, and it would give me private access to Fiona's ghost.

"Good news?" Carina was staring at me.

"Yes! I can move in today. Finally!"

Finnegan looked up from his work and smiled. "We'll be neighbours."

My smile fell. Okay, so I wasn't really that upset, but I didn't want him to know that. Also, having him next door meant he'd be *next door*, too close for comfort. Why did he have to be so hot? *Stupid man.* I did not want to make an idiot out of myself. If he realised I thought he was gorgeous, he'd never stop making fun of me. That was a distraction I didn't need. *He* was a distraction I didn't need.

"Don't look so happy about it, Lightning. Just think, if you need to borrow a cup of sugar, you can come to me and avoid Mrs Collins."

I couldn't help the small smile that invaded my face. "Okay, so you make a good point. Avoiding her is at the top of my list of things to do. Josie's also offered me help any time I need it." I scratched my forehead. "Do you think Mr MacPherson would mind if I took a couple of hours to get moved in?"

Carina shrugged. "I'd check wit' him, but I don't t'ink he'd care. One of d'ose hours would be your lunch hour. Besides, if you're getting your articles handed in, he wouldn't give a sheep's boil whed'er you wrote d'em at midnight rad'er d'an ten in d'e morning."

"True. And I have worked a couple of nights."

"D'ere you go. You've answered your own question."

I packed up my stuff and checked in with Mr MacPherson. He didn't mind. *Yay!*

I practically jogged back to the pub, excitement zinging through my body. Yes, there had been a dead body in my apartment, but it was gone now, even if her ghost remained. Funnily enough, ghosts seemed to be less frightening than an inanimate body. I was looking forward to getting my stuff put away—no more living out of suitcases for me.

I ducked into the meals area to let Meg know I was leaving. There were a handful of people here already, but it was a bit early for the lunch crowd.

Meg looked up from wiping down a table. "What are you grinning about, missy?"

"I've got the okay to move in. I'm so excited. Sorry to be leaving you though. Thank you so much for making me feel so welcome." I sort of wanted to give her a hug, but it wasn't as if I were leaving Manesbury. I was only going up the road. And since when did I want to hug people? Maybe the people I'd surrounded myself with before weren't worth hugging. Something to ponder later.

She grinned. "That's wonderful. We'll miss you though. I hope this doesn't mean you don't want to hang out with me any more."

"Of course not. If you're happy to hang out with me, it's all good."

"Do you need any help moving?"

I chuckled. "I think I can handle two suitcases."

"Are you going to walk them all the way?"

"It's not that far, but you make a good point." It would be lucky to be half a mile, but the cases were unwieldy.

She smiled. "That's settled, then. I'm driving you. I'll meet you at the back door in ten."

Wow, that was so nice of her. "Thank you! That gives me time to pack up. You're awesome."

She grinned. "I know."

I raced upstairs, got my stuff together, and made sure I left the place tidy. The less work for Meg and her staff, the better. I was just about to open the door when Meg's grandmother appeared. "You leaving us, love?"

"Yes. My apartment's available."

"Can I ask you a favour?"

"Um, okay. I don't know if I can help, but I'll try." Did she need help leaving here, like Patrick? Last time I'd spoken with her, she'd said she'd chosen to stay, so it probably wasn't going to be that. And look at me, being all comfortable with spirits as if they were live people. Once I'd been ready to believe in myself—and ghosts—it didn't take long to adjust.

"Meg's really taken a shine to you, and she's going through a rough time. I was hoping you could check in on her, be there for her."

Going through a hard time? I knew she was looking into getting back into dating, but other than that, she hadn't opened up about her personal life or her past. I smiled. "I'm sorry to hear that, but I was going to stay friends with her anyway, so I can definitely say yes. I would be happy to be there for Meg."

"Oh, thank you so much. You're a dear, Avery."

"I like to help if I can, and Meg's a great person."

"Aye, that she is. Safe travels, Avery. Good luck in your new home."

"Thanks. Good luck... here." I chuckled. What did you wish for a ghost who apparently was where she wanted to be?

I lugged my bags downstairs and made my way to the back door. Bailey was serving someone at the bar and gave me a subtle nod as I passed. I waved. His expression didn't change. He was a closed book, that one. Another attractive man I'd do well to take no notice of.

It took no time at all for Meg to drive me to the flat. No sooner had she pulled out of the driveway than she was parking at the lane's entrance near Mrs Crabby's. She helped me get the bags out of the back of her Land Rover, and we each wheeled one up to Mrs Crabby's. "I'd love to stay and help you get settled in, but I have to get back to the pub. Lunch hour is always madness."

"That's okay. You've been a massive help as it is. I appreciate it." I thought about what her grandmother had asked. "What night is your night off?"

"Well, tonight is good. Dad's still helping out, so I can escape."

"Why don't you come round, and we'll have dinner here? We can have a mini house-warming party. Do you like spag bol?"

She smiled. "Love it. I'll bring the wine."

"You're on. See you at seven?"

"Excellent." She gave me a quick hug. Before I knew what had happened, she'd jumped back and was walking to the car. How sweet, but I hadn't had a chance to reciprocate. I hoped she didn't think I didn't appreciate the hug. *Argh. Guilt.* I'd have to let her know later.

I dragged one bag up the stairs and unlocked the door—no one had asked for the key back, which was great because it meant I didn't have to deal with Mrs Crabby. My day was going relatively well—why ruin it now?

I turned the handle. *One. Please don't be a dead body. Two. Please. Three.* I pushed it open. Yay for empty apartments. I grinned and wheeled my bag through the door. Funnily enough, creepy feelings didn't assail me. I wasn't sure how it was going to feel, but maybe because I'd met Fiona's ghost, knowing her body had been here wasn't such a drama. Before I could really check the place out, I hurried downstairs to grab my other bag before someone—okay, Mrs Crabby—complained about the bag on the front porch.

Once I'd gotten that suitcase inside my flat, I shut the door and surveyed my domain. An old, red Persian rug lay in the centre of the space, over fawn-coloured timber floors. A grey three-seater couch faced a small TV on a low sixties-style table. I scrunched my nose and eyed the couch. It was less than pristine. A brown stain on the seat closest to the door was definitely something to avoid. A few threads hung down along the bottom at the front. I could probably pick up a better one for a hundred pounds from the internet, but I wouldn't bother till I knew I was staying. And I had no idea if Mrs Crabby would let me throw this one away.

A round timber table with four plain timber chairs sat in the corner near a window. The kitchen was to my left—a small separate room with green seventies benchtops and old appliances. It was big enough for one person, so that was something. At the back of the kitchen was a door with a skeleton key still in the lock. I opened it. A small deck—large enough for a petite circular table and two chairs opened to the incredible vista of fields and distant forest. Stairs from the deck led down to the garden.

Other than that, there was a pink-tiled bathroom straight out of the fifties, and one bedroom. The bedroom had the same timber floors as the living area, a double bed, two-door free-standing wardrobe, and a stomach-height chest of six drawers— three drawers on each side. I opened the wardrobe to make sure nothing was lurking there, and an avalanche of mothball air swarmed over me. I coughed and shut it quickly. *Yuck.* It definitely needed airing out, so I pushed up the window, admired the rural view for a moment, then pulled the wardrobe door open again. I'd hang my clothes up later. Assuming the drawers were infested with mothball grossness, I opened those and checked for the little white balls of ew. I found four, threw them away, and left the drawers to air out as well.

There was no linen, which wasn't so bad—I didn't want to sleep in something old and not clean… like the couch. Hmm, was there somewhere in town I could buy that stuff? I guessed I'd soon find out.

"Avery!"

I jumped and screamed before slamming a hand over my mouth. I pivoted around. Fiona. "Jebus, woman. You scared the absolute you-know-what out of me." I tried to slow my breathing.

She laughed. "Sorry. It was an accident."

"Do you remember anything else?"

She frowned. "No. Sorry. I find that sometimes, when you say something, you trigger a memory. Maybe if you ask me specific questions, I'll remember more."

"That's not a bad idea. I can't right now, though. I need to get this place sorted so I can just relax later. I have a friend coming over for dinner as well. Do you think you cannot pop in until she's gone? If you do, I'll have to ignore you because, if you can remember from your time in a living body, people who think they can see ghosts are often ridiculed by the rest of society."

She smiled. "Yes, that's fine. I understand. Okay, well, I'll just fizzle out of sight."

"Fizzle?"

"Yeah. It's strange. In order to let you see me, I have to concentrate and want to be seen. When you can see me, it feels kind of like I'm a glass of water that's just had a fizzy tablet dropped into me."

"Like a Berocca?"

She nodded. "Exactly."

"What does it feel like when no one can see you?"

Wrinkles appeared on her forehead. Her eyes glistened with tears. "It's scary sometimes. There's nothing, and it feels so... empty. If I want to see your flat and the front garden, have things how they were when I was alive, I have to concentrate. 1 don't want to be this way forever, but I don't know how to go anywhere else, except that field I mentioned last time, and my sister's dreams a couple of times, but that sapped my energy. I'm working on going home, so I can see Simon, but I haven't managed that yet."

Oh, wow, that sounded horrible. Heaviness settled into my stomach. I was sad for Fiona but also scared for myself. I didn't want to die at the best of times, but knowing there was definitely some kind of scary, void element to it made it even worse. Possum poo. "I have no idea what I'm doing or if I can even help, but I'll try."

She gave me a sad smile. "Thank you, Avery. I appreciate it."

"If you want to hang around and be all effervescent while I'm gone, feel free."

"Thanks."

I left Fiona to haunt my place and went into the village. The supermarket would hopefully have what I needed. It was like winning the lottery when I found two sets of sheets for the double bed... except one was scarlet, and the other was brown. Not my first choice... or second, or even third. Maybe I'd buy one set now and grab some white sheets next time I was somewhere that had some taste. I settled on the brown because it didn't remind me of murder and blood. At least the tea towels and towels were aesthetically inoffensive. I managed to grab white ones, as well as the food I needed for tonight and just general stuff. It would be nice to make my own breakfast and eat it in private. I wasn't a fan of people watching me eat. Probably a leftover from my days when Brad would criticise me for putting my elbows on the table, or having a crumb on the corner of my mouth. *Stupid Brad.* He even said my chewing was too loud, but it wasn't. His was. And I wasn't even joking.

After I put everything away, I sat on the disgusting lounge, but not on the stain. At least the fabric didn't smell. The pictures of this place online had made it look a bit fresher than it was. Some of the paint was peeling, and there were a couple of hair-line cracks in the plaster—not that the place was falling down, but maybe this was why people hadn't wanted to rent it. And maybe, unlike me, they could afford better. But the online photos had definitely been touched up.

Oh, well, it was what it was, and it was home… for now. I'd just have to make it work. For once in my life, I was pretty sure I could.

# CHAPTER 15

After getting my spoils home from the supermarket, I washed the sheets and hung them on the communal clothesline in Mrs Crabby's backyard. The view from her narrow but long garden was almost as spectacular as from my bedroom. Huge, boundless sky, rolling fields bordered by forest as far as one could see, and a paddock of sheep.

Once I'd done that, I was free to continue my investigation. Where to start, though? As I walked back to the office, I pondered things. I could stake out Simon's place, see if he was still seeing that woman, but I could end up sitting there for days and still not discover anything, and I'd already played the "doing the story" card with him. My next stop would be the estate agency. Maybe I should question her boss, tell him I knew about him coming onto Fiona, see his reaction. It would ensure I'd never be allowed in there again. I sighed. This was way harder than it looked in the TV shows.

The other thing I could do was check out the agent selling that piece of land, see if he wanted it enough to kill her. It would help to know what was in her diary. Being an agent, surely, she had one. That was something I didn't know—when was the last time someone saw her? *Idiot me.* Why didn't I think of this before? I supposed moving to a new place and realising for sure I could see ghosts was enough to knock the common sense and training out of me for a bit, not that I'd made a habit of solving murders back in Sydney. But I did know how to research, and I did know what the steps were—generally—for a murder investigation.

*Right.* I'd have to speak to Fiona again. I turned around and headed back. At least everything was within a ten-minute walk around here.

When I got home, I didn't bother sitting down—this was hopefully only a quick stop. I'd told her she could hang out when I was gone, and she was standing by the window gazing out to the street below. She turned and looked at me. "What are you doing back so soon?"

"I thought of something else to ask you. Did you have a work diary? Do you remember what your last appointment was on the night before I found you? Did you go to the gym after work? Has anyone been bothering you, like strange men?" Maybe someone like a stalker had killed her, someone who wasn't on anyone's radar?

She shook her head. "I didn't go to the gym that night, and no one unusual has been bugging me, and before you ask, I wasn't having an affair either." She looked at the ground for a moment, maybe thinking about Simon's indiscretions. Finally, Fiona looked up. "I do have a diary, but surely the police have it."

"Well, they might, but that doesn't do me any good. I can't exactly go in there and ask to see it."

"True. Um, I had a late appointment with the vendor of the land I didn't want to sell. He was still trying to convince me to sell it, and Mr Schmidt told me I had to try and work something out. He really didn't want to lose him as a client." She smiled. "That's more than I've been able to remember for ages."

"Did you go anywhere else after that?"

"Just home." She licked her lips. "I had a late cup of tea with Simon. He'd already had dinner by the time I got home." She turned back to the window and gazed out. "We really made a mess of things, but I don't know where we went wrong."

I didn't know what to say. It was too late for her to fix anything now. Would she feel sad forever, or was being dead like being alive—feelings faded over time? "Do you remember where you were the next morning, before I found you?"

"No. I was obviously supposed to be here and then wherever the urgent thing was. I have no idea what it was." She hit herself in the forehead with the heel of her hand a few times. It made no sound, and I wondered if it hurt.

She turned to look at me again and rubbed her forehead. Maybe it had hurt. "I have no idea. Sorry. And if it was a last-minute thing, it wouldn't be in my diary."

"It's not your fault. This hasn't been a total bust though. There are things I can work with."

"Are you sure?"

I smiled. "Yes. Don't worry; we'll get to the bottom of it."

Her expression said she wasn't so sure; then she turned and looked back out the window. She had much to think about. If I were killed, I'd want to know who and why. I'd probably be more than a little crapped off about it too. When I said bye, she didn't answer, but I didn't take it as her being rude—she obviously had a lot on her mind.

At least I knew what I had to do now, but I didn't have a car, and the bus service here wasn't super frequent—a bus every hour in each direction. I looked at my phone. Aaaaaand it was leaving in one minute. Right, there was no way I'd get there. Which was why I went straight to the pub. I'd promised to look out for Meg, but she was being more helpful to me than I was to her. And I hated asking anyone for help. If it wasn't for solving a murder, I would've waited an hour for the stupid bus.

The lunch rush was over, but a few people sat around drinking. Meg and her dad were standing behind the bar, having a chat. Meg didn't notice me till I was standing in front of them. "Avery! How did the big move go?"

I grinned. "All set up, groceries are in the fridge, sheets are on the line. I'm ready to cook you dinner later."

"Awesome."

Her dad smiled. "It's about time someone cooked dinner for this one. She works her behind off here."

She gave her dad a "why did you have to say that" look. I laughed. "It's fine. You looked after me so well when I was here; it's only fair that I reciprocate." I swallowed. Maybe I should just wait for the next bus. She was obviously busy, or at least spending time with her dad. Putting her out was a bad idea. "Okay, well, I'll see you later."

Her brow wrinkled. "You didn't just come to tell me you'd settled in. If it's one thing I've learned over my time working in a pub, it's how to read people. Now, spill. What is it?"

Bloomin' hell, she was good. I gave her a sheepish look. "Argh, you got me." I licked my bottom lip. "I hate to ask, and I know that sounds pathetic since I'm asking anyway, but I was wondering if you could do me another favour?" Argh, I was being a bother, but until I got my own car, I was going to have to be sometimes. Maybe I should look at getting one soon. Surely there'd be something that worked for around a thousand pounds.

"Hit me." She smiled. Of course she did. She was so nice.

Now to lie, but it was for a good cause. And it wasn't a complete lie. The article was important, but at this stage, helping Fiona was my top priority. I was just lucky I could cover it with the work story. "I'm working on an article about Fiona."

Her brow wrinkled. "Oh, I thought you'd already handed it in."

"Ah, yeah, but this is a different one, more about who killed her."

Meg's dad stopped smiling. "Don't be getting my daughter into trouble now."

"Oh, um. I won't. I just needed a lift somewhere. I don't have a car. I promise she won't be in any danger. I just wanted to go back to the estate agents she worked for and ask her boss a few questions."

He didn't take his gaze from me. "She worked for Schmidt, didn't she?"

"Yes."

He folded his arms. "Schmidt is as dodgy as they come."

Estate agents had a bad name at times, but from what I'd seen, Fiona was trustworthy. I couldn't explain what I knew though…. *Imagine me saying, "I was chatting to Fiona yesterday and…."* *Ha ha.* What a quick way to lose a potential friend. "Well, that's why I want to talk to him again. Last time I spoke to him, I didn't get to have a long conversation."

Meg's dad looked at her. "Be careful. Don't let this one drag you into anything." I could understand his concern, but it wasn't as if we were dealing with the mob. I was going to ask Schmidt a few questions, and they were even related to his business. He reminded me a bit of my father—overbearing and bossy—and now I wasn't sure if I liked him any more.

Meg shook her head. "I'll be fine, Dad. Avery's the one asking the questions. I'm just her chauffeur."

"Well, just be careful. Use your noggin."

"I will." Meg looked at me. "Let's go."

I smiled, thankful she wasn't going to freak out just because her dad was—there was nothing to freak out about, for goodness' sake. "Thank you."

We hurried out the back to her car. I figured she wanted to rush just in case her dad wanted to keep going on about it. When we got in, she turned to me. "I'm so sorry about Dad. He doesn't mean to be overprotective, but he worries. Ever since Mum died...."

"That sucks. I'm sorry. I do appreciate your help. I'm happy to give you petrol money too."

She gave me a "no way" look. "Don't be silly. It's not like we're driving across the country. You can just cook me dinner every now and then." She waggled her brows, and I laughed.

"Deal."

As she dropped me out the front of the building, I regretted not calling first. What if he wasn't in? Maybe the agent who was competing with her would be in. At the very least, I could ask the receptionist what she thought, although that would be trickier: (a) because she didn't like me, and (b) because she was at work and would be stupid to say anything against the people she worked with where they could hear her.

I wiped my sweaty palms on my skirt and went inside.

The receptionist was different to last time. A woman in about her fifties sat at the desk on the phone. Her red hair was swept up into a chignon. She tapped her pen on the table, over and over. Was she related to MacPherson? He was constantly moving or tapping. She gave me a polite nod and gestured me to sit in one of the chairs against the wall. Instead of sitting, I perused the listings in the window again.

They'd all been replaced, Fiona's name and contact details removed from all of them. The commercial land had the name of the new agent, Mr Crowley. Looked like he'd gotten what he wanted. But if she hadn't wanted it anyway.... Why had Schmidt insisted she work with the vendors? Yes, she was their best agent, but properties sold themselves to some extent.

"Can I help you?"

I spun around. "I was wondering if Mr Schmidt was in."

"Can I ask your name?"

"Oh, sorry. I'm Avery Winters. I just had a couple of questions for him about Fiona's work here. I wrote an article on her the other day, but my boss wants another one, so I need more information." I slid my hand into my bag and crossed my fingers.

She picked up the phone and pressed a couple of buttons. "Hello, Mr Schmidt. I have a woman here to see you.... An Avery Winters." She nodded. "Okay, yes. Bye."

She smiled. "He said he'll see you now, but he only has a few minutes." I'd heard that before.

"Great. Thank you so much."

"It's just through there, and—"

I cut her off with a smile. "I remember from last time. Thank you."

"Oh, good." She smiled and lowered her gaze to her computer.

Adrenaline warmed my stomach. How was he going to react? Was I going to be thrown out? I didn't want to waste what was likely going to be my last opportunity to get information from this office. I paused at the door, took a deep breath, then opened it.

Schmidt stood. "Come in, Miss Winters. To what do I owe the pleasure of a second visit?"

His smile was oilier than I remembered. When I reached the desk, he held out his hand, and I shook it. His hand engulfed mine. I didn't miss the painful squeeze at the end of it. Establishing his authority, maybe, or trying to impress me with his strength? "I missed a couple of questions last time. I'm hoping you can answer them for me. I realise your time is very valuable since you run such an exclusive agency."

He sat and gestured for me to do the same. The light in his eyes brightened a level. A bit of flattery got you everywhere with some people. "If I can, I will."

When I sat, I perched on the edge of the seat, ready to leave. There was no use getting too comfortable. I resisted the urge to push my chair back and increase the distance between us. "Ah, I hate to ask you this question, but I wouldn't be doing my job properly if I didn't." His expression went from oily and proud to wary. "I heard a rumour that you and Fiona were having an affair. I wouldn't normally ask, but you are rather attractive"—oh how I lied—"and it would match my hypothesis that her husband was probably the one who killed her. I've heard he's the jealous type. So, did you have an affair with her?"

Different emotions played across his wide, square-jawed face —surprise, caution, curiosity, and, finally, his chest puffed out. He cleared his throat. "Well, I don't like to brag, but Fiona did have a thing for me. We didn't make it official, though. I'm married." He held his large hand up to reveal a gold band. "She chased me, and it was flattering, but I had to turn her down."

I smiled coyly. "You're such a gentleman. Do you think you hurt her feelings? I mean, us women have fragile egos. Rejection can be hard to take." The ridiculous crap that came out of my mouth sometimes even surprised me.

He smiled. "I doubt you'd know about rejection, a blonde little minx like yourself."

*Minx*?! *Argh.* I pushed the anger and shudder down deep. I was playing the game, and I should've known he would bite. *Just smile.* If I could hold my disgust off for long enough, I might discover something important. I looked down in an effort be demure, before looking back up at him through my lashes. *Kill me now.* "Okay, you got me." Yeah, right. My ex-boyfriend ditched me as soon as the water got rough. The way he told it, me being hit by lightning was more of an inconvenience to him than it had been to me. "Um, did she want to get back at you because you rejected her? Like, did she refuse work just to upset you? Women can be such cows sometimes." If I could trick him into talking about that deal she didn't want to take, I might get somewhere.

His lips pressed together, and a glint of anger flecked across his eyes. "Well, if I'm honest, she was acting strangely before she died. She was okay with taking on the sale of the land, but when I rejected her, she came and said she didn't want to do it, that it was too much work. To get the deal, she'd agreed on less commission, and I think she regretted her decision. She wanted a way out. I have another agent on it now, and he's more than happy to do the job." He smiled, shark that he was. Was that the story he'd given the other guy, or was it just that she died, so he could happily pass it along? "It was a shame she felt that way. As much as she was trouble sometimes, she was my best agent. I really am sorry she's gone." Hmm, sorry for the loss of a good employee, or sorry for the loss of someone to perv at? The jury was out on that one.

Had he killed her out of frustration? She was strangled, and his hands were more than large enough to do that easily. Maybe he was scared she'd go to his wife and tell her he'd made a move? I'd have to ask her about that later. Hopefully she'd remember. "You are so sweet. She was lucky to have such a considerate boss. Well, I think I've got everything I need." I stood. "Thank you so much for speaking to me with no notice. I appreciate it."

He stood, his eyes roving up and down my body. *Gag.* "We could continue this conversation over a cup of tea, if you'd like. I know this great little café."

"That's so kind of you, but I have to decline. My boss is expecting me back. He needs me to make him his tea every afternoon. He gets so cross if I'm late. Have a good afternoon."

Before he could suggest any other days to get together, I opened the door and hurried down the hallway. *Yuck.* I couldn't help congratulating myself on my ability to liberally spread the bull manure. I gave the receptionist an enthusiastic wave and grabbed an A4 leaflet off her desk without stopping. "Thank you!" Then I was out the door and looking for Meg's car.

Luckily, she'd found a parking spot a minute's walk up the street. I got in. She smiled, but as I slid into the passenger seat, her smile faded. "What happened? You look... not happy?"

"Mmm, you could say that. Fiona's boss is a turd. He's an inferior form of the male species. A creepy liar." Oh, possum poo. Had I just said too much? I shut my mouth. *Don't say anything else, Avery.*

"Tell me what you really think." She chuckled. "But seriously, what happened? Are you okay?"

"Yeah, nothing really happened. He'd barely finished telling me he was married before he was asking me out. And he did that thing guys do where they look you up and down. I'll admit, I was flirting a little bit, but more complimenting him on stuff to get him to talk. He totally ran with it, though."

"Oh, so you maybe can't blame him 100 per cent?"

"Hmm, maybe. But maybe not. I mean, just because someone flirts with you, doesn't mean you ask them out. And I wasn't being overly flirty—it wasn't as if I shoved my boobs in his face. I didn't tell him I wanted to date him—I just buttered him up a bit. Not to mention, he's the one who's married and about twenty years older than me."

"Fair enough. Sounds like you used your feminine wiles. Did you expect he wouldn't react?"

"I was hoping he wouldn't, but I did need that information. The police haven't found Fiona's killer yet, and I wanted to know if he had anything do to with it." *Gah, stop talking before you say something you'll regret.*

"Did you get the information you wanted?"

I shrugged. "Well, he didn't exactly come out and say he killed her." I made a face at her, then smiled. "But I did get information I didn't have before, so it was worth being creeped out."

"Good for you, Avery." Her expression turned serious. "I know my dad was annoying back at the pub, but I feel like I should repeat what he said to me—be careful. If he is a killer, you don't want him setting his sights on you."

The happiness at my kind-of success soured in my mouth. "Yeah, you're right. I'll be careful. Don't worry. I shouldn't need to talk to him again, but there is someone I do need to talk to."

"Who's that?"

"The agent who took over some of Fiona's portfolio. There's a commercial block of land that seems to be at the centre of some disagreement. It would do to talk to him but not in the office—somewhere Mr Schmidt won't see me."

"Where are you thinking?"

I looked out the window. People walked past, enjoying their day, oblivious to the fact that an innocent woman had been murdered. How many stories was I oblivious to? That's why I'd become a journalist—I wanted to shine light into the dark corners, expose unfairness, show the bad people for who they were. We weren't always aware of the people close to us who were trying to undermine us at every turn, and I had to admit that I didn't see my ex for who he was until it was too late, but if I could save even one person from tragedy, I'd do it. "I'm thinking I need to go to that auction."

"Which auction?"

I held up the piece of paper. "This one."

"When is it?"

"Tomorrow." Was this a bad idea?

Meg grabbed the paper. "This land is near where I used to live, and it's about five miles from Manesbury." She looked at me. "You're going to need a lift, and I insist on taking you. I want to make sure you're safe."

"I can't ask you to drive me again. I'll prepare better and take the bus. Besides, I am safe. I've been doing this job for a few years, and I haven't come to grief yet."

"No. I'm driving you. You can cook me dinner tomorrow night, too, if you want. Dad's decided to stay on for a few extra weeks, which means I'm free whenever I want—I just have to let Dad know because he's spending time visiting friends while he's here as well as hanging out with Bailey and me."

My cheeks heated. How could I turn this down? But I was imposing way too much. Before long, she'd realise I was a pain in the bum and distance herself. That was it; after this time, I wouldn't ask her any more. "Okay, deal. I am sorry though. I just have to find a cheap car."

She clapped her hands. "Oh, Bailey can help you with that. He's the master of finding a bargain, especially with cars. He found my Land Rover. We got it really cheap, and he and his mate did some work on it. It's never broken down on me. It's been an awesome car."

Argh, someone helping me again. But I'd be stupid to knock back her offer. The sooner I got my own car, the sooner I could stop asking everyone for a hand. "Okay. But make sure he's okay with that. I hate imposing."

"Are you kidding? He'd love to help you." She smirked. "He thinks you're hot."

My eyes widened. "He does not. Stop it." I put my hands over my ears. "I don't want to hear it. La, la, la, la, la."

She laughed. "Okay. I'll stop embarrassing you now. But I'm not lying."

"Did he actually say that?"

She shrugged. "Not in so many words, but I can tell."

I rolled my eyes. *Argh, poor Bailey.* He'd likely be just as mortified as me right now if he knew. Besides, heterosexual guys found lots of girls hot. It was in their nature. It didn't mean anything.

"Aaaaanyway, thank you for your offer. It's more than generous… on both counts."

"Any time, Avery. Any time." Now our discussion was over, she started the engine, indicated, and pulled out into the street. I'd been so lucky to find a friend like her. But could someone become a friend so quickly? I hadn't made a new friend in years, so I had no idea.

I supposed I'd find out in time. I just hoped she thought I was worth it because I honestly didn't know.

# CHAPTER 16

W as today the day I was going to get essential information regarding Fiona's death? I was hoping. I dressed in my baby-pink skirt and tailored jacket and wore a white camisole top underneath. I paired this with nude peep-toe heels. I didn't always wear heels because even though they looked great, they were ridiculously uncomfortable. It was a mile walk to the office, so I put the shoes in a plastic bag and wore sneakers. I wasn't totally immune to pain.

Despite the fact that it was summer, the top temperature today was only going to be eighteen degrees Celsius. That was an average winter temperature in Sydney, so I definitely needed the jacket. The charcoal sky threatened more rain. We'd had a downpour about half an hour before I left the house, but the weather gods had seen fit to give me a decent window of non-rain to get to work. I did have an umbrella, thanks to Meg. She'd grabbed it from their lost property box. This one had been sitting there for a year, so she was certain no one was going to claim it.

Dinner last night had been awesome. Meg was wonderful company, and we got along well. She'd left at eleven, and then I'd called to Fiona, just in case she had any other information, but she didn't respond. Crazy as it was, I worried about her. Could bad things happen to ghosts when they were in that in-between realm? Was there someone I could even ask about this stuff? I'd have to look into it, but not in this village. The last thing I needed was to weird people out and become an outcast.

As I reached the home stretch, a high-pitched grating sound came from the road to my left. I jerked around. A red car slid out of control. *Bang!* I cringed as it crashed into a white car that had stopped for the postal van picking up the mail. My heart raced, and my breathing came faster. *It's okay, Avery. No lightning is coming.* Despite my PTSD, my first instinct was to run and help—that had been how I was before the accident. Now I hesitated. Time to force some deep, slow breaths while I counted to fifteen. Once my brain was on board with the fact that I wasn't in any danger, I did the journalistic thing and pulled my phone out of my bag and started filming. I was sure that was a crappy thing to do, but I needed more stories this week, and this was definitely a story. Two other passers-by had run to help the white car jammed in the middle. I rushed across the road to the red car.

An old lady with a helmet of grey permed hair sat there looking around the car. I knocked on her window. She turned and opened it. At least there was no blood. "Are you okay?"

"I— I think so." She was a slim woman who wore her wrinkles elegantly, along with her white blouse and pearl earrings.

"Does anything hurt?"

She sat a moment, probably taking stock. "My knee."

I stopped filming. "I'm going to call an ambulance." I dialled and gave them the details.

When I got off the phone, the old woman stared at me, worry in her eyes. "You're not going to leave, are you? Can you wait with me?"

"Of course I can. I'm Avery. What's your name?"

"Dorothy. I was off to a doctor's appointment."

"What happened?"

"My foot slipped off the brake, and by the time I got it back on, I was too close."

"Ladies, is everyone all right?"

I turned. Gah. Finnegan. He'd better not steal this story off me. "We're fine, thanks, and I've called an ambulance.

"What happened?"

"What does it look like?" I was not giving him any details. Maybe I was being petty, but better to be safe than sorry. That wasn't a cliché for nothing.

"Someone hasn't had their coffee this morning." He turned his grin on Dorothy. "I hope she's being nice to you."

Dorothy managed a smile. "She is. Avery promised to stay here until the ambulance comes."

"Well, I'll wait with you both." He gave her one of his swoon-worthy smiles. He just couldn't help himself, trying to charm every person he came across.

"Don't you have work to do?"

He shrugged. "It's a slow day."

I narrowed my eyes, but I couldn't exactly accuse him of anything. He hadn't stolen this story… yet. Instead, I turned back to Dorothy. "How's the knee? Is it feeling worse?"

"About the same, thank you, Avery. I'll be okay."

Finnegan nudged me to the side and smiled down at Dorothy. "This is becoming a bit of a habit. Does this mean they'll take your licence away?"

She frowned. "Yes." Her eyebrows drew down. "Dolts. Who do they think they are? None of these have been my fault… not really. My foot slipped."

Finnegan looked at me, a small smile and a raised eyebrow telling me what he really thought. He looked at her. "I hear the bus is a nice way to travel."

She screwed up her face. "Pfft. Buses are dirty, and people smell. All those germs."

"Maybe if you play your cards right, I'll give you a lift sometimes." He winked.

Her expression softened. "Oh, that would be wonderful. Thank you."

Time to get back to work. I lifted my phone. "Do you mind if I take a photo for the paper? It's my job to report on the goings-on about town."

She smiled. "I guess so. It won't hurt my insurance claim, will it?"

"Not unless you were planning on lying to them."

Her hand went to her chest. "Of course not."

"Smile." I stifled a chuckle. That was such an odd thing to ask someone in this situation, but for some reason, I thought it would make the article funnier and cute. Yes, I was a weirdo. She smiled, and I took a couple of photos.

A siren wailed in the distance, getting louder with each second. "I think your ride's here, Dorothy. Can I have your last name, for the article?"

"Patterson."

"Thank you." I turned and glared at Finnegan, a warning not to steal my information. He put his hands up in surrender, his expression that of someone mortally wounded by the suggestion he would do anything underhanded. I didn't believe that act for a moment—not that he'd proven to be someone who was always underhanded, but if the last place I worked was anything to go by, he'd steal my articles as soon as smile at me. My ex had done that... twice. He claimed it was more important for him to get the bigger scoops because he had to justify his place as assistant editor. He'd won an award for my story about police corruption. I'd worked on it for months. He'd told me it wasn't the best writing he'd ever seen, but he'd fix it. Stupid me trusted him. He put it into the paper as his own article with me as co-writer. Why had I stayed with him after that? I'd been pathetic—that's why. He reasoned it by saying we'd soon be married, and I'd have our children, but he'd need to be the breadwinner, at least in the medium term, so it would benefit both of us if he were earning more.

I'd been had.

Never again.

As the ambulance pulled up behind Dorothy's car, Finnegan looked at me. "Are you okay by yourself here? I do actually have to get back."

"Not to write this story, I hope."

"No. I have something from yesterday afternoon. Promise." He did look convincing. I had no choice but to trust him.

"Yes, I'm fine. I want to make sure she gets into the ambulance okay."

He gave Dorothy a wave as the paramedics reached us with their bed on wheels. "Good luck, Dorothy."

"Thank you, Finnegan." Seemed as if everyone knew everyone around here… except me. How long would it take for me to meet everyone and start fitting in? I'd almost met more ghosts than I had real people here. I smiled wryly. This was definitely not the situation I'd envisaged for myself five years ago… not even a year ago could I have foreseen this.

As the paramedics got to work, I stepped back and filmed. They talked to Dorothy before opening her door and checking her over. One of them took her blood pressure and pulse. Once that was done, they helped her out of the car and put her on the bed. Two tow trucks arrived on the scene as well.

I paused filming to bid Dorothy adieu, then recorded as they put her in the ambulance and drove away. I briefly checked in with the other driver, Max, who was complaining of a sore neck, but other than that, he was okay. He'd been on his way to work.

Right. That was my story for the day... if Finnegan didn't steal it.

I jogged to the office and didn't bother to say hello to Bethany—she always ignored me, and I didn't have time. At least I hadn't seen Finnegan take any photos of the scene. Hopefully that meant the story was all mine.

I said a quick hello to Finnegan and Carina, then got straight to work. Within an hour, I'd written the story and uploaded the photos and the video, then sent the email to Mr MacPherson. *Done.* When I looked up, Finnegan was gone. Oh, wow, I must've been in the zone.

I checked my phone. Just after ten. The auction wasn't till one, so I had a bit of time. Maybe I should pick up another story or go for a wander to see if one presented itself as it had this morning. Maybe today would be my lucky day?

Carina got up from her chair and came over. "Hey, Avery. How's everyt'ing going wit' d'e flat?"

I smiled. "It's great, thanks. A bit dated, the kitchen and bathroom, but all in all, it's good. Everything works, and the view out the back is super pretty."

She smiled. "Sounds nice. How've you been finding everyone?"

"Um... okay." I wouldn't tell her how crabby Mrs Collins was —she was probably already aware, and I wouldn't tell her what a cow Joy was—she could be her best friend for all I knew. The less I said, the better. "Meg's been so kind. She's helped me out more than once."

"Meg's a good one. You can't go wrong wit' her." She leaned closer, her expression serious. "I just want you to know d'at if anyone gives you strife, I'm here for you. You make sure to let me know. Okay?"

I blinked. Why was she being so nice? We hardly knew each other. Did this mean she didn't want me to be driven away like the last guy? I smiled. "Thank you. That's kind of you to offer. I appreciate it." I'd never take her up on that, of course, but the fact she'd offered meant a lot. It was certainly more than I'd ever expected when I decided to move here. I was more looking for a place far away from the parental units, but also somewhere I had a clean slate. If people were neutral towards me, it was an improvement.

MacPherson came through the door. "Kelly, Winters. How goes it?"

"Just grand, t'anks." Carina gave me a wave and headed back to her desk. *Yikes.* Was I in trouble? What had I missed?

MacPherson pinned his gaze on me. His serious expression didn't look good, but then he cracked a smile. "Nice work on that accident this morning. An exciting story with a happy ending. Keep it up."

"Oh, thanks."

He gave a nod and left. Okay, that was a flying visit. At least I wasn't in trouble. *Phew.*

"Excuse me." A young boy's voice floated in from the doorway.

*Huh?* I looked around and scratched my forehead. Just when I thought I wasn't going crazy, I started hearing voices. Just great.

"Oh, sorry." A boy, maybe about eight years old, dressed in brown shorts and a grubby white T-shirt, stood in front of my desk. "Are you Avery?"

I glanced over at Carina who was concentrating on her laptop. I looked back at the boy and nodded as subtly as I could while still getting my message across. I also gave him a small smile.

"Patrick wants to know if you've spoken to his friend yet."

Possum poo. I shook my head. And what was going on here? I was under the impression that Patrick was stuck by himself. Maybe other ghosts who weren't constrained could visit him. I had no idea what this meant or if it even mattered—at the very least, I had no brain power to deal with this right now when another ghost was standing in front of me asking questions.

I stood and looked at Carina. "I'm just going out to stretch my legs. Be back shortly."

She looked up from her work. "Knock yourself out."

I smiled. Her accent always cheered me up. I clearly didn't have enough Irish accents in my life. I slid my phone out of my bag, placed my gaze on the boy, and jerked my head towards the door. Hopefully he got what I was saying. He nodded and turned around, then walked out. *Okay, good.*

I followed him down the stairs and out the front door. Once I was outside, I put the phone to my ear to pretend I was having a conversation with a dead child. Bloody hell. What had my life become? The cool splatter of raindrops pattered annoyingly on my face. Of course I forgot my umbrella. *Best get this conversation over and done with quickly.* "Who are you?"

"I'm Charles."

"How old are you?"

He squinted at me as if weighing up whether to tell me or not. "Seven, but when I carked it, I was almost eight. Two weeks away from my birthday." He pouted—obviously still peed off about it.

This seemed really invasive to ask, but was there conversational etiquette when communicating with the dead? "How long ago did you die?"

He counted on his hands, raised his arms, then let them slap on the sides of his legs, which made no sound. I shuddered. That was definitely creepy. "I was born in nineteen thirty-eight. My family's all dead now. They came and said goodbye when they went, but I didn't want to go with them. I weren't ready."

"Oh, okay." Maybe he didn't like his parents the same as I

didn't like mine. I certainly wouldn't be following them in the afterlife. Wherever they went, I didn't want to be.

"You can tell Patrick that I haven't spoken to his friend yet. I've just had a bit of other stuff to do, but I'll get to it soon."

He cocked his head to the side. "When?"

"I don't know. Hopefully in the next few days." If I didn't chicken out. I still had no idea how to approach Patrick's friend without upsetting him and looking like a freak who was trying to cause trouble.

He looked me up and down, his penetrating gaze finally resting on mine. The expression on his face was too observant and considered for a seven-year-old. I needed to remember that he was, really, much older than me. But how much had he learned after he died? He'd still tried to count on his fingers before, which meant he was still a child. Maybe he'd always been a cluey person, wise beyond his years, and that's why he wanted to stay around? "You're a chicken." He bent his arms and put the backs of his hands onto his waist and flapped. "Bock, bock, bock, b-gawk." Yep, he was definitely still a kid, although I could see me doing that to someone too.

I laughed. "Yeah, maybe I am. I haven't worked out the right way to tell his friend. I don't want to upset him, and I don't want him to think I'm crazy and trying to cause trouble. This is a delicate situation. Tell Patrick I'll come and see him soon. Maybe he could give me an idea on how he should best be told."

"Okay, fine. Bye." He gave a wave and disappeared.

I lowered my phone to my side and stared down the laneway towards the high street. Now what? Was this kid going to stalk me until I got the job done? Great. And, just in case you weren't clear, that was sarcasm.

My phone rang, and I almost dropped it. Damned surprises. "Hey, Meg. How's it going?" Oh no. Was she about to tell me she couldn't take me to the auction?

"Hey, Avery. Just letting you know I'm still good for today. I'll be ready to leave at a quarter past twelve. By the time we get there and find parking, it'll be quarter to one, and the auction starts at one. I don't want you to miss anything."

"Thanks. You're a champion. There are a few properties going up for sale, though. We might be sitting there a while."

"I don't care. It'll give us time to sus the room out, maybe observe that agent in his native habitat."

"Okay. I'll make sure I get to the pub just before quarter past. And thanks again."

"My pleasure. This is going to be fun!"

"Ha, yeah. I hope it doesn't turn into a snoozefest."

"Nah, this investigating thing is exciting. Anyway, gotta go. See you later."

"Bye." I headed back into the office. It was time to focus on what I wanted to get out of today's auction visit. Patrick's problem would have to wait. Guilt tap-danced around my stomach, unsettling it. This helping-ghosts thing was way more complicated than I could've imagined. But I was a problem-solver. I could totally handle this.

The lies we told ourselves.

# CHAPTER 17

I walked through the door from the pub's entry hallway to the bar area, my fingers crossed that Meg's dad wouldn't be there. He'd given me a hard time last I'd seen him, and whilst I understood that he cared about his daughter, it irked me that I was being blamed for putting her in danger.

Damn. He was there. He placed a tray of what looked like clean glasses on the bar and looked up at me. "Hello, Avery."

Hmm, there didn't seem to be any animosity there for a change. Phew. "Hi. Is Meg here?"

"She'll be back in a minute. She's gone to the loo."

"Okay. Cool."

"I hear you're going to an auction."

"Yep, and we'll be in a room full of people. Nothing will happen to Meg… unless the roof falls in or a terrorist decides to crash the auction."

He raised a salt-and-pepper eyebrow. "Very funny. I did want to mention something, though." He must've seen the muscles in my jaw bunch as I jammed my back teeth together. "It's nothing like last time. Don't worry. Just a bit of extra information for

Avery the journalist. Meg told me what you're up to with the auction."

I relaxed slightly. "Ah, okay. Thanks."

"The commercial land your agent is selling… it used to have industry on it. When I was a lad, they got rid of it and demolished the buildings because of the pollution. That land's been sitting there all this time. You might want to look into whether the land was remediated or not."

"Oh, wow. Thanks. That would make an interesting story if it hasn't. Then I'd get two stories in one."

"Glad to help."

"Avery!" Meg hurried in, glancing from her dad to me and back again. Her gaze finally settled on me. "Is everything okay?"

I grinned. She was trying to be subtle. "Everything's fine, thanks. Your dad was just giving me a bit of background info on that land the agent is selling. I'm going to check it all out after the auction."

"You can probably get a copy of the contract if you register to bid."

"Hmm, maybe I will. Thanks."

She grinned. "Any time. Are you ready?"

"Yep."

She kissed her dad on the cheek and led the way out the back entrance to her Land Rover. The drive was pleasant enough, even though it was drizzling. I enjoyed checking out the countryside, and Meg was always good company.

The car park at the auction centre in Exeter was only half full, but most of the cars were expensive—BMWs, Range Rovers, Mercedes, and even one Rolls Royce. I'd never be able to afford one of those cars, let alone a whole house. *Ah, to be rich.* It was still the dream, though, to have enough money to buy my own flat. I was still young, so maybe I was a bit hasty in saying that I'd never be able to afford one.

Meg found a car space, and I laughed. "Thanks for putting my door next to a new Range Rover. Do you trust me to get out without denting it?"

She laughed. "Do you need me to move the car?"

I judged the distance. "I think I can just make it." I'd only been half joking. There was room to get out, but sometimes things went wrong, and if there was a margin for error, I'd need all of it. I let out a relieved breath when I negotiated exiting the car without mishap. "Phew."

She laughed. "You're a weirdo."

"Yeah, yeah, and you don't even know the half of it." And she didn't. Yeah, I see ghosts and talk to them.... Ooookay.

Neither of us had bothered to bring umbrellas, so we jogged to the auction-room door, which was tricky in my heels. I would've changed out of them after leaving the office, but I wanted to look the part, and I was pretty sure sneakers weren't high-end fashion when paired with a business suit.

As soon as we entered the tile-floored entryway, a tall, slim woman in a black suit, her long silky hair making me think of a shampoo commercial, asked for our names and numbers. "And will you be bidding today?"

Meg and I looked at each other. As long as I didn't actually hold the paddle up, I couldn't get in trouble. At least it wasn't bidding by eye twitches—knowing I shouldn't eye twitch would make me eye twitch. It would be a total disaster where I found myself buying something I could never pay off. Could they arrest someone for that? "Um, yes."

"Which property?" I gave her the address for the commercial land, and she wrote something next to my details. "Your lot is number four today. Good luck. And don't forget to hold it up, and be clear when you're bidding." She handed me a paddle with the number ten on it. "Just go through that doorway and take a seat." She pointed to the next door on our right.

"Okay, thanks." I smiled, and Meg elbowed me. "Oh, before we go in, can I grab a copy of the contract? I forgot mine, and I'd like to have it on me, just in case."

"Yes, of course." She reached for one of the black binders on the table next to her and grabbed out a thick document. "Here you go."

"Thanks."

As we walked off, Meg said, "Ooh, I hope we get it." She grinned.

"Mmm hmm. That would be awesome." I shook my head. She was way too into this.

We found chairs towards the back—the better spot to watch everyone. The agent who'd taken this job from Fiona was standing towards the front, whispering with another black-suited man. He looked exactly like his headshot in the brochure. Did they all think wearing black made them look more important? Who knew? I was tempted to go and talk to him now, before everything started. He'd probably be tied up with the purchaser afterwards. Although, if I hung around with the excuse of wanting to talk to him, there was no telling what else I might find out by listening to the other people here. Maybe some of them had known Fiona? I figured people from estate agents within an area probably knew each other.

A few more people filed in, all with paddles in hand. An older gentleman, who looked a bit like the Kentucky Fried Chicken guy without the weird little tie, sat next to me. "Good afternoon, miss."

I smiled. "Good afternoon."

"Which property are you bidding on, then?"

He wasn't holding a paddle. Did he own one of the properties? Was it the one at the centre of the disagreement between Fiona and her boss? "Ah, that commercial land."

Meg rubbed her arms as if she was cold, then nudged me with her elbow. "Who are you talking to?"

Cat's bum. I shut my eyes and took a deep breath, then turned to Meg and smiled. "Just practicing what I'm going to say to Crowley."

She stared at me a moment before smiling, as if she were weighing up how honest I was being. "That's a relief. I was beginning to rethink our friendship."

I swallowed. Maybe I should stop this friendship before it started. It was going to end in tears one day anyway. Eventually, I was going to do something I couldn't explain away. Then it would all be over, and she'd probably tell Bailey, and everyone else she knew, about how crazy the new chick in town was. If I kept to myself, my secret was less likely to get out. Unfriending was easy on social media. How was I going to do it in real life?

"Avery, are you okay?"

"Ah, oh, um…."

She laughed. "So eloquent! No wonder you need practice before speaking to that agent."

"Ha ha, very funny."

A voice came over the loudspeaker. "We're about to start. Please be seated and have your paddles ready. I'm Brian Fisher, your auctioneer for today." He ran through the bidding rules, and he didn't need to tell me twice not to raise my paddle if I didn't want to bid. The fact that they even had to explain something that simple was ridiculous. Maybe they should make people take an IQ test before attending.

I glanced to the seat next to me. The ghost was still there. He gave me an understanding smile. I returned it, but I didn't dare say anything else.

"Property number one on our schedule is a Grade II listed stone farmhouse." He described the property and started the bidding. I swallowed my surprise. One million four hundred and twenty pounds was the opening bid. It did have some land with it, but only enough for a hobby farm. Sheesh. Meg's eager gaze pinged from bidder to bidder. She was really enjoying it. When the hammer finally fell at one million eight hundred and seventeen pounds, she clapped.

She turned to me. "Wow, that was fun!"

"Mmm hmm. How long has it been since you've been to a party?" I chuckled.

"You could be right. But, seriously, this is fun. Imagine having that kind of money and just snapping up whatever property you wanted."

I sighed. "I won't because it'll just be torture."

The next property was a two-storey terrace in the centre of a nearby town, which sold for nine hundred and thirty thousand pounds. The following property passed in, and then it was "our" turn. I made sure the paddle was on the floor under my chair. There was no way I was having any accidents.

Colonel Sanders looked at me. "I thought you were bidding?" I shook my head and pressed my lips together just to make sure I didn't say anything. "So, why are you here?"

*Curious little ghost.* At least if I didn't answer him, there was nothing he could do.

The auctioneer introduced the land and described it as an incredible opportunity for ground-floor retail and two levels of residential above. An opportunity not to be missed at any cost. If it was so great, why didn't Fiona want to sell it? Did she not like the owner? I flicked my gaze around the room. Was the owner here watching, or were they out the back waiting? *Hmm....*

No one put up their paddle for the first couple of minutes. Tough crowd. After enthusiastic prompting from the auctioneer about the rare golden opportunity, a man two rows in front of us held his paddle up. Opening bid: two million seven hundred thousand pounds. *Jebus.* That was crazy money, not to mention the commission Fiona would've gotten.

The auctioneer nodded at someone near the front who I couldn't quite see. "Two million eight hundred thousand. Do I hear two million nine?"

The guy near us raised his paddle, and so it went. A third person entered the fray.

"We have three million seven hundred and fifty-two." He looked around. "Do I hear three million eight hundred?" Nope. No takers. He looked over at Crowley who gave a subtle nod. "I'll be happy to take another ten thousand, then. Three million seven hundred and sixty-two?" Silence. "Going once at three million seven hundred and fifty-two...." His dramatic pause didn't incite any sudden paddle waving. "Going twice at three million seven hundred and fifty-two.... You'll be missing the development opportunity of the century if you miss out today. Land of this calibre rarely passes through this auction house. This is your last chance." *Come on. Nobody wants to pay more. Just give it to them already.* He raised his gavel. *Come on.* The suspense. It was like being constipated. There was a point at which you just had to say you were done and move on. He slammed it down, the crack echoing through the room. "Sold!" He called out the bidder number, and that was it. Done. Thank God for that.

Meg wriggled in her seat. "That was so exciting. We should come to auctions more often."

"Has anyone ever told you you're weird?"

"Yes. I take it as a compliment."

"Of course you would." I couldn't help my grin. It would be way safer to stop this friendship from developing, but she was fun, and I'd miss her. I blinked. That admission surprised me. There was only one person I missed after leaving Sydney, and that was my sister. There was no one else from my old life who stirred up any lingering positive feelings. A little worm of self-pity burrowed into the shrivelled skin of the apple in my chest that I called a heart. When you didn't use something for a while, it spoiled. It was unbelievable that there wasn't just brown mush there. *Make the most of it while you can, worm.*

The auctioneer announced the next property.

The ghost next to me stood. "Lucky you didn't get that one. I smell a rat."

"Um, Meg. I need to go the bathroom. Can you keep an eye on Crowley?" I wanted to talk to the ghost. Maybe he knew something, or maybe he was having a bit of fun with the live person? I wouldn't know till I knew. And, yes, that made perfect sense.

"On it."

As I stepped past the ghost and through him, I shuddered. There was nothing to feel, but I *knew.* I whispered, "Come with me."

At the back of the auction room was the sign for the bathrooms. When I reached the door, I looked back. He'd followed, thank goodness. I went through into the short common hallway leading to the bathrooms and pulled my phone out of my bag. I held the phone up to my ear and looked at Colonel Sanders. "Is there something wrong with that land?"

He laughed, and his eyes crinkled at the corners. "You really can see me. You were a bit hot and cold in there, so I wasn't sure."

"I didn't want my friend to think I was nuts. She can't see you."

He shook his head slowly, bemusement on his face. "In all my years coming to these auctions, no one has ever noticed me."

"Well, I can see you, and I appreciate your warning. What's wrong with it?"

"I heard that smug salesmen talking to the owner earlier. I'm not sure exactly what's wrong, but they were skiting that they're going to get away with it, that by the time the new owner found out, the agent and the seller would be long gone." His fists balled. "Despicable practice. In all my years as an agent, I never lied or ripped anyone off. An agent's job is to find the right buyer for the right property. If you do your job correctly, you have repeat business for years. I served my community, not swindled them."

"How long did you work as an agent?"

"Fifty years. I worked until the day I died, and I loved every minute of it, even the difficult clients. I saw them as a challenge, and not once did I have an unhappy client or purchaser."

"If only everyone was like you. Thanks for the information. Is there anything else?"

"No. That's it."

Hmm, was he stuck here? Should I ask? It wasn't as if I had time to help every ghost I came across, but I'd wonder if I didn't ask. "Are you stuck here?"

He laughed. "No. I wander about wherever I want. I just enjoy these auctions."

"Okay, just checking. I better get back out there, and thanks again."

"My pleasure." A bowler's hat appeared on his head. He took it off and bowed with a flourish.

I grinned and slid my phone back in my bag. "Bye."

Another auction was going on by the time I stepped out, and I stayed where I was until it finished. That must've been the last one for the day because everyone stood and meandered outside. I found Meg in the hallway we'd originally entered from. "Where is he?"

She gave a nod to a closed door at the end of the hallway. "That must be where they sign all the contracts."

I swallowed. If there was something wrong with the property that they'd managed to cover up, should I run in there and stop them signing? But what if the ghost hadn't told the truth? Cat's bum. I should have asked him more questions. Maybe he had history with the seller or the agent? And if I stopped the sale, could they sue me if I was wrong?

Meg poked my shoulder. "Earth to Avery. Come in, Avery."

"Oh, sorry. Just thinking things through. I guess we just wait. There probably isn't another way out of here, so we could sit in your car and just watch the front door." If they had covered things up, getting proof and establishing my innocence wouldn't be easy. As much as it galled me, I'd have to sit this one out. If they had ripped someone off, hopefully I could prove it before they ran away with the money.

"Okay. That'll give us a chance to read the contract too."

"I suppose so. Let's go."

We headed outside into the drizzle and hurried to the car. My toes ached. High heels were such a punish. As soon as I hopped into my seat and shut the door, I slid them off. *Sweet, sweet relief.*

Meg pinched her nose. "Oh, lady, they pong."

My cheeks heated. "They do not!" Did they stink and I couldn't smell it because I'd created it?

She burst out laughing. "Oh my God, you should see your face. Sorry, hon. I was kidding."

"Oh, for goodness' sake. You owe me chocolate or something."

"We've got a lovely chocolate pudding on the menu. I'll bring some for dessert tonight."

I gave her my best grumpy face. "Hmm, I'll consider forgiving you."

"What if I bring four? Two each."

I held out my hand for her to shake. "Deal."

She laughed. "You strike a hard bargain."

I was about to answer when Crowley walked out of the building. "He's out. Be back soon." I slid my torture devices back on and got out of the car. He looked like he was headed for a BMW parked near the entrance. I made a beeline for it. His hand was reaching for the door when I got there. "Mr Crowley."

He looked at me and produced a too-big fake smile. "Hello. And you are?"

I held my hand out for him to shake. "I'm Avery Winters. I've heard such good things about you."

He shifted his shoulders, and his smile became genuine. Compliments were like dog treats. They usually got a positive result. "Why, thank you. Can I ask who's singing my praises?"

"Your boss, for one. A friend of mine has a property they wanted to sell, and she asked me to find an agent for her. She knows I know Schmidt… we go back a fair way. We were actually supposed to catch up for lunch this week, but I'm a bit busy. Anyway, when I was speaking to him, he said I can't go past you."

His forehead wrinkled. "You can't what?"

*Huh?* Oops, I'd Aussied it up too much. "Oh, sorry. I was paraphrasing. He said you were the best person to deal with. And after seeing how well today's auction went, well, I'm sold." I giggled at my own joke, hoping he took me for a slight idiot. People usually underestimated me on first sight—being blonde and petite put me in the nice and harmless category, which I was in every other situation outside of work, but when it came to my job, I usually got to the truth, whether people wanted me to or not. If only I had the same confidence when it came to my actual life.

"Oh, well…." He glanced around the car park, then back at me. "When is your friend looking at selling?"

"As soon as possible. Her father died and left her quite a large house. It's six bedrooms. A little dated. The house next door sold a year ago for two million pounds. The market's improved since then… or so the papers say." Man, was I talking crap. Oh well, if I was wrong, it would just reinforce the act I was putting on.

He rubbed the back of his neck and looked at his car before looking back at me. "I'm a bit rushed for time right now. Can I give you my card, and you can call me tomorrow?"

"Oh, I'm sorry for keeping you. Do you have like a celebratory lunch or something?"

He swallowed, his Adam's apple bobbing. "I have to pack for a business trip. Do me a favour, and just wait for me to call you. If it's not tomorrow, it will be the next day."

"Do you have a conference? How committed to the job you are!"

His forehead wrinkled. "Ah, yeah, that's it. So I'll be busy."

"Oh, I also wanted to say that Schmidt told me about your colleague, Fiona. I'm sorry about what happened."

He blinked, maybe trying to catch up at the quick pivot of subjects. "Ah, yes. Nasty business that."

"Schmidt told me that you were doing so well with the commercial land, and that he was happy Fiona wanted you to have it." *Lies, lies, and more lies.* Should I be scared at how easy I found it?

His lips pressed together, annoyance flashing through his gaze. "Fiona was a fool. She didn't know a good deal when she saw it… or, rather, she wasn't capable of making good decisions. She lost out of an excellent commission. If it wasn't for me, our office would've lost it." He looked over my shoulder, then back at me. "Now, if you'll excuse me, I really have to go." His fake smile was back. "Good to meet you, Miss Winters." In other words, it wasn't good to meet you; in fact, it was downright annoying, and you've ruined my day. I wasn't sure why…. Maybe it was my mention of Fiona? There seemed to be no love lost there. But he'd been champing at the bit for most of the conversation anyway.

"Likewise. I'll wait for your call." I smiled and held up his card. "Oh, you don't have my number. Do you have a pen, and I'll write it down for you?"

He huffed out what seemed to be an annoyed breath and yanked a pen out of his top jacket pocket. "Here." He shoved it at me.

I smiled innocently. "Thank you." I held out my hand. "Do you have another card I could write it on?" He stared at me, his shoulders slumping. He reached into his pants pocket and handed me another card. "Thanks!" I wrote my number down and handed everything back. "Enjoy your conference."

"I will." He didn't bother smiling because he was too busy throwing his door open and falling into his car. I'd no sooner turned around to return to Meg's car than he was speeding through the car park. Hmm... interesting. An estate agent running away from work. How unusual.

I hopped into Meg's car. She swung her gaze from the fleeing BMW to me. "What was that about? He seems to be in a hurry."

I shut my door and put my seat belt on. "I have no idea." Which was something I was kicking myself for. "I did mention Fiona, but he was trying to leave almost from the moment I introduced myself."

"Maybe he knows you write for the paper?"

I bit my lip, considering. "No, that's not it. He didn't recognise my name." I sighed. "It probably has nothing to do with anything. He's probably got an appointment for a colonic irrigation and doesn't want to be late?"

Meg's mouth dropped open before she burst out laughing. "Oh my God, Avery. You're hilarious. But I suppose that would explain how keen he was to leave. So, what now?"

"I don't know." The contract was open in her lap. "Find anything interesting in there?"

"Maybe. I went to the page that lists historical contamination, and there was nothing."

"Nothing? I thought your dad said it'd been vacant so long because of that."

She shrugged. "Maybe they cleaned it up?"

"You would still think there would be a report on that... unless they do things differently over here. Back in Sydney, they would've included it."

"Well, I haven't gone through the whole thing. Maybe you should just read through it later." She handed it to me. "Let's get out of here. Sitting in car parks is not really my thing." She started the car and drove to the street. On the way back, I had plenty of time to ponder my conversation with Crowley, and I concluded that it definitely didn't add up. But did that have anything to do with Fiona's murder, or not?

Unfortunately, I had no idea how to figure that out. But I wouldn't let it stop me.

# CHAPTER 18

Back at the pub, I got out my laptop and looked up the address for Simon Daniels's ex-mistress. She had one of those pre-set names at the bottom of her email, so I knew her full name. I had no idea where she worked, but I'd see if she was home, and if she wasn't, I'd hang out there until she was. Fortunately, she lived about five-minutes' walk from a bus stop. I'd taken enough of Meg's time driving me everywhere, so I decided to brave public transport.

Two bus changes and the walk later, and I stood under my umbrella, out the front of a small, white, pebble-dash semi-detached home, the pitter-patter of the rain echoing next to my ears. Boy that stuff was ugly—the pebble-dash, not the fact that the home was attached on one side. Whoever thought that lumpy stuff was a good idea had no taste whatsoever.

I checked my Apple Watch—5:42 p.m. The records indicated that she lived with another woman. They had different surnames, so I assumed she was house sharing. Would one of them be home, or would I have to stand out here for hours? There was only one way to find out.

Huddling on the small front porch, I knocked on the door. My heart raced. My mouth dried up. Would Emily react violently to my questions? No one liked to be called out for being the other woman, and if he'd broken up with her and stayed broken up, she was likely to be hurting. It was always at this point in my research that I was grateful for my martial arts training. I was a brown belt in Hapkido—a Korean martial art. It was only a few belts away from black—which was actually years of hard work— but it meant I had a good grounding in self-defence and striking —not that I was planning on punching anyone. Which reminded me; I hadn't done any fitness or training since I'd been here. I'd lose my skills if I didn't use them. Note to self: find a dojang to train at.

Footsteps sounded from inside the house. I'd stalked Emily's Facebook, so I knew what she looked like, but she had all her other information set to private. "Who is it?"

"My name's Avery. I'm looking for Emily."

The door opened, and Emily stood there in a grey tracksuit, her hair wrapped in a towel. "I'm Emily. What do you want?"

Hmm, not exactly the friendly type, although could I blame her? She'd obviously just got out of the shower, and I was a stranger. "I was hoping to ask you a few questions about your ex, Simon Daniels." I'd be more likely to get information out of her if he had stayed away from her and she was still angry with him. Hopefully the gods of luck were watching out for me today.

Her expression darkened, and the door moved forward. I stuck my foot in it, stopping it from closing. She gritted her back teeth together. "I have nothing to say to you. Now get your foot out of my door."

"I spoke to him after Fiona died, and he admitted that he was sorry he'd broken up with you." Oh my God, I was becoming a compulsive liar. Back in Sydney, I'd tried to stick to the truth, and if I missed getting the information, I'd find another way, but over here, I'd lost all semblance of honesty. Had the lightning strike taken that away from me as well? Not that I would lie to friends or try and rip people off, but lying to get information was easier. I was so going to hell.

She put her hand on her hip and tilted her head to the side. "Well, he should've thought'a that earlier."

Damn. She wasn't giving me much. Might as well come right out with it. "Do you think he killed his wife?"

She stared at me. And stared. She bit her lip. Ooh, was she going to say something? *Please say something.* "He didn't like her. That's why he was fooling around with me, but then she made him break up with me, but she wasn't putting out. He messaged me a few times, but I didn't want him back. He made his choice. I'm moving on."

"What do you mean, 'didn't like?' Was it hate or just mild dislike?"

She tapped her foot on the floor. "Hmm, maybe a six out of ten. He hated that she made more money than him. He hated that she spent all her time at work. He hated that she didn't let him get away with crap." She shrugged. "And I don't care. Would you please take your foot out of my door before I call the police?"

"Okay. Thanks so much. You've been helpful." I slid my foot out of the way, and the door slammed shut in my face. I cringed. *Yikes.* But at least I'd gotten some information… more than I thought I'd get. Now, to go home and figure out how it all tied into Fiona's death, if it did at all. I had a long time to think about it on the return trip, but I was no closer to an answer when I got home.

Meg came round for dinner, payback for her driving me around. She also brought all the chocolate pudding goodness as promised, which made her my favourite person. After dinner and dessert, we sat on the gross couch and looked through the contract. I wasn't sure if it would help Fiona's case any, but if there was a crime going on here, it would give me a good lead to another article. Not to mention that once curiosity assailed me, I'd dig and dig like a Labrador who'd been told not to destroy the garden. Speaking of dogs, I missed Tess, my ex's Maltese terrier. She was the best thing about our relationship, and now I could never see her again. I swallowed the surge of tears trying to make a break for it.

Meg's brow furrowed. "Avery, are you okay?"

"Oh, um… yeah. Just sad about the dog I had to leave behind." I sniffled. Time to change the subject. Talking about myself gave me hives. "Anyway, it doesn't look like there's any reference to past contamination or a clean-up. What's the council like to deal with?"

"They should be helpful. I think you're right in wanting to go there." She sipped her wine. "But what if that agent and the owner have done something wrong and they find out you're looking into it? Aren't you worried?"

"No. Someone has to uncover things if they're ripping people off. Besides, how are they going to find out I'm poking around? Apparently Crowley is going away to a conference tomorrow."

"That's right. Hmm…." She swirled the wine around in her glass. "You'll probably need a lift to the council. It's a few miles away. What time do you want to go?"

My cheeks heated. I felt like such a useless leech. "It's fine. I can catch the bus. I'm up on the timetables. I did an article on it, you know."

She laughed. "Yes, I saw that. I also read the piece you did on

Fiona. That was really beautiful. You have such a way with words."

My cheeks got even hotter. "Thanks." I wasn't used to such open praise. My parents hardly ever read any of my articles, and if they did, they were more critical than my editor. My ex was also never impressed, and the couple of times he liked what I did, he stole it and claimed the credit. *Grrrrr.*

"And I am driving you. Buses are gross. Besides, I have nothing to do tomorrow."

"What about work?"

She shrugged. "Dad told me to take tomorrow off. He knows I need a break."

I drained the rest of my wine. I didn't want to be a bother, but I also wasn't going to say that, because then she'd just argue more, and I didn't want to make a big deal out of it. I gave her the best smile I could muster, considering what a pain in the bum I was. "Okay, thanks."

"And you don't even have to cook me dinner tomorrow night. I have a date."

I sucked in a breath. "That's awesome! Who's the lucky person?" I had no idea if she solely liked guys, so I figured that was the best way to ask.

"A guy I met at a beer tasting a few weeks ago. He's had my number ever since but didn't call till yesterday. I forgot to tell you earlier. Anyway, he seems nice enough, but then, they all do at first."

"Hmm, not all. I've heard some horror stories. I once did an article on the dangers of online dating. One girl agreed to a date, and when she showed up, he took one look at her, told her that her boobs were too small and left. Another guy showed up to a date and was nothing like the profile pic, which the woman later found out was a model pic from online. Seriously, how did he think he'd get away with that?"

She laughed. "I have no idea, but this guy's okay. Other than being glacially slow at finally asking me out, he was polite and funny and attractive. Not that I'll get my hopes up, but one date is better than none."

That was debatable, but I didn't want to hail on her new shiny thing. "Good luck. Do you want me to call you twenty minutes in, in case you need an excuse to leave?"

She grinned. "Such a sceptic. And, no, don't call me. If I want to leave, I'll just leave."

"Wow, good for you."

She drank the last of her wine. "Okay. I'm off, but what time tomorrow?"

"I'll spend the morning in the office, just so they know I'm around, and we can go at about twelve?"

"Sounds good to me. I have a hair appointment at nine, and it will probably take all morning. If I'm running late, I'll text you."

I smiled. "We have a plan. Thanks."

We said our goodbyes, and she left. As soon as I shut the door, Fiona appeared and paced back and forth, her hand on her lapel, lines of distress on her forehead.

"Are you okay? What's wrong?"

She stopped and looked at me. "I've lost my pin."

I cocked my head to the side. "What pin?"

She ran her fingers down her lapel, over and over. "The one that's usually here. I won it for being the top-earning agent three years running. It was the first one they'd ever given out."

I stood and went to her. I lifted my hand to grab her lapel, but my fingers found nothing. Bloody hell. These ghosts were as solid as a real person to my eyes, but they weren't physically there. Goosebumps peppered my arms and nape, and I shuddered. How had my life gone from normal to crazy town in less than a year? Oh, that's right, lightning strike. "There's certainly nothing there."

"Maybe it fell off when whoever it was killed me? I've thought really hard, and I know I was wearing it the morning I died. And, Avery...."

"Yes?"

She licked her bottom lip. "I'm scared. It's getting harder to stay here when I want. I'm spending more and more time in the nowhere place, and I don't like it." Fear radiated from her eyes, and my heart went out to her. Was the answer to her suffering figuring out who'd killed her? Maybe she needed to let go of this world in order to go to the next? Or was it not a world but a reality or dimension? I couldn't comprehend it. When I believed in nothing, dying seemed like the worst thing... not existing... but when I really thought hard, living forever was also horrifying, especially if you had to be by yourself. I hoped if there was somewhere else waiting for her that it was a place she wanted to be.

"Hold on. You might just be waiting for the killer to be caught, and I'll do what I can to make it happen quicker." I paused because I hated hurting her, but I needed to tell her what I'd done. "I went and saw Simon's ex. She was adamant that they're not together, but she seems to think he was really unhappy with you, like, maybe more than you thought."

She stroked her lapel again. "I still don't think he could've killed me."

"Are you sure that's not just because you loved him? Thinking your husband could be capable of killing you has to be confronting and horrible. I'm just saying... maybe really think about it."

Conviction held her back straight. "No. He definitely wouldn't. I'm as sure as I can be. He was never violent. Yes, he was unhappy, but he's not a confrontational kind of person, which is probably why he had an affair rather than come and talk to me about how he felt."

Okay, so I wasn't going to change her mind. At least she was sure, and he'd supposedly had an alibi. Maybe I needed to get on board with that too. Still, if he had her lapel pin, it would be a given that he'd killed her. How could I figure it out? Maybe I could risk visiting him one more time, tomorrow evening. "Okay, Fiona, I won't push it. Is there anything else you remember about the morning you died?"

"I remember feeling annoyed, but that's it. Honestly, it's like my brain doesn't want to remember." Could I blame her? She was strangled. The feeling of fighting for air and not being able to get it was petrifying. I gulped in a few extra-deep breaths. Yep, no way would you want to remember that in any detail at all.

"Okay. Well, feel free to stay here. I'm going to bed."

She looked around nervously. "I might for a while, but there's another ghost who visits when you're not here. She's a bit angry."

For cripes' sake. Now I had a cranky ghost to worry about? At least they couldn't physically touch me, but could they move stuff around? Maybe I'd find a lamp hovering, ready to conk me on the head in the middle of the night. That would be fun... not. For the first time since moving in, I wanted to be back at the pub. I'd been safe there. *Stop, Avery!* The last thing I wanted was to spiral into the cesspool of dread I'd suffered after being struck by lightning. I swallowed my fear. It wasn't going to beat me again. I was stronger than that. I'd survived my ex, my useless parents, being struck by lightning, thinking I was nuts, and now seeing ghosts. I'd successfully moved to the other side of the world for goodness' sake. I wasn't going to cower now.

I gave Fiona a sympathetic look. "Stay safe. I'll do everything I can. Goodnight."

"Night, Avery. And thank you. You really are an angel."

I hated to tell her I wasn't, but if it helped her, so be it. Now I just had to live up to those undeserved expectations. I wasn't sure how I was going to do that when I was probably going to be incapable of even getting a good night's sleep, but the least I could do was try. And try, I would, even if I was destined to fail.

# CHAPTER 19

The next morning, after getting about four hours' sleep —opening your eyes every ten minutes to check no one was staring at you was not conducive to sleep—I had coffee at home before heading to work. I hadn't been back to the café after being ripped off by that stupid cow. My pride had been dented, but more than that, I wanted to retaliate, and in a small town, that was not the way to go, so avoidance was my weapon of choice, or non-weapon, as the case might be.

Just as I reached the office, handbag strap across my chest, laptop bag in hand, one of my to-do things automatically crossed itself off my list. Although, by the look on Simon Daniels' face, maybe I didn't want it crossed off.

As soon as he saw me, he stomped towards me, flinty anger sparking from his gaze, his jaw set, hands balled into tight, punchy fists. I stopped walking and readied to drop my laptop bag and defend myself. Adrenaline warmed my stomach, and I adopted a loose fighting stance, one foot in front of the other. Thank goodness I'd worn my low court-style shoes today.

Although stilettos could've done some damage, I wasn't sure how well I could balance on those.

He stopped a couple of feet away, thank God. His voice was loud, and people passing by stared but kept going. *Yeah, thanks for your concern.* "How dare you go and see her! She told me you harassed her. And how did you even find out?" So many accusations, and I wasn't going to deny any of them, nor was I going to answer his question. "You'd better not put any of that in the paper. I'm not even seeing her anymore, for God's sake." He stepped closer, within striking range. My muscles tensed. "I've put a complaint in with your boss. And if you go anywhere near me or my ex again, I won't be held responsible for what happens. Got it?"

My heart hammered, and I tried to slow my breathing. Bloody adrenaline. I'd be all jelly after this too. Man, I hated that. "Are you threatening me? Maybe you did kill your wife. It's not like you were happy with her." Oh, for Jeebus's sake, why did I have to say that? What if he hadn't killed her, and I was baiting a truly grieving husband? But then again, he had just threatened me. Whether he felt justified or not, that was abysmal behaviour. And maybe my goading would get an accidental admission of something.

His face reddened. His fists shook, but they were still at his side. *Come on, then, buddy. Go for it, and see what you get.* Maybe my defiance showed in my eyes, or maybe he finally realised we had an audience, but he stepped back. "Don't ever contact me again. Keep your crooked journalism away from me and my ex, or else." He turned and walked down the street. The bystanders seeped away, not one offering me help—a couple of them even looked at me like *I* was the scumbag. *Fine.* There were always going to be stupid people. I held my head high as I buzzed the office intercom.

"Hi," I called as I went through. Silence, which was typical.

All was normal with the world, at least in this office. The aftereffects of the adrenaline made my legs shaky, and I was happy to plonk into my chair.

Finnegan and Carina were both in. They looked at me. Finnegan narrowed his eyes, then got up and came over. "Are you okay? You look a little… rattled."

I took a deep breath, trying to slow myself down. *You're fine, Avery. The big, bad man is gone.* "I had an altercation outside. I'm fine. Nothing really happened."

He raised a brow. "Was it an altercation, or was it nothing? It can't be both."

Carina hurried over at *altercation.* Her concerned stare raked over me. "What happened? Do you have any injuries?" Her eyes widened. "It didn't have anyt'ing to do wit' d'at angry guy did it?"

I smiled in an attempt to reassure them of my wholeness. It didn't look like they were going anywhere till they got an explanation, so I'd better spill. "You mean the guy who just came in here and complained about me to Mr MacPherson? Yes."

Finnegan gave me the once over, his expression serious. "Are you sure he didn't hurt you? Do you want me to call the police?"

I shook my head. "No. He's upset. He's wife just died, and I probably wasn't very nice either just then."

Carina twirled some of her blue hair around a finger. "He started it, I'm assuming?"

"Yes. He was angry that I went to see his mistress."

"But she has an alibi." It didn't surprise me that Finnegan knew about her. He had an easy information source in his dad's best friend.

"Yes, but alibis can be manufactured. And, look, I didn't think she'd say much, but I didn't ask her about where she was. I don't think she killed her."

"So, why did you go?" Finnegan had crossed the line from caring to nosey.

"None of your business."

Mr MacPherson strode through the door and stopped short, his gaze bypassing my companions and stopping at me. "We need to have a talk. My office. Now." He turned and left, his footsteps echoing ominously as he went back along the hallway.

Possum poo.

Finnegan gave me a frustrated look and went back to his desk. Carina was all about sympathy. I wasn't sure which was worse. I could do without the attention right now. "You'll be all right, hon. Mac will stand behind you. He supports his team."

I stood and brushed my hands down my skirt. "I'm sure everything will be fine. Thanks for the encouragement." I didn't want her to think I was ungrateful. "Best not keep him waiting." I gave her another "I'm fine" smile and left.

My heels click-clacked loudly. The little girl appeared as I reached MacPherson's office door. She looked up at me. "Are you in trouble?"

"Maybe."

She patted my arm, and a tingle travelled along it. My eyes widened, and goosebumps replaced the tingle. Holy hell. What did that mean? I swallowed. "Ah, thanks. What's your name, by the way?"

"Erin."

"Lovely to formally meet you, Erin." I gave her a genuine smile.

"Lovely to meet you, too, Avery." She grinned, revealing two missing front teeth. Sadness settled through me. She was so young. What had she died of? Was it rude to ask?

"Avery! Get in here!"

I jumped. The door had been ajar. Hades. Had he just heard me "talking to myself?" Erin mouthed, "Sorry." I shrugged, then pushed the door open and shut it behind me. I willed my legs to take me all the way to his desk, but I didn't sit, just in case he liked to chastise people while they were standing.

He tapped his finger on the table and looked at me as if searching for someone. "Who were you talking to out there? Were you on the phone?"

I swallowed. "I was talking to myself, making sure my voice was working properly after having such a fright outside. When I'm nervous, my throat can close up." *Oh, really, Avery. The queen of bull faeces.* I did have to acknowledge that I was proud of my ability to think quickly, no matter how stupid it sounded. If I pretended it was true, he'd buy it. People wanted to believe others were telling the truth, and if someone was mainly honest, their default would be to assume someone else was telling the truth too. That was how scammers managed to fool so many people. Man, I hated scammers.

He stared at me for a beat too long. "Right, okay." He gestured to the seat. "Sit." I did. He pushed his chair back and stood, then paced back and forth behind his desk. I wasn't sure if he was trying to intimidate me, or he couldn't stand to be still. I had a suspicion he might have ADHD. He was always tapping, or moving, or being overly enthusiastic—not that that meant he did have it, but he was noticeably more active in quiet environments than anyone I'd ever met.

I didn't want to sit here all day. If he was going to give me a warning, I wanted it over and done with. "I'm sorry Mr MacPherson. I needed to question Mr Daniels' mistress for a story I'm looking into. He was very upset, I know. He threatened me outside, so I wasn't very charitable in what I said. If he'd been nice about it, I might have apologised. Are you going to give me a warning?"

He stopped pacing and spun towards me. "He threatened

you? That's not on, Winters, not on at all. Did you notify the police?"

"Ah, no. I think he's just upset about his wife. If he contacts me again, I will."

He scratched his chin. "Right, well, if you want, I can call them. No one threatens my staff and gets away with it."

I blinked, not sure where this was going. He seemed awfully understanding and protective for someone who was probably going to give me a warning. "Ah, thank you. I'm sure everything will be fine. I don't want to make a big deal out of it."

"He could be a killer, Avery." He made a good point. "But I won't call the police unless you want me to."

"Not right now. If I hear from him again, I will, but he warned me to leave him and his mistress alone, so I don't think he'll be bothering me again… unless I do what he's told me not to."

"And will you?"

"At this stage, no. I don't think the mistress has anything more to say to me anyway."

"Right." He sat again and picked up his desk phone. "Hello, Bethany. Can you bring me a tea? Thanks." He hung up and looked at me. "I called you in because Mr Daniels complained about you seeing his mistress. I told him that it was a free country and you'd done nothing wrong. He wanted me to discipline you for harassment, but I refused. I thought I'd call you in here as a courtesy, to let you know he'd complained."

Well, that was a surprise. "Oh, okay. Thank you. After what happened outside, I thought I was in trouble."

He laughed. "Trouble? For doing your job? Never! And you're sure you're okay?"

"Yes, thanks. Is that all?" I hoped that didn't seem rude, but I needed to go for a walk and dissipate the nervous energy turning into lactic acid in my muscles. "I don't want to take up any more of your time. I'm sure you're busy." Maybe that softened it.

"Yes, that's it. Actually, so far, you're doing a good job. I like your voice, which is what got you this job in the first place. You've written some humdingers in Australia, and your boss gave you quite the glowing recommendation."

I smiled. Hannah, the woman who ran things at the previous company, was tough but fair, and being a woman, she knew how difficult it could be. When my ex had submitted my story as his own and added me as a contributor, she'd called me in and asked me about it, thinking that I'd actually done most of the work. I downplayed it and gave him the credit—admitting he was a jerk and stealing my stuff would not only make him look bad, but I hadn't wanted him to break up with me. Pathetic, right? "Wow, thank you. I appreciate you saying." I smiled. "So far, I'm enjoying working here. I hope I can keep putting in good articles."

"I'm sure you will. And if that man gives you any more trouble, come and see me."

"I will. Thanks." I stood, gave him a nod, and left. Well, that wasn't what I'd expected. When I'd first arrived and heard about the previous guy being shafted—or quitting, or being driven to quit, depending on who you asked—I thought I was in for a rough time. Maybe moving here really had been the best idea I'd ever had.

After going for a walk, I covered the supermarket specials. They had ads for that sort of thing, but according to Carina, supporting local business was on their agenda. While I was there, I couldn't resist buying their chocolate-fudge ice cream that was half off, and after tasting it, I made sure to say something special about it in my piece. With my budget, it wasn't often I splurged on the good-quality stuff, so I waited for sales. I took my spoils home, wrote the article, submitted it, and by then, it was time to walk to the pub. Meg hadn't texted me, so I assumed her hair appointment was running on time.

I entered the bar area, expecting to see her. Bailey looked up from clearing a table. He gave me a chin tip. I supposed calling out across the room half filled with patrons wasn't professional. I returned his chin tip and sat at the bar. Might as well look busy while I was waiting. I pulled out my phone and checked it—no text. She shouldn't be too long then.

I figured I'd check Instagram, see what my "friends" from Sydney were up to. None of them had contacted me for months. As soon as Brad broke up with me, I'd become a persona non grata. I won't lie—it sucked. Had they just put up with me because I was dating him? Was I generally unlikable? I wasn't the life of the party. Maybe that was it? They were all loud and showy. I didn't like to be the centre of attention. They probably saw that as boring, and they were probably right. Looking at their pictures ached in a way I wasn't expecting. Was it time to unfollow them, leave my old life behind well and truly?

"How's it going, Avery?"

I jerked my head up. Bailey smiled at me. Damn those matching dimples on either side of his mouth. I smiled. "Hey, Bailey. I'm good, thanks. How are you?"

"Good. You waiting for Meg?"

"Yep." I looked at my watch. "She's ten minutes late. She's not usually late, is she?"

"Nope, but it was a hair appointment. You never know how long she's going to be when she's in date mode." He smirked. "Do you want anything while you're waiting?"

I shook my head. "All good, thanks."

"Well, if you need anything, just let me know." He grinned

and moved away to serve a customer. I was way out of practice with flirting, so I wasn't sure if he was just being polite when he said if I needed anything to let him know, or if anything was suggestive. *Seriously, Avery, get over yourself.* Even if he was flirting—which he most likely wasn't—men were bad news. I needed to stand on my own two feet, get to know who adult Avery was without someone else there to insist on what she should do, wear, and how she should be.

"Avery! Sorry I'm late."

I swivelled on my bar stool—ah, how I loved a swivel chair. "Ooh, look at your gorgeous colour." She had shortish hair. How long could colouring and styling that really have taken?

She held up her hands. "I got fancy schmancy nails too. Figured I might as well." She fluttered her lashes. "And tinted lashes."

"Ah, so the works." I laughed. "You look gorgeous. That dude is going to think he's the luckiest guy ever."

"Why, thank you. Are you ready to go?"

"Yep."

"Then let's get to it." She waved at Bailey as we left, and Bailey and I gave each other a nod. His even came with a small smile. *Ignore the cuteness. Ignore it!*

Meg babbled the whole way there, obviously excited about her upcoming date. It was nice to just nod and look out the window but not have to talk. The last few days had been exhausting, and the less energy I had to expend, the better. I also didn't mention the altercation with Mr Daniels this morning because I didn't want to talk about it, and Meg was sure to ask a gazillion questions. She'd probably find out about it on the village grapevine later anyway, and I'd answer her concerns then.

We arrived at the council building, and Meg parked. "Do you mind if I come with? I'm kind of curious, and Dad wanted to know what we found out too."

I shrugged. "If you want. Might be good to have you there. We can discuss the information later... if there is any." As much as this could turn into an interesting article and possible police investigation, I could be chasing ghosts. I chuckled to myself. Ha ha. Maybe they had cleaned up the site, or maybe it was never as contaminated as Meg's dad had thought? But, at this stage, it was all maybes, and I dealt in facts. And since I was curious, I wouldn't let it go till I captured those facts. My parents had always accused me of being the dead curiosity cat. They never approved of my job and told me it would kill me one day. Totally irrational, but there was no arguing with them. I was sure they'd find fault with whatever profession I'd chosen because I wasn't good enough for any job... except maybe working at the supermarket like my mother. Not that it wasn't an honest job, and a vital one at that, but I desired more out of life. I wanted to expose the bad guys, report on good stuff as well, cheer people up. My job was a mixture of entertainment and justice, which was one reason I loved it so much.

It was oddly comforting to have Meg at my side as we went into the council and to the front counter. They probably had a similar system to back home, since we were a colony, but you never knew. The blonde, bespectacled lady at the counter smiled at us. "Hello, ladies. How can I help you?"

I'd brought the contract. I put it on the counter. "I'm just researching this land. My friend's uncle was thinking of buying it, but he's overseas at the moment and wanted us to dot the i's and cross the t's. He thought this land may have had previous contamination, but it's not mentioned in the contract. Would you be able to check?"

"Oh, that's interesting. I can see what I have in the system. It might take a few minutes, if you don't mind waiting."

"We're good." Meg and I both smiled.

The woman tapped away on her keyboard. Unfortunately we

couldn't see her screen, but I did trust she'd be honest. Although, what if someone at council had fudged things for a bribe? This might be harder than I thought. If there was anything to find, we might never find it.

After a few minutes, her brow furrowed. She looked at us. "Can I get you ladies to wait here? I just need to talk to someone."

"Yeah, sure." My gut did a little flip, the one I got when my research took me somewhere potentially exciting. I looked at Meg. "I wonder what she found."

Her eyes were bright. "You might have stumbled upon something important, Avery. Which wouldn't surprise me. You're smart."

I didn't want to burst her bubble and remind her that we hadn't even known each other for a week and that she might be jumping the gun on her assessment, so I just smiled. "Ah, thanks." It might be time to change the subject while we were waiting. "So, how many hours, minutes, and seconds before your date?"

She grinned and looked at her phone. "Five hours, forty-five minutes, and twenty seconds. Ooh, now it's seventeen seconds." She poked her tongue out at me.

I laughed. "How long has it been since you've been on a date?"

"Five months. Before that I took a dating hiatus for six months."

"Bad break-up?"

Her smile fell. "You could say that. Anyway, I'm pretty much over it now, but it took time." She obviously didn't want to elaborate, so I wouldn't push her. She'd tell me when she was ready.

Finally, the council lady returned, a moustachioed man with her. His orange cardigan looked like a seventies' throwback, even though he was only in his thirties. She introduced him. "This is Peter Falks. He runs our remediations department."

I smiled. "Nice to meet you, Mr Falks. I'm Avery Winters. This is my friend Meg."

He gave us a nod but no smile. Hmm, were we about to be fobbed off? "Hello, ladies. Ellen here has told me you're looking for information on a property you thought might be contaminated."

I nodded. "Yes. Is there anything you can tell us?"

"I have no records here. We archive them after five years. The last entry I have for this property on our computer database doesn't mention anything, so I'm afraid I can't help you." He smoothed out his moustache with two fingers. When he did it the third time, it made me think he was patting himself. I shook my head to rid it of the thought so I wouldn't laugh. If I didn't know better, he was nervous. There was something he wasn't saying. "So, if that's all, I'll leave you in Ellen's capable hands." Instead of turning to leave, he folded his arms.

I narrowed my eyes. Why come out to see us? Was he ensuring we left? He knew something for sure. "The person who wants to buy this property has a lot of money, and if there's anything wrong with it, he won't hesitate to sue the council." Meg looked at me, her eyes wide. I wasn't sure if she was impressed or horrified I'd gone in so hard.

Peter went from smoothing his moustache to smoothing his vest. Oh, he was hiding something all right. "There's no information on our system." He wasn't getting away with it that easily.

"Did someone delete it?" I sniffed the air. "Do I smell a bribery scandal, Peter? Should I ask for an inquiry into this council and the way it keeps its records?" Maybe I was overdoing it, but I might only have one chance at this guy, and I wasn't wasting it. They said honey caught more flies, but a fly swatter often did a good job too.

Meg grabbed my upper arm. "I'm sure we don't need to resort to that, Avery." I gave Meg a "not now" look.

Peter cleared his throat. "I can assure you that we operate above board here."

"So what aren't you telling us?" I tapped my foot, making it loud enough to be obvious. "Because when I'm finished here, I'm going to call my friend's uncle's lawyer. He can put in a formal request to the council for all the information on this property going back fifty years."

Ellen pivoted her gaze from me to Peter, worry clear on her face. "Do you want me to call security?"

He stared at me, possibly tossing up how serious I was. I hardened my gaze. *Make no mistake, buddy, I won't give up.* His swallow was loud enough that I heard it. He said quietly, "No, but can you give me a minute with them?"

Her brow furrowed, but then she understood. "Okay. Yell out if you need me." She turned and made her way far enough down the counter that she could still serve people but couldn't hear what we were saying.

Peter leaned forward, his arms resting on the counter. He lowered his voice. "I could get into a lot of trouble talking to you, so I'll make it quick. We have no records here, but when I got this job about six years ago, I did see something about this property. The address rings a bell. If you want to look into it, you should ask them to pull the information from the archives. The man running things back then retired two years ago. His name is Bob Fairly. Please leave me out of this. Whatever it is, I had nothing to do with it."

I could push him further, but my gut told me that he'd given up what he knew. My gut was also trying to tell me something else, but I couldn't be sure it wasn't just that it needed food. "Thank you, Peter. I promise not to mention you when I talk to the lawyers, and I'm sure if they find anything, you'll be kept out of it since you didn't do anything. Thanks for coming clean."

He grunted, and I almost didn't hear his reluctant "Pleasure," when it floated across the counter. He turned and walked away.

I was pretty sure that was awe shining from Meg's face. "Wow, you were incredible." She shook her head. "If I didn't see it with my own eyes, I wouldn't believe it. You're a real toughie when you want to be."

I smiled. "Not so tough in my personal life, but when it comes to work, I'm a bit of a magpie."

"Magpie?"

"I swoop and peck and attack. They don't see me coming, and when I'm finished, they're traumatised." I smiled.

"Remind me never to get on your bad side."

"I doubt you could. You're too nice. Okay, let's get going. I have somewhere else I need to stop. I hope you don't mind, but it is on the way back."

"Where?"

"The police station. I need to speak to Sergeant Bellamy."

"Not a prob."

I made a mental note to buy her a bunch of flowers with my first pay cheque, or electronic funds transfer of wages, if I was going to be specific. She'd done so much for me, and I had no other way to thank her, well, other than cooking dinner, and that wasn't exactly a gourmet experience. She'd stop doing me favours sooner rather than later if that's all I had to offer. Not to mention the guilt I carried with me every time I asked her for help.

On the way there, I sat with the contract in my lap. "So, Meg, what do you think?"

"I think you're onto something. Is that why we're going to see Sergeant Bellamy?"

"Ah, no. That's about something else." After Fiona had told me about the top-agent pin she'd been sporting the day she died,

I went to her social media and checked out her pics. Every work photo of her where she had a jacket on, that pin was there, on the right lapel. I'd had the benefit of seeing her lying on my floor —not that I remembered whether the pin had been there then or not. But I could say that I hadn't seen it. It would be my excuse to bring it up. Hopefully the police would take it seriously. If it was at her house, maybe they could make a case against her husband, or it might at least make them look more closely at him, alibi or no alibi.

Meg dropped me out the front and drove off to find parking. I crossed my fingers that Bellamy would be open to hearing what I had to say. I walked in to find the same female police officer as last time manning the front desk, or was that womanning? "Miss Winters, what can I do for you?"

"Hi. I was wondering if I could see Sergeant Bellamy. It's just quick. I have some information for him regarding the Fiona Daniels case."

"I'll just see. Could you wait a moment?" She turned away and left before I answered. In other words, you'll have to wait a moment. Why did she put it politely? I was more annoyed than I would've been if she had just told it how it was. Politeness could backfire if you weren't careful. Expectation was everything.

Thankfully, when she returned, Bellamy was with her. He didn't buzz me through, though. He spoke to me through the security glass at the front desk. "Hello, Miss Winters. I understand you have some information regarding Mrs Daniels."

I didn't know much about police protocol, but surely this should be done in a more formal setting. Already he wasn't taking me seriously. Cat's bum. "Yes. I just wanted to say that when I found the body, I noticed she wasn't wearing the pin that she has on in literally every photo of her at work in the last year. I was wondering if, maybe, it fell off when she was attacked? And that, maybe, if you found it at her house, it might point the finger back at her husband." Talk about having to make things obvious.

"Thank you, Miss Winters. Is that all?" Bellamy's stern expression didn't waver, and I wondered how much of it was practiced normal police face and how much of it was annoyance that I dared suggest that they hadn't paid full attention to things.

"So, will you check it out? It just seems kind of important to me, and if I write another article on it, it would be great to be able to say how thorough you were and how wonderful you were to listen to silly little me and my concerns." Oops. I wasn't making friends right now, no matter how friendly my tone was. I really should learn how to be more subtle. That was certainly not my strong suit.

His face darkened. Yep, definitely annoyed. He spoke through gritted teeth. "Yes, we'll check it out. Can you tell me where you saw photos of her at work?"

"On Instagram and Facebook. There were even a couple of videos of her on her company's website. They're from earlier this year as she walks the viewer through properties for sale. It seems like she never takes it off. From what her boss said, it was a pin given to her and no other agent because she's been the best sales-person there for a few years in a row. Her sister mentioned it to me too. She said she always wore it to work." Now I'd have to call her sister and fill her in, cover my bum. It wasn't as if I could tell him Fiona herself had told me. That would've gone down exceptionally well. "Maybe you could look through security footage from that morning, see if Fiona was wearing the pin when she left the office?"

The policewoman behind him didn't look nearly as annoyed as her boss. The way she was looking at me was... cautious mixed with, dare I say it, curiosity. It wasn't quite respect. I was probably only an annoying reporter at the end of the day, and no one wanted their professionalism called into question, especially in front of their own staff, but he only had himself to blame since he wanted to speak to me out here. I couldn't be responsible for the harm he brought to himself.

"Right. Is that all?" he asked.

"Yes, thanks, Sergeant Bellamy. Thank you for taking my concerns seriously. I appreciate it, and I'm sure if Fiona were still alive, she'd appreciate it too." Hopefully he'd see that I wasn't trying to be a cow—I was honestly trying to help. "There's a killer out there, and I, for one, would be happier knowing they were out of commission."

He cleared his throat. "Yes, well, I can't argue with you there. Good day, Miss Winters."

"Good day, Sergeant."

As I made my way back to Meg's car, despondency slumped my shoulders. Even if they took me seriously, would this help find her killer? If whoever it was had thrown the pin away, it might never be found. It was literally like looking for a needle in a haystack. It seemed the more I discovered, the more that came into question. My earlier enthusiasm was waning, and I had no idea if I had the energy to keep going to the end. The problem was, I couldn't let Fiona down. Once I promised someone something, I saw it through. And I'd promised her I'd find out who killed her.

Note to self: be careful what you promise people because one day, you won't be able to deliver. I just hoped that day wasn't barrelling towards me like an out-of-control truck.

# CHAPTER 20

T hat afternoon, when I was back at home, I called Alice, Fiona's sister, and explained about the pin. "Do you think you could pay Simon a visit and ask about it? Would that be too suspect?"

"You're right that she always wore it at work. The few times I caught up with her for lunch during the week, she was wearing it. I remember because I chewed her out about not wearing the locket but she always wore that."

"I guess she was proud of what she'd achieved." Maybe it also made her feel more capable in front of her male colleagues, in case they needed reminding that a woman could do the job just as well as they could... or better. Hmm, maybe that's one reason Crowley didn't like her. He probably thought she was rubbing his face in it.

"She was proud. That job was everything to her. Anyway, I'm not sure how I'll go visiting Simon. He's made it clear that he doesn't want to see any of her family. Other than relaying information about the funeral arrangements, he won't talk to us. Trust me—I've tried."

"What? That's weird."

She sighed. "I think it's because they were having problems, but it just makes me more suspicious. Oh, and I found out from a mutual friend that he's changed his flight to the day of the funeral. He jets out that night. I just… I can't."

"I'm sorry." What else could you say to a grieving woman who suspected her brother-in-law of murdering her sister?

"Right, well, I'm going to get going. I'll let you know if I manage to see him. Bye, Avery."

"Bye." Well, that wasn't great. Maybe this missing pin was a dead end. And the fact Simon was leaving earlier made this all the more urgent. If he had killed her, he was close to getting away with it. I imagined he had no plans to return. There was something else that was bothering me, but it was something to do with our visit to council.

I sat on the couch and opened the contract for that land sale again. What had I missed? I flicked through. When I saw it, it slapped me in the face, and I sucked in a breath. How had I missed this before? I had a pretty good memory. Maybe I hadn't taken it in properly when I read the contract the first few times.

The owner of the land was listed loud and clear a few pages in. Anderson Fairly. Fairly wasn't a common surname, so chances were, he was related to good old Bob who happened to be in charge at the council when the records conveniently disappeared.

*Interestinger and interestinger.*

Now what? Maybe I should call MacPherson, see what resources he had access to in terms of lawyers and friends that could do him a favour. I couldn't afford to pay a lawyer to send a threatening letter to council regarding the land. I could, however, get in touch with the purchaser. But would they listen to me? I only had a suspicion and circumstantial evidence.

Hmm.

Did the council have a preferred-companies list when it came to soil testing, businesses they contacted when contamination was suspected? I could call them. How helpful they'd be, I had no idea, but it was worth a try. Unfortunately, it was after five, so I'd have to wait until tomorrow. I googled the property address and contamination, but nothing came up. A historical photo did appear, showing a service station with a smaller industrial building at the back, so at least there was my proof that it hadn't always been clean, vacant land. But nothing else—no articles or resources on the actual contamination.

Fiona materialised, standing in front of me. "Avery, you're here."

"Yes. I'm sorry to report that I don't have any new information, but I did tell Sergeant Bellamy about your missing pin."

"Thank you." She didn't smile, though. Her eyes held a sheen of fear. "There's a young boy out the front. He says he needs to speak with you."

"A ghost boy or a live boy?" If he'd spoken to Fiona, he was likely a ghost, but it didn't hurt to ask. Maybe there were more people like me?

"A ghost. Do you know him?"

"I might. How come he can't just come up?"

"Unless he has a special connection to your house, he can't just come in. You have to invite him."

"Oh. How did you find out? Is there like a handbook you wake up with when you die?" Okay, so that was a lame joke, but I was curious. Besides, he'd visited me at work, and I was pretty sure no one had invited him in.

"Ah, no. I tried to visit next door, but I couldn't. The only house I can get into is this one, and the other night, I managed to go home, but I couldn't stay long. It was as if I was being sucked back here."

"Right." What else could I say to that? There were rules to the in-between, and I had no hope of figuring them out. I couldn't even work out what in Hades was going on in *this* world.

No sense keeping my stalker waiting. He was probably here to hassle me about dealing with Patrick's stuff. The problem was, it was full daylight outside, and I didn't want to be seen talking to myself. But if I invited him in, would he have access to me whenever he wanted forever more? No, no, no, that wouldn't do. I'd spent a lifetime to get to the point where I could live in peace by myself, and one ghost having access to my house was more than enough.

I hurried downstairs as quietly as I could—I didn't want to alert Mrs Crabby and have her come out to spy on me. When I reached the front fence, sure enough, Charles was waiting for me. I sat on the fence as if I were enjoying the afternoon and gave him a subtle wave.

"Patrick wants to know how long this is going to take. A day can feel like forever in our world, especially when we're stuck."

I made sure my voice was quiet. "Have you ever been stuck?"

"Yes. It took me a while to decide how to move on."

"How come you could enter my work, but you can't come into my house?"

"No one lives there. It's not a sacred space. Houses are sacred spaces, but places people work, they're kind of soulless. There's nothing to protect."

I chuckled. "Places of work certainly are soulless. Interesting that the universal powers that be recognise that."

"So?" He squinted up at me. "When are you going to get the job done? You're really slow; you know that?"

Irritation grated chunks out of my patience. "I have other things going on right now. Not to mention that I have to deliver the message the right way or it won't help anyone. Do you have any suggestions on how to tell Patrick's friend his message without having him attack me or just shut the door in my face?

He might think I'm the world's biggest charlatan trying to cause trouble."

"Oh, yeah. You could be right. So, do you have a timeframe I can give Pat?"

I sighed. I barely had time to think about what I was having for breakfast tomorrow let alone what I planned days in advance. I'd need to pick a day I had the mental energy to deal with what I had to do, and tomorrow was not going to be it. "I don't know. Not tomorrow, and maybe not the day after. Maybe on the weekend? I need time to figure it out. Tell Patrick I'm sorry, but I will get to it. I promise."

He cocked his head to the side and narrowed his eyes. "All right. I'll let him know. I'll be back to see you after that if he's still there."

I shook my head. "You're like a bulldog. You know that?"

He smiled, and his chest puffed out proudly. "Yep. Bye, Avery."

"Bye, Charles." I turned to go back inside, and Mrs Crabby opened the door and stepped out.

"Why were you sitting there talking to yourself? You'll have everyone thinking I gave a nutter lodgings. *Are* you crazy? Do you have schizophrenia? If you do, I can't have you staying here." She pressed her lips together and gave me a "well?" look.

For mighty Zeus's sake. Just what I needed to deal with. I'd barely moved in, and now I might have to leave again? To be fair, even I thought I'd been crazy before I realised ghosts were real, but it was none of her business. And if I didn't have this place, I had nowhere else to go. Being homeless was not a life goal. "I have to interview someone tomorrow, and I'm nervous about it. I wanted fresh air as well, so I thought I'd practice out here." I smiled. "And, no, I don't have any mental illnesses." That I knew of....

She scowled. Trust was obviously not in her vocabulary. "I'm watching you." She turned, went back inside, and shut the door behind her. I heard the lock turn and click into place. Thank God I'd brought my keys with me. Note to self: don't ever lock yourself out because you'll never get back in.

She appeared at her window, frown in place, and pointed a finger at me for good measure, then shut the curtain. I snorted. That was probably her entertainment and exercise for the day. She should thank me for motivating her. I'd have to think of other ways to annoy her later. I could be like her personal trainer.

A person walked towards me from the alleyway, and I knew it wasn't a ghost, unless Finnegan had died since I'd seen him last. I considered running inside, but it was too late—he'd seen me. "Hey, Lightning." He waved and headed straight for me.

"Hey, Vinegar. Annoying as ever, I see." He knew I hated that name, and as much as I'd thought vinegar was a clever come-back, it didn't seem to bother him. I'd have to try harder.

"Oh, how you wound me. Enjoying the view, I see." He waved at the dirt expanse sitting between our row of terraces and the two houses across the way.

"Yes. It reminds me of you—it's bland and sounds good crunching under my shoes."

"You don't know what I would sound like crunching under your shoes."

"True, but I can imagine. Dirt is less offensive though, so I do like dirt a little better."

He smiled a gorgeous smile, one that lanced straight through my heart and to other places. I pretended he hadn't affected me because he knew what he was doing. His gorgeousness obviously got him places with everyone else, but it wasn't going to work with me. I wasn't *that* much of a pushover... at least, not anymore. Out with the old Avery and in with the new. "I don't believe you for a second, Lightning."

"Not my circus, not my monkeys." I stood. "Enjoy staring at

yourself in the mirror later. I have work to do." I grinned, turned, and made my way inside, thankful the key worked on the first go and I didn't look like an idiot fumbling the getaway.

Back upstairs, I made a list of everything I had to do, in order of importance. I wasn't ashamed to admit that last on my list was "annoy Mrs Crabby." Although, I'd probably already achieved it. I'd cross it out, but, really, it wouldn't hurt to annoy her again. First on my list was calling all the soil-testing companies in Devon. Hopefully one of them would have the information I needed.

Second on my list was finding more evidence against Fiona's husband. How I was going to do that, I had no idea. Fiona wasn't much help any more, and Bellamy wasn't talking. I really had zero clue what I was doing. And I couldn't even stalk Simon Daniels because I had no car. Not to mention that if I had more connections in this village, I might be able to expect people would talk to me. As it was, trying to interview anyone would be like asking Mrs Crabby to sing me a lullaby to help me fall asleep.

Third on my list was finally speaking to Patrick's friend, but I had so much to do that I doubted I would get to that this week. I felt like I was letting Patrick down, but without doing it right, I would mess it all up, and maybe he would be stuck here indefinitely. Hades. If only I knew how all this afterlife stuff worked.

I put my pen and paper down and set to making dinner. That was one thing I wouldn't stuff up too badly, and right now, I needed all the successes I could get.

# CHAPTER 21

The next morning, I made my calls from home. I didn't want Finnegan stealing my thunder. If he got wind of what I was looking into, he might just decide to research it himself. It was nine forty-five, and I was on my twelfth company. Who knew so many companies did soil sampling? "Hi, I'm Avery Winters. I was wondering if I could speak to someone about a soil sample your company did a few years ago."

"Yes, Avery. Do you have the address?" I gave it to her. After a minute, she said, "Yes, actually, that was one of ours. You're in luck. The person you need to speak to is here. I'll put you through to Adam London. Hang on a moment."

Wow, that was too easy. Did they not have confidentiality agreements? Or maybe not, since it's supposed to be public knowledge and council was notified at the time. Or maybe it was done so long ago that it's not seen as confidential any more?

"Adam speaking. How can I help you?" He sounded friendly enough, if not a bit older, maybe even retirement age. Was that why I was lucky he was still there?

"Hi, Adam. I'm Avery. A friend of mine wants to buy some

land, but it's been flagged at council as being contaminated, and I wanted further information. The council told me to give you guys a call." I was such a fibber, but I didn't see how else I was going to get this information.

"Of course, Avery. I have the address here. I'm just pulling up the file now. Ah, here it is. Do you want me to email it to you?"

My mouth dropped open. I definitely hadn't expected this level of cooperation. "Yes, please. That is so kind of you. I just have one more question."

"Shoot."

"Do you follow up on remediation or have anything to do with that?"

"No. We just submit our report and give four recommendations for firms which are accredited to do that. That list will be in the file I send you. Is that all?"

"Yes, thanks, Adam. You've been a massive help. Thank you so much!"

"My pleasure. Goodbye, Avery."

"Bye." I hung up, a huge grin on my face. I'd done it; I'd gotten strong information. This could potentially lead to some serious charges being brought against the Fairlys. Their name wasn't indicative of how they operated—fair, they were not. Now to look through the file and contact the remediation companies and see if I was leaping to conclusions.

Holy moly, this file was potentially explosive… or at least the soil was. They found high traces of zinc, cadmium, benzene, and lead, and lesser traces of some other dangerous chemicals. There was even asbestos. They recommended that it was unsafe and shouldn't be built on until the soil was removed and replaced. Building on it was illegal and would attract huge fines. Not to mention how sick people would get if they lived and worked on the site. The groundwater could also be contaminated. Had it flowed to nearby waterways?

The plans on the land weren't just for retail but also residential. What if young kids played outside and dug stuff up? Lead poisoning was horrific, and by then, they might be able to sue someone, but it would be too late in terms of health damage. And was the owner about to take the purchaser's money and leave the country? It wouldn't surprise me. Knowing the way crooks operated, he probably had everything in his wife's name so the courts couldn't touch any of his assets in the event they did sue him. Colonel Sanders had mentioned they were planning to take things and run from what he overheard the day of the auction.

Anger narrowed my eyes and gritted my teeth. I squeezed my hand into a fist, wishing I could punch the owner and his brother right now. Hapkido them to a pulp. The first rule of hapkido at our dojang was never initiate conflict. Would my instructor be too upset if I broke that rule this one time?

I went through the list of four remediation companies mentioned in the report and called each one. None of them had been employed to clean the site, and the conversation I had with the CEO of the last company told me everything I needed to know. "As far as I'm aware, the property hasn't been touched since the report. It's sat vacant. I do look every couple of years, see if the work's been registered, but it hasn't. I even chased it up with the owner once when we had a quiet patch. He said he didn't have the money and was waiting until such time as he had it."

"How long ago was that?"

"About four years ago. Thankfully, we got busy about six months later, and I haven't been in touch with him again, but I would've heard if someone landed that job. It was a big one. Everyone in our industry tends to keep tabs on each other."

"Okay, then. Thanks so much, Mr Oliver. I appreciate your help. Bye." I hung up. My stomach warmed with excitement.

Was I about to blow this story wide open? I grinned. This would totally earn me story of the week. It was a shame they didn't have a story of the month because this would qualify. I hadn't reported on anything this juicy for over a year. The fact that nothing was listed at council was my only stumbling block. Maybe it had all been done, and I just needed to look for it—it wasn't impossible that it had been remediated, and Mr Oliver didn't know anything about it. It was time to ask for help.

I called MacPherson. "Hi, Mr MacPherson. It's Avery."

"Morning, Winters, and call me Julian. Not calling in sick, are you?"

"No. Just working from home this morning. I had a bit of research to get through, which is why I'm calling. Would you be able to order some information from council? It's supposedly an archived file, but the information I'm looking for shouldn't be more than five years old. Do you think you can help?"

I could hear the smile in his voice. "Yes, I certainly can. I have a lot of sway in this area—no one wants to get on the wrong side of the newspaper. One call and I can have something covered on the national TV news as well."

"Excellent." I gave him the address and told him what I needed. "Oh, I'm sure I don't need to ask, but can you not mention anything to Finnegan?"

He took a moment to answer. He chuckled. "Not a problem. You thinking this will be a story-of-the-week winner?"

"I sure do. I hate to push, but how long until you can get that information?"

"Right now. I'll make the call and let you know." The phone went dead. Stupid lack of goodbye. That bugged the hades out of me. But I wasn't going to complain if he got me what I wanted.

I stood and paced the living area. Had I stumbled onto the fraud of the decade? Well, maybe I was overstating things, but it was still exciting. If I was right, this would lead to arrests and a safer public. The purchaser wouldn't lose their money either. And it wasn't a small amount of money to lose.

I was just about to take my nervous energy out to the back deck when my phone rang. "Hey."

"Hello, Avery. Those records you wanted don't exist. Is this a case of there's nothing to find, or do you have proof those records should exist?"

I smiled. "I have proof. I have to go, but thank you so much for looking into it. Bye."

"Let me know how you go."

"Will do." I hung up before he could ask me anything else. I wasn't sure exactly what to do now. Should I find out who the purchaser was and hand copies of everything to his solicitor? And who would tell me the person's name? Wasn't that private information? I could tell the police, but it wasn't an urgent type of crime. I googled and found that I should contact Action Fraud. But would they act straight away, or would my report go into some queue and take months for someone to deal with?

"Avery, I'm glad you're here."

I started. "Zeus's pyjamas, Fiona. Stop scaring me." I didn't appreciate the galloping heart. If my heart raced, I preferred it to be from something fun like hapkido.

She clutched one side of her jacket lapel. Were those tears on her cheeks. "He's... he's with her... right now." She burst into tears.

I stood and was going to hug her, but there was really nothing to hug. How was I supposed to comfort a ghost? "I take it you're talking about Simon and his girlfriend?"

She sniffled and gave me a hard look. "*Mistress.* I'm not even in the ground yet, for heaven's sake."

I stood close to her. "I'm sorry I can't give you a hug. That sucks." I shook my head. "That rat practically attacked me yesterday and insisted they weren't together. She denied it too."

"Of course they did. He probably wants everyone to feel sorry for him. Boo hoo, poor Simon's wife died. How will he survive?" She called him a couple of choice names that I agreed with.

Hmm, I didn't want to upset her, but it was worth asking since I was having trouble getting information every other way. "I'm assuming you saw them at your place." She nodded. "Did you happen to look for your pin? If you could find it, it would pretty much confirm that he killed you."

She started crying again, and I had to wait a couple of minutes for her to stop. Seemed like the dead experienced emotions just as strongly as the living. I wasn't impressed that heartache carried beyond the grave. Seriously. Give us humans a break.

Finally, she sucked in a few shuddering breaths and wiped her eyes. "I know I said he couldn't have killed me, but you should've heard what he was saying about me to *her*. He s- s- said he was glad I was g- g- gone so they could be together." She hiccupped. Jebus, that was brutal. What a pig.

It was harsh to ask her to return, but I didn't see that we had a choice. "Do you think you could go back and look? I did mention it to the police, about the pin, but I don't know if they're looking into it or not. I have a feeling they don't take me too seriously." Okay, so it wasn't just a feeling. It was more of a fact.

She wrung her hands together. "Later? When I saw them, it shocked me. I managed to stay for a bit, but then they started talking about me. The more upset I got, the harder it was to hang on. I didn't even mean to come here, but I found myself leaving there and getting thrown into the darkness before popping out here."

I gave her an encouraging smile. "The powers that be knew

you needed to be here, somewhere safe. Maybe wait a while, then." I tamped down my rising frustration. It was looking more and more certain that he'd killed her, but he was getting away with it, and before long, he'd leave the country and totally escape punishment. As much as that was the most important point, I couldn't help the twinge of anger needling me. How dare they both lie to my face. I was not going to be kind in my article when I reported on the police arresting him for murder. So there.

She sat on the other end of the couch, on the towel that covered the brown stain, not that it mattered—she was incorporeal, after all. "Thank you, Avery. You're so kind. I don't know how I'd get through this by myself."

"Any time, Fiona. I'm happy to help." Was this why I'd been given the gift of seeing the dead? It wasn't the best gift I'd ever gotten, but helping people was a fairly noble undertaking. I wasn't a fan of the pressure though. Trying to prove someone was a murderer was difficult enough for the police, let alone a reporter with no contacts in a new country. I'd just have to make the best of it and not think about how I'd feel if I failed Fiona.

My phone rang. MacPherson again. "Hello, Avery speaking."

"Winters, I have some information. My mate from the council called to tell me he'd found something—the original request for soil testing. He assures me that if the request exists, all that other information should exist too. The only reason it survived the apparent cull of the other material is that it was filed in the wrong box. It was filed in the same street name, but wrong street number. Thank God for mistakes, hey, Winters?" He chuckled.

"Yep, yay for mistakes. Is he going to send it through?"

"Yes. I've asked him to cc you in."

"Great, thanks."

"So, are you going to tell me anything else about this investigation?"

"Not till I have all my ducks in a row. You won't mention anything to Finnegan, will you?"

"No. This is all yours. I'm sure he's working on other things that are equally as interesting. Must go now." The line went dead. What was it with him? It was as if he hated goodbyes so avoided them altogether. I hated surprises, unless they were good ones, so being surprised every time someone hung up was irritating to say the least, and I couldn't avoid it, unless I suddenly hung up on him next time. *There's a thought.*

He'd hung up before I could ask him about finding the purchaser's information. We had to stop the sale from going through before they lost all their money rather than just the deposit, which would still be in the vicinity of three hundred thousand pounds. Yikes.

I picked up the contract and looked at the solicitor's information. Then I went to my computer and set up a new Google email in a fake name. I called the seller's solicitor.

"Perkins and Hollow. How may I direct your call?"

"Hello, this is Annie Jones from Schmidt Estate Agency. Can I speak to the secretary dealing with the Fairly conveyancing matter?" I didn't want to get stuck talking to a solicitor. They'd be much cluier and not send me anything.

"I'll just put you through." *Ah, hold music from the eighties.* Pat Benatar screamed down the phone.

"Good morning. Susan Piper speaking."

"Hi, Susan, this is Annie Jones from Schmidt Estate Agency. Mr Schmidt has requested a copy of the signed pages of the contract for the Fairly conveyance, and I can't find them anywhere." I lowered my voice and pretended to be stressed. "I don't know if the other receptionist misfiled it, but if I can't produce it, I'll be on my second warning. I can't afford to lose my job, and this time, it wasn't my fault. I swear. I know they would've sent you guys a copy, and I was hoping you could email it. You'd be saving a girl's life." Who knew I could be so dramatic?

"Annie, that's fine. I can certainly email it. I'd hate for you to get into trouble. I can do that right now. Where would you like it emailed?"

"Anniejones.schmidt@gmail.com. And you're a total star. Thank you so much, Susan. I owe you one. If there's ever anything I can do for you, please let me know."

"Bye, Annie, and have a lovely day."

"You, too, Susan. Bye." I pressed the red hang-up button. *Please don't realise the email is complete and utter cow poo.* I sat on the couch, a silent Fiona watching me, and willed my email to ding with a new message. Yes, there it was! I looked at Fiona. "Success!"

"I hope you can have that kind of success getting Simon arrested. Quick thinking though. That's the land I didn't want to sell, isn't it?"

"Yes, it is. I did ask you about it the other day, but you couldn't remember much except that you didn't want to sell it. It appears that the land is contaminated. Did you find out somehow?"

She bit her bottom lip and stroked her lapel. Her brow wrinkled as she stared into space. "That rings a bell." Her eyes widened. "Yes! I knew from growing up in the area that there used to be a service station and an industrial property on that site, and I wanted to make sure it was clean, but then the council had no information. I didn't find anything with the Google search, so I went to the library to look at old newspapers and such. I found an article claiming the property was contaminated, and there was a protest to stop the owner from developing it. All that had been scrubbed from the internet. When I went to Schmidt about it, he told me to stop being silly, that the company needed the commission." She shook her head. "When I went back to copy the article to cover myself, just in case we were ever sued, it was gone. I should never have told Schmidt where I got it." Her eyes widened. "What if Schmidt killed me?"

I raised a brow. "Well, I originally thought he might have killed you because you turned him down a couple of times, but maybe this was why?"

She sighed. "But, then, Simon is still happy I'm gone, so it was more likely him. I had no evidence, and Schmidt knew I'd sooner find another job than dob him in. I just didn't want to cop the blame if anything happened. When he insisted the office would still sell it, I made him promise to leave me out of it, and I promised to forget about it." Her shoulders slumped. "I should've told someone. It was wrong of me to let them go through with it."

"Well, if he thought you were going to stay quiet, I can't see him killing you. If every crooked estate agent killed to get people who knew stuff out of the way, there'd be a hell of a lot more dead people." Funny but not funny. So many scams abounded in the world that it was hard to keep track. "Do you think he killed you?"

She cocked her head to the side and thought for a while. When she turned to me, conviction shone from her eyes. "No. That morning, I went into the office, but I left alone, and I did leave. I came here to check everything was in order and that the place was still clean before I had to go somewhere else. At least, that's how I remember it."

"Okay." I needed to check that Schmidt had an alibi. How I was going to get that information out of Bellamy, I had no idea. Unless Finnegan knew the answer. He'd been researching this case after all, and Bellamy might have given him some inside info. The question was, what would it cost me?

Fiona stood. "I'm going to go back, see if I can find that pin. Wish me luck."

"Good luck, Fiona. If I'm not here when you get back, hang out, and I'll be here later. You can do this."

She nodded, determination mixing with the tears in her eyes. "Thanks, Avery. Bye."

If she could be brave, then so could I. It was time to go and see Finnegan.

*Good luck, Avery. You're going to need it.*

# CHAPTER 22

When I walked into the office, Finnegan looked up from his desk. "Hey, Lightning. I hear you're sniffing out a good article."

I narrowed my eyes. "How much do you know?"

He held his hands up in the universal surrender gesture. "Nothing. Julian just said you were onto something, but he didn't expand."

I relaxed my shoulders back down most of the way, but I wasn't ready to be 100 per cent casual about it. He might know more than he was letting on. I put my stuff on the desk and looked over at him. "I did have a question to ask you, about Fiona Daniels's case."

He sat up straighter and stared at me. It seemed I had his full attention. Unfortunately I couldn't guarantee I would get his full cooperation. "I know that Bellamy is your dad's best mate, and I was hoping he fed you some info, like whether Fiona's boss, Schmidt, had an alibi for the morning she was killed."

He pulled an exaggerated shocked face. "You *were* listening!"

He stood and pointed at me. "You little liar, Lightning. You lied… to my gorgeous face."

I snort laughed. "Yes, I did. Imagine that. And you're not gorgeous, just so you know."

"She doth protest too much." He smirked. "So, you need my help." He wandered over and stood on the other side of my desk. "What do I get in return?"

I folded my arms. The desk was not enough of a barrier to deflect his stupid charms. Maybe he'd wear a balaclava if I asked. It would be way less distracting. "You would get the pleasure and warm fuzzies from knowing you'd helped a fellow journalist."

"I'm not much for helping people. Sorry. I'd rather get the warm and fuzzies because you traded a piece of information I might need."

I was probably stepping into dangerous territory, but I didn't see that I had a choice. "What information would that be? You've got all the connections over here. I've got nothing."

"How did Meg's date go last night?"

I blinked. I had not seen that coming. "Um… I have no idea. I haven't spoken to her yet." Zeus's pyjamas, did that make me a bad friend? I'd meant to call her, but I was saving it for later, in case she'd slept in, and then I'd gotten caught up in everything.

"Ba bow. Wrong answer. Try again."

"I can call her now, if you like? Do you have the hots for her or something?" Not that I cared, but I was sure Meg would like to know. And, okay, so I was lying a teeny-tiny bit, but since I did not want to date anyone, it would be selfish of me to not want Meg to be happy. *Mmm hmm, you tell yourself that, possum.*

"Wouldn't you like to know." He waggled his brows.

"Well, be nice, or I'll tell her you asked."

His smile fell faster than a ravenous drop bear. "Okay. Call her and ask…. Please."

Before I dialled, I had one more question. "Can you answer my question, or don't you know?"

He feigned a wounded expression. "What kind of monster do you think I am? Of course I know the answer."

I pointed at my eyes with two fingers on one hand and pointed back at him while mouthing, "I'm watching you." Then I called Meg, hoping I wasn't being a horrible friend by getting private information out of her and sharing it with someone else, although, I could just give him a very shortened version that wouldn't have her hating me when she found out because I *was* going to tell her. I'd rather lie to Finnegan than Meg. Not that I wanted to lie to anyone, but I was fairly certain that betraying a friend would get you unfriended pretty quickly. And because I worked with Finnegan and dealt in information, it would be way easier to make it up to him. It would only annoy him when he found out that I'd told Meg, but I would hurt Meg much more if I blabbed her personal information to others. She answered. "Hey, Meg. It's me, Avery. Just wondering how the date went."

"Ooh, I was going to call you, and you didn't have to say your name. You're in my phone."

I smiled. "Cool. So… spill."

"He was really nice and such a gentleman. He was funny, cute, likes the same food as me. His favourite dessert is the same as mine, would you believe? And he paid for dinner, dropped me home, and gave me a super sexy kiss without pushing for anything more. He even texted me this morning to check I'd had a good time."

I grinned. "He sounds lovely. That's so awesome. When are you going out next?"

"I'm not sure. He's got a busy week at work, but he's going to let me know in a couple of days. So far, he seems promising. But let's not jinx it."

"Okay, but I'm so happy for you. Anyway, I'm at work, but I wanted to check in and get the goss."

I could hear the smile in her voice. "Thanks, Avery. Maybe pass by here on your way home, and we can have a drink."

"Okay. Will do. See ya." I placed my phone on my desk and met Finnegan's anticipatory stare. *Oh, Meg, please forgive me, for I am about to sin.* "She had a great time. The guy was nice, respectful, paid for dinner, and he wants to see her again." At least it wasn't super private info.

Funnily enough, he didn't seem upset by that. "That's good. Thanks for letting me know."

"Why did you want to know?"

"I can't tell you. Sorry. It's a secret. It would require more information from you."

I rolled my eyes, then wanted to slap myself for showing any kind of reaction. He would love that he'd annoyed me. "Of course it's a secret." I waved my hand as if it was of no import. "Can you answer my original question, please? Did Schmidt have an alibi?"

"Yes. He was in the office all morning. The receptionist corroborated it, and they obtained information that showed his phone as being in the office the whole time as well. You know how phones ping towers?"

I gave him a "stop mansplaining" look. "Oh my God, yes of course I know. Jebus, Vinegar." I shook my head.

He smirked. "Just making sure."

"Well, thanks for answering."

Curiosity lit up his gaze. "So, why are you still interested in that case?"

"It hasn't been solved, has it?"

"No, but that's yesterday's news. Besides, as soon as they figure out who it is, Bellamy will call me, and I'll run the story."

"Is that right?" And this was why I was still asking questions.

Plus, I cared because I knew Fiona, and I couldn't stand to leave something unanswered. This case would've bugged me whether or not I could see ghosts. When you find a dead body in your flat, you tend to be super curious about how it got there.

"Yes, that's right. So don't waste your time."

I didn't bother to hide what I thought about that question. "Just a little word of advice—I hate being told what to do. In fact, it will just make me more determined. Also, while you're sitting on your hands, lazily waiting for easy information, I'll be working it out, and I shall beat you to that article."

He raised a brow. "Is that so?"

"Yes."

"Wanna bet on it?"

I smiled. He had no idea that I had inside information, but then again, maybe the police were close to solving the case, and they did have a lot of information I didn't have—solid, provable-in-court information. There was a chance I was all bravado, and I was going eat dirt on this one. Still…. "Okay. Name your wager."

"You have to spend one full day researching one of my stories for me if I win." He grinned, entirely too pleased about the prospect.

I considered it. That would be irritating but not the end of the world. "Okay. And you have to ask Bellamy to give me inside information on the next case that comes up that I want information on."

He blinked. Obviously, he couldn't guarantee it, but I'd make him try. He licked his bottom lip. "Um, I'm not sure I can do that."

I cocked my head to the side. This wouldn't be as good, but maybe it would still help. "Okay, then. You have to pass on all the information he gives you, and if you're not working on the same case, you have to ask him for me anyway."

"Hmm…." He stared at me, maybe trying to ascertain my willingness to budge. I smiled as if I'd won. That usually put people off. "Fine. You have your bet." He held out his hand, and I shook it. It was difficult to ignore the zing that travelled up my arm at his warm touch. It was probably only because I'd been celibate for many, many months, and I was only human. But a zing was a bad reason to start anything with someone you didn't like or trust, and, honestly, any man would be a mistake at this time in my life.

"It was your bet, but whatever."

It was his turn to roll his eyes. "Such a stickler for the truth." Ha, if only he knew how much I'd been lying lately, my nickname would change from Lightning to Pinocchio.

"Totally. Anyway, thanks for the information. I risked a lot to tell you about Meg's date. I feel like I've broken her confidence."

"Did she ask you not to say anything?"

"No, but still…."

"You did the right thing. I'm just looking out for her. That's all." He looked over his shoulder, at his desk, then turned back to me. "Time to get back to work, Lightning." He returned to his desk, and I sat. Blocking all thoughts not related to the things I was working on, I got out a pad and pen. Sometimes it was easier to think on paper than on a screen. I wrote down the facts of Fiona's case. Who were the suspects, and why did I think they were? Which ones had alibis? So far, her husband, his girlfriend, and Fiona's boss were my prime suspects, and they all had alibis. Right. That was short and sweet. So, according to my piece of paper, a stranger killed her. Nope. Someone was lying, but who?

I glanced over at Finnegan, who was concentrating on his screen, his fingers tapping away at the keys. Would he answer another question for me, or would it turn into a whole drama requiring reciprocal information? If it did, I had nothing else to tell him, and if he asked me to feed him more information on

Meg in the future, I wasn't going to do it. I sighed. That was a no go, then.

I was in dead-end city with that, so I might as well work on the article. This was going to be a doozy. I pulled out my laptop and turned it on, then went straight to Susan's email. Once I notified them, I could start writing my article. I'd only have to wait for confirmation on what action they'd be taking before I could finish it. Once it was with the police, I could say "the police are investigating" blah, blah, blah. I'd have to be careful about the estate agents though and word it as if they didn't know about the whole scam. I was fairly confident that courts didn't accept "a ghost told me" as a reliable information source, and the last thing I wanted was to get sued for defamation.

I wanted to call the solicitor anonymously, but they were more likely to follow up with me if they knew exactly who I was, and if I needed to meet with them in person, there would be no hiding who I was. I went to the stationery room—so Finnegan couldn't eavesdrop—and dialled the number.

"Samson, Smith, and Temple. How may I direct your call?"

"Hi, my name is Avery Winters. I was wondering if I could speak to Mr Temple, please."

"May I ask what this is regarding?"

"The conveyance of a commercial development site. You're acting for the purchaser, Frank Poole."

"Thank you. Just a moment, and I'll put you through." She put me through to his personal secretary, Rebecca, and I had to repeat everything. Why did they double up? What a waste of time.

"I'll put you through to Mr Temple now. Have a lovely day."

"Thanks. You too."

"Paul Temple speaking."

"Hi, Mr Temple. My name is Avery Winters, and I needed to discuss something important about a matter you're working on."

"Rebecca mentioned the Poole conveyance at Fentonshire. Is that correct?"

"Yes. I'm a journalist, and I was looking into the property before it sold. There were rumours it was contaminated. I've ascertained that it was, but the council records seem to have gone missing, and I can't find anywhere that it was ever remediated. I thought your client should know. The evidence points to the seller being fully aware of the condition of the land." Silence. After a few beats too many, I thought I should check he was still here. "Hello? Mr Temple?" Maybe he'd hung up.

He cleared his throat. "That's a serious accusation, Ms Winters. What evidence do you have?"

"The council has confirmed there are no records regarding the reports of contamination, yet I have the report right here. I've also been sent a request form that was filed in the wrong box at council, which indicates they did initially have concerns about this land. As I said, I've looked into this and have a lot of documentation. I've spoken to a firm which was bidding for the remediation work, but they were turned down, and as far as they know, nothing was ever done. The council has no records of a report on any remediation work either. The seller's brother used to head up that department at council."

"Well, if you can send all that through, I'll take a look. In light of this, my client will need to confirm that the land is clear before he settles on the property. Thank you, Ms Winters."

"My pleasure. I do have a favour to ask. Can you please keep me in the loop? I'm assuming you'll get another company to confirm whether or not the property is clean. I'm writing an article on this situation, and I'd like to offer the reader a conclusion, so what action, if any, will be taken. If your new tests prove the soil is clear, I guess I'll have no story, but it looks pretty on the nose at the moment."

"Of course. I'll check with my client that he's okay with this, and he might ask that his name is kept out of the article, but at this stage, I have no problem with letting you know what happens."

"Thank you so much. I look forward to hearing from you. I have your email here, so I'll email those documents and all my contact details. Thanks for taking me seriously."

"It would be neglectful of me not to. Thank you for bringing it to my attention."

"No problem. Have a good day."

"You too, Ms Winters. Bye."

"Bye."

I sent the email off, and that was that. I smiled. He'd taken me seriously. How refreshing that I hadn't had to send all my proof off first. I'd been there before.

Right, now that was done, onto problem three—Patrick.

I still had no idea what to do. Why was this so hard? I could write Craig an anonymous letter, but then I wouldn't know if he'd ever read it, and Patrick needed confirmation. Maybe I could talk him into meeting me at the spot Patrick died, and Patrick could answer whatever questions he had via me. That would be fairly convincing that I wasn't a scammer, wouldn't it? But how to get him to turn up? Maybe he'd be willing with the stuff Patrick had already told me, things no one else would know.

My inbox dinged. An email from MacPherson. Another hopeful local wanting their story told. Well, it wasn't as if I had any other leads to follow today. Back to the grindstone. I wrote the details down and stood. At least it was Friday. The weekend was one sleep away, but that also meant that I'd have to wait longer to find out about the commercial land. I sighed.

Time to go and interview a Mr Maloney about his giant courgette. What a fabulous life I led.

# CHAPTER 23

Monday morning rolled around after an uneventful weekend, which I mostly spent by myself avoiding Patrick and any other ghosts except for Fiona. I needed a break, and strolling the grassy hills and forest near my place provided just the relaxation I needed. I even managed to practice some of my hapkido in the back garden—if I didn't use it, I was going to lose it.

The first thing I did when I got to the office was type up the article about Mr Maloney's gigantic courgette. I titled it *Mr Maloney Shows off his Giant Courgette*. I chuckled as I sent it off to Mr MacPherson. Afterwards, I checked my other emails and found one from Mr Temple.

*Ms Winters,*

*Thank you for contacting me on Friday. The information you provided has proven to be informative, and we will be following up this week. We've ordered urgent soil testing, which is taking place this morning. The results*

*should take about a week to come through, and my client was happy for me to keep you posted.*
    *Kind regards*
    *Paul Temple*

I smiled. Maybe I was wrong, but I was more likely to have stumbled upon a scam, and now they were looking into it, I could relax, knowing Mr Poole's money wasn't going to disappear.

Now what? I had no new leads on Fiona's murder, and I was actively avoiding doing anything about Patrick's situation, but with nothing to do, there was nowhere for me to hide from my guilt.

Possum poo.

Fiona's funeral was in two days, which meant that's all the time I had to figure things out before Simon potentially got away with murder. Impatience vibrated through my legs, and I stood. Sitting here doing nothing wasn't an option. *Dammit.*

What was more important—the article I wanted to write, revealing Fiona's killer or actually catching Fiona's killer?

I sighed. No matter how much I wanted the story, ignoring what was right was a step too far, even for me. I called the man I least wanted to talk to. Finnegan. Pressing the Call button gave me stomach cramps.

"Lightning! Did you miss me over the weekend?"

I rolled my eyes even though he couldn't see me. It was an automatic reaction to the waffle that leaked from his mouth. "Like a hole in the head. I actually have a proposition."

"You're propositioning me, and I'm not even there in the flesh to enjoy the look on your face. I'm just about to come in. See you soon, and you can proposition me properly. Bye."

Argh! What a pain in the bum. I couldn't help smiling though

—he was joking, and if I let him get to me, he'd enjoy that even more. I needed to take him for the joker he was.

True to his word, he walked into the office within a minute and a half. As soon as he stepped in the door, he came to my desk and grinned. "You're eager."

"What?"

"You're standing up, ready to jump into my arms." Rather than being cute, his dimples were being highly offensive right then.

"Whatever you reckon. Sorry, but I don't have time for this right now." My face was pretty clear on how I felt about it. So much so that his smile fell. It was as if I'd just told him Santa wasn't real. The tiniest part of me succumbed to the guilt of being the reason he was no longer cheery. I had that effect on people.

"Oh, my mistake. I'm not the one who called you and said they wanted to proposition you."

"You need your hearing checked. I said I had a proposition." I held up my hand. "And before you go off on an idiot tangent, I need help. I didn't want to ask you, for obvious reasons, but I don't have time to muck around... Fiona doesn't have time."

His forehead wrinkled. "Fiona?"

"Fiona Daniels, the murdered woman."

"But she's already dead. You're not making any sense."

"I think he killed her... well, he's the most likely suspect, and he's leaving the country on Wednesday, straight after the funeral. And he's taking his girlfriend with him. Fiona's sister told me that he bought a one-way ticket." Okay, so she didn't really know he had a one-way ticket, but I didn't want Finnegan fobbing me off.

He scratched his chin. "What do you need *me* for? I don't think I can help."

I resisted the urge to step from foot to foot. He wasn't making this easy, and we didn't have much time. "You have information, or at least maybe you can warn Bellamy. Can he stop Simon Daniels from leaving the country?"

"Not unless there's evidence to suggest he murdered his wife. His alibi checked out."

"Can you ring Bellamy for me and ask if they discovered whether or not Simon had her real estate pin?"

"Her what?"

*Argh. Deep breaths.* "She always wore her award pin—Agent of the Year, of three years, actually. She wasn't wearing it when I found her. But she never took it off. He was supposed to check the security footage of the office that day and see if she was wearing it. She went into the office that morning before she came to my place."

He gave me an assessing look and folded his arms. "And how do you know all this?"

"I spoke to the receptionist and her boss. I'm a journalist, remember? And I don't need to remind you that I found her. I saw her lying there… dead. That poor woman. Her husband might be about to get away with it. Don't you care?" As much as collaborating with him hurt, I wasn't even going to rule out begging. Desperate times and all that.

He dropped his arms and huffed a huge breath. "Fine. And what do I get for helping you?"

"Nothing. I've spilled all my information. I'm sure you'll steal the story once everything comes to light, but I don't care any more. If he gets away with it, well…." Fiona will be stuck in my apartment and the creepy in-between forever. But I couldn't say that. "It would be awful. And what's to stop him killing his girl-friend once he gets sick of her?" I wanted to grab his shoulders and shake the stuffing out of him, but that wouldn't help, so I jammed my back teeth together instead.

"So, you're giving me the go-ahead to write the story if it pans out that Mr Daniels is the killer?"

Stupid circumstances. But what did it really matter? There would be other stories, and I still had my contamination article to write… if I didn't get stiffed on that too. I pushed that out of my head because now wasn't the time. "Yes. You can have the damn story. I can eat Ramen noodles if I don't get any bonuses for a while. It's fine." I wasn't above exaggerating to make him feel sorry for me.

Surprise registered in his gaze before he tamped it down. Maybe he didn't want to offend me by feeling sorry for me, or maybe he thought I was lying to get him to drop the article? I was trying to manipulate him, so I supposed he wasn't far off the truth on that point. "Okay, I'll help you. Despite what you think about me, I don't want a killer to go free either, and I can guarantee that none of the police do either."

"So, will you call him?"

"I have a better idea—we'll go and see him. Come on. I'll drive."

I shut my mouth as quickly as it had fallen open. He'd come through, even though he'd demanded a price. At least the cost to me wasn't too high. The day I sacrificed the truth for a story was the day I'd quit.

And I was far from ready to quit.

In fact, I was just getting started.

🙖🙖🙖

PC Lizzy Adams was yet again at the front counter. As soon as she saw Finnegan, she grinned. "Here to see the sergeant?"

"You bet." He gave her his dimpled grin, and she pressed the buzzer to let us straight in. If there were such a thing as reincarnation, I was coming back as a hot guy so I could get whatever I wanted.

Lizzy didn't even escort us to Bellamy's office. Finnegan had free rein around here. The two officers at their desks waved as we passed. The younger one grinned. "You've got some moves, Fin."

Finnegan stopped and chuckled. "You know it. How'd you get on the other night? Saw you with a good-looking lady." He was probably toning down the description for my benefit. I wasn't going to lie—I appreciated it.

The officer's grin diminished to a smile. "I got her number. Taking her out for a meal on Friday night."

Finnegan gave him a thumbs up. "Nice work, my man. Love to stay and chat, but I have this one here with the whip." He nodded at me, and the two officers grinned and gave knowing nods. I held in my disdain.

"Right you are. See you later, Fin."

He held up his hand to give a half wave and continued to Bellamy's office. He knocked—surprise, surprise that he didn't just barge in as if he were the boss. "Come in!"

Finnegan opened the door and stepped back to let me walk in first. If he kept surprising me like this, I was going to have to reassess some—not all—of my negative critique of the man. "Hi, Sergeant Bellamy." I gave him my brightest "I hope I'm not being a bother" smile.

At least he returned it. "Miss Winters, what a... lovely surprise." He gestured to the seat, then looked at Finnegan. "And, Fin, what are you both doing here?"

Fin and I sat, and he took the lead. "We're here about Fiona Daniels, actually. Avery has something she'd like to say."

Bellamy beat me to it. "If you're here about the pin, I have nothing to report. We haven't had a chance to look at the security video again, but we paid Mr Daniels a visit, and he let us search his home. It wasn't there. I meant to get PC Adams to call you, but I've been up to my neck in work."

Cat's bum. Some of the fight bled from me. This wasn't going exactly as I'd envisaged, and we'd only just sat down. Still, all wasn't lost yet. "Were you aware that Simon Daniels is leaving the country on Wednesday, straight after the funeral... with his *girlfriend?*" I couldn't keep the judgement out of my voice, even though I was supposed to be a professional journalist.

He stared at me, looked at Finnegan, then back to me. "No, I didn't know. We did ask Mr Daniels not to leave the country, but since we have nothing on him, he is free to go."

"Can you figure out a way to keep him here? At least until you find some evidence."

He raised both bushy brows. "You are aware what you're suggesting is illegal? We can't invent evidence, which is what I'm sure you're suggesting. We do things above board here."

"I'm sure you do. I wasn't asking that... exactly. What happens if he leaves, and then you figure it out? You'll never get him back."

Bellamy gave Finnegan a withering look, and the question was obvious—Why did you bring this woman here to bother me? Why? The sergeant didn't even bother to rearrange his expression when he turned back to me. "What are you suggesting we do then? Hmm?" He folded his hands together, placed them on his table, and twiddled his thumbs. People actually did that? Interesting.

Finnegan and Bellamy both stared at me, waiting, waiting, waiting. *Come on, Avery, don't crumble under the pressure.* "He threatened me. I'd like him charged." I blinked at my own genius. It had taken me forever to think of it, but I finally came through. *Yay me.*

Bellamy's lazy expression disappeared in a puff of activity as he sat up straighter and his hands flew to grip his chair arms. "What? When? Why didn't you report it to us?"

Finnegan nodded, and I couldn't be certain, but I think his expression was mildly impressed. "I was there just after it happened, and Lightning was rather shaken up."

"Lightning?"

Finnegan grinned. "She was hit by lightning once." I gave him a dirty look.

Just what I needed—someone else asking me questions on a topic I did not want to talk about. I chopped it off before it began. "I'd prefer not to talk about it. Some people don't know when to shut up."

Bellamy chuckled. "You've got that right, Miss Winters."

"Please, call me Avery."

"Okay, Avery. So, what happened, and when?"

"It was last week on Thursday. He complained about me to my boss; then when I got to the office, he was waiting outside in the street. He yelled at me, almost attacked me, and told me that if I went anywhere near him or his girlfriend again, I was going to cop it. I think his exact words were, 'I won't be held responsible for what happens.'"

Finnegan leaned forward, outrage emanating from his eyes. Was he exaggerating to help my cause, or did he really feel that way about my attack? "When she came upstairs, she was shaking. It was obvious she was terrified, but she felt sorry for him because he'd just lost his wife, so she didn't want to call you. I told her she should, but since she didn't want to, I wasn't going to argue—she was upset enough as it was. You can confirm all this with Julian because he asked her if she wanted him to call you as well."

"Right. Well, then. Let's get the details. I'll take down your statement, everything you can remember. Once that's done, we'll pay Mr Daniels a visit. But we're rather busy today and tomorrow, so we probably won't be able to pick him up until after the funeral. I think that we should let him attend his wife's funeral—the police aren't monsters, and I don't think you are either. Am I right?"

I smiled. He was good at this sneaky stuff. They could probably only hold him overnight, but this would be enough to scupper him from leaving straight away. Then it would take time for him to find another flight. We'd bought ourselves at least another day, which was better than nothing, and maybe with a bit of luck, the police could order him to hang around for a few days until they decided what, if anything, they were going to charge him with. "Sounds good to me. I'm glad you have empathy. I wouldn't want him to miss his wife's funeral either. His holiday, on the other hand…."

Finnegan looked at me and shook his head, a ghost of a smile on his face. "Remind me never to get on your bad side. You have an evil streak a mile wide."

I smirked. "Who says you're not already on it?"

Bellamy laughed. "Oh, she's got your number, Fin." Bellamy looked at me. "Nice to see a woman who can resist this one's charms. Goes to show he's human after all."

Finnegan gave Bellamy a wry smile. "Well, my father's not exactly perfect, and the apple doesn't fall far from the tree." The last was said with a tightness I'd never noticed before. Bad blood?

Bellamy's mirth disappeared. "We all have choices, lad. You fell a lot further from that tree than you think." Well, that was weird coming from his dad's best mate. So strange. I glanced at Finnegan. Maybe his life wasn't as perfect as I'd thought. I'd been so caught up in my own mess that other people's pain had escaped my notice. It was a good reminder that most people had stuff going on that they hid well. It wouldn't hurt me to be kinder to Finnegan—not that I'd let my guard down, but I would acknowledge he was still just a person, not some monster out to love and leave every woman he came across. Everyone didn't always have an ulterior motive for being nice.

Finnegan grunted in answer. "Anyway, I think we have a solution to this assault matter. Thank you."

"My pleasure, lad."

The ghost of the long-dead policeman from the other day

appeared, again standing behind Bellamy's chair. He looked at me. "I told you he was a good officer. You just needed to give him a chance." I gave him a quick smile. Bellamy and Finnegan could figure I was smiling at what Bellamy had just said. What I would really love would be to have a proper conversation with the ghost. Maybe we could come to some arrangement whereby he gave me information about what was going on at the station. He could be a good source of inside info. I didn't see how I'd ever get to talk to him though. The station was heavily surveyed—by police and cameras. I'd look like a right weirdo talking to myself, not to mention that no one would be likely to leave me by myself anywhere here.

Bellamy looked at me. "Is that all?"

While I was here, I might as well ask. "So, you're certain that Simon, his girlfriend, and Fiona's boss—Schmidt—all had solid alibis for the morning she was killed?"

The sergeant took a deep breath, and his expression became the generic, serious police officer one that he likely showed to every stranger on the job. He was shutting me out. "Yes, Miss Winters."

"Please, call me Avery. I know you have to keep things confidential, but I'm here as an advocate for Fiona rather than a reporter. I'd be happy to sign something to say I won't repeat what I hear here."

"That's not the point, Miss Winters." Hmm, so we weren't going to become best buds. Looked like Finnegan would retain that privilege.

"I'm just trying to help. Are you any closer to catching whoever is responsible?"

"We have evidence, but we can't link it to anyone yet. Now, that's more than I should've said, but I want to assure you that we're working very hard on this. I also want to remind you that I'm trying to work with you by picking up our friend on

Wednesday afternoon. I could bring him in now, and he'll be out by tomorrow morning. Is that what you want?"

I sighed. "No. Fine. Thanks for doing at least that." What else could I say? It wasn't Bellamy's fault that I couldn't figure this out. If only Fiona knew more about what had happened.

"Well, if that's it, I have work to do." Bellamy stood, as did Finnegan. They shook hands.

I stood. "Thank you, Sergeant. I appreciate your help."

I led the way out the door. Hopefully something else would come up between now and the day after the funeral. Maybe I could goad Simon into actually hurting me. If he grabbed or punched me, we could get him held longer for sure.

Once we were outside and walking to Finnegan's car, he stopped and gently grasped my arm, halting me. "What are you thinking about? You're awfully quiet."

"Ah, nothing. Just going over the case in my head." I looked at where he held my arm, all too aware of the warmth of his hand. He let go.

"I'm not sure what you've got going on up there." He glanced at the top of my skull. "But be careful. We're dealing with a murderer, Lightning. Let the police handle it."

"I will."

He gave me an assessing stare. "Forgive me for being sceptical, but I don't believe you."

"Are you saying I'm a liar?" I wasn't offended by his suggestion, more impressed that he could read me so easily, but I wasn't going to let him know that.

He grinned. "You're leaving me nowhere to go with that, and I don't feel like getting into trouble, so I'll leave that well enough alone." His expression turned serious. "Just like you should with the Daniels' case."

"Touché, Vinegar. Touché." Even though I'd given up my right to the story—if or when the murderer was exposed—this visit hadn't been for nothing. "Thank you for helping me. Bellamy wouldn't have seen me if it wasn't for you. And I'm sure Fiona would say thank you too."

He shrugged, and was that a blush on his cheeks? "It was nothing. I was glad to help; plus, you've given me dibs on what could turn out to be a pretty smashing story. I didn't just do it out of the goodness of my heart. I'm not that nice." He turned and walked the rest of the way to his car. I followed, his warning—maybe not the warning he'd meant to stick—echoing in my brain.

*I'm not that nice.*

If I ever forgot that, I'd only have myself to blame when it all went wrong. Unfortunately, I was known for being a sucker, and no matter how much I told myself I didn't like him, I kind of did. *Noooooooo, Avery. Shut this down right now.*

Maybe this was just a blip because he'd shown some kindness—no matter that he was getting something in return, he still didn't have to help me, and I could see through his bravado. And it was probably just a tiny crush—after all, even the sergeant thought he was good-looking. My reaction to Finnegan was normal for a heterosexual woman. It would fade in time. Wouldn't it?

*Dream on, Avery. Dream on.*

# CHAPTER 24

That night, after telling Fiona that Simon wouldn't be able to go anywhere straight after the funeral, I slept better than I had in ages. She'd been grateful and relieved. She said it had given her a chance to keep looking for the pin. Once she found it, she'd tell me, and I'd pass the information to the police.

Then we'd have our killer locked up for good.

Tuesday dawned, cloudy, cool, but not raining. As usual, I packed my heels in a plastic bag and wore my sneakers. I placed the bag, my handbag, and my laptop bag in a knapsack. There was someone I needed to visit before work. Patrick.

I still hadn't solved the problem of telling his friend—or, maybe, I hadn't found the guts to risk being labelled a cruel person if it all went to hell. To be fair, I didn't know if just telling his friend would free Patrick or if his friend had to believe the message and benefit from it before Patrick could leave his stifled existence. Whatever stage I was at in the avoidance of telling his friend, I still owed Patrick an update and explanation.

The crisp morning air smelled of jasmine, and the walk was

quite pleasant. Traffic whizzed by—the hordes off to work. At least I got to enjoy a bit of exercise and nature before braving the office. It was best to focus on the positives because Patrick wasn't going to be happy that I hadn't done anything yet.

None of the excuses I'd tried out in my head came to me when I finally saw him. "Hey, Patrick."

He smiled. "Hey, Avery. Long time, no see."

Guilt rumbled through my empty stomach—once I'd decided to come here, I'd been too nervous to eat. "I know. I'm sorry. I don't have any news. The truth is, I don't know how to tell your friend, and I'm a coward." See, I could be honest when the situation called for it.

Patrick stared at me, and his smile faded. "Oh. I guess I knew since I'm still here."

"But do you know for certain you'll go onto somewhere else once he gets the message?"

He shrugged. "Not 100 per cent, but I'm pretty sure. It just feels right, like that's what's stopping me." He cocked his head to one side. "I did have an idea. It might even make it easier for you."

"Oh, do tell." How horrible was I that the poor ghost had to figure this all out for himself! I was useless. *Useless Avery. Pathetic Avery. Avery Who Never Listens.* My parents had lots of names for me. At least they couldn't get to me here.

"Colin and I used to joke sometimes about sending each other letters via the newspaper when we died. We'd been best friends for so long that we couldn't believe something like death could separate us." His laugh wasn't even brittle—he actually found it funny. "In a way, we were right. I've been thinking about it a lot since you came along. I've had the answer all the time, but I just didn't know, and now you're here, you can help."

"But we were at that stage before. You asked me to help. That was your answer."

He shook his head. "No. That was the lazy way out. I have something more specific."

"Okay. Shoot."

"After his grandparents died, we used to talk about how cool it would be if they could at least send letters, which would be called letters from the dead. Like, you'd get up in the morning and check the letterbox. "Hey, Mum, I've just got a letter from the dead. So many people think their loved ones come to them in dreams. This is just a version of that, I guess. I managed to get into Colin's dreams once, but it didn't make a difference—he didn't know it was real, and it's really hard to do. There's no way of proving it's not just the person wishful dreaming."

"You make a good point. And when you wake from a dream, you forget some of it too. It's not concrete enough."

"Yes. Anyway, all that stuff I told you before, can you put it in a letter from me and send it to the paper? Could you title it *A Letter from the Dead to Craig*?"

"I don't decide what goes into the paper. MacPherson—my boss—might think it's too weird. And even if I did get it in the paper, how would I get Craig to read it?"

"Could you deliver the paper to him? Tell him that Patrick wanted him to read it? I'm sure he'll know as soon as he reads it that it's true. Explain what I said about the letters from the dead. At least it'll be anonymous."

"But how will he know that I know it was meant for him?"

"We'll put his surname on it."

My eyes widened. "Isn't that a bit too personal? Everyone will know it's for him."

"So?" His gaze was hopeful.

I didn't want to give him any empty promises. Maybe this way could work? "But why can't I just deliver a letter? And why does it have to be in the paper?"

"You said you didn't want to deliver it. This way, you don't have to tell him anything except that Patrick wrote that he wanted him to know—his name's on it for God's sake—and you wanted to make sure he got the message, just in case it was legit. You won't have to admit you can see ghosts. You're just the middleman from the paper. And you won't have to hand him the actual letter, which someone could prove you wrote in the first place. We don't want that." His face relaxed, and his lips curled into the smile you got when reminiscing about good times. "One of the bullies at school made it into the paper once for scoring five goals in football in one match. After that, Craig and I both wanted to make it to the paper." He frowned. "And we did make it into the paper." He gestured to the tree. "For this. That's not how I want my story to end. Having this letter in the paper will be a proper send-off, leave everyone with a happier message." He grinned. "And I get my final five minutes."

I licked my lips. I supposed it could work. At least I wouldn't have to explain where I got the information from. I'd just have to make sure it made it into the paper, and he read it. I smiled. "Okay. I think that all makes sense. We'll give you a proper good-bye, one that leaves readers and your mate with tears of joy and peace rather than grief. I'll write myself an email and send it from the library at Exeter. I'll go in this morning." Now that we had a plan, as silly as it might be, I wanted to execute it and cross it off my list. This was slightly better than me turning up at his door with a message from Patrick. I wasn't going to be outed as a crazy person if we did it this way, and I couldn't argue that it seemed fitting.

Patrick grinned, and relief radiated from him. "Thank you so much, Avery! You're an angel. I feel like this is going to work. You can use the stuff I told you before and add this." I scrambled to get my notebook and pen out of my bag and took down the extra information. When we finished, his smile evaporated—not that he was unhappy. It was more like he was contemplative. "If this works, this will be the last time we see each other."

I blinked, the burn of tears ambushing me. I hardly knew Patrick, but sharing such moments of import in his afterlife, I couldn't help but feel a strong connection. I wouldn't exactly miss him, but maybe I would, just a little. "I'd hug you goodbye, but...."

His grin returned. "I know. Thank you, Avery. I don't know what happens next, but if I have any shred of memory left, you'll occupy a part of it."

I smiled. "Thanks, Patrick. I can honestly say that I'll never forget you. Safe travels. Maybe we'll meet again one day."

"Maybe we will." He waved as he did me a favour and dimmed, until he vanished, avoiding a prolonged and awkward farewell. As I turned and headed for the bus stop, I let the tears flow freely. Now I just had to get this right.

◎✖◎

Three hours after hopping on the bus to Exeter and the library, I'd sent myself the email, grabbed brunch, and had returned to the office. Finnegan and Carina were out, so I sat at my desk and dived straight into work. The sooner I approached MacPherson about featuring this letter, the better. After reading it to check it said everything Patrick wanted, I printed it out. Not that I hadn't already read through it ten times at the library before I sent it, but mistakes liked to hide and jump out at the last second. I grabbed the two-page letter off the printer and headed for MacPherson's office.

My knock was immediately greeted with "Come in."

As soon as I stepped into his office, I halted. Oooookay. MacPherson was juggling three balls in the middle of his office. "Is this a bad time?"

He caught the balls one by one and slid them into his pant pockets, then smiled. "Not at all. Come, sit." He went around to his side of the desk and put the balls in one of his drawers. "Is everything okay?"

I sat and smiled. "Everything's fine. I wanted to show you this letter. It's anonymous and was emailed to me today. It gave me goosebumps, to be honest. I think we should feature it under the heading 'Letters from the Dead.'" I handed it to him.

MacPherson leaned across the table to grab it from me, his expression curious. At least he wasn't saying no straight away. If he did reject it, I was going to take it to Craig anyway and tell him that I'd received it from who-knew-where, and I felt that I should pass it onto him. Either way, this was happening. Maybe that's what I should've just done in the first place? Why was I so stupid? Fear. It made life difficult whenever it appeared.

As MacPherson read through the email, I hugged myself and tapped my finger on my arm. I also crossed my legs and swung the top leg up and down. *Please say you'll feature it.* "I think we can make a thing about it, as in an emotional piece. We can talk up the mystery of where the letter came from too."

He finished reading and placed the pages on his desk. It took him a moment before he looked up at me. Were those tears shining in his eyes? He cleared his throat. "I remember when that accident happened. Walsh covered it. Terrible tragedy. But I don't know…. This could stir up a lot of angst for his family, and it's obviously not from Patrick. Who would write such a thing?"

"I don't know, but it seems heartfelt. Maybe his parents would find it comforting, especially if it's saying things they need to hear. Besides, a lot of people believe in ghosts. His ghost could have written it."

He stared at me, his eyebrow raised, his face in a "you've got to be kidding" expression. MacPherson drew a deep breath in through his nose and let it whoosh out of his mouth. "It will certainly get people's attention. It's got mystery—who wrote it—emotion, and a goodbye. It's a risk, though. We could cop flack, as I said."

I wanted Patrick's wish to come to fruition, but getting this in the paper wasn't the be-all and end-all—giving the note to his friend was. And I was ready to step up and stop being a wuss. This time, I wasn't going to say anything. I'd let fate decide as it would.

MacPherson jumped up. "We'll run it. If we have to print an apology later, we'll do it, but I don't know that anything will happen. Maybe you're right, and there's things in there they need to hear."

Warmth spread through my chest. Patrick was one step closer to finding peace. I also knew for a fact that there were things in there for his parents. Even though Patrick's main intent was to help his friend because he felt he was suffering more than his parents, he still had a note for them in there. "Will it go in tomorrow's edition?"

"Yep. I'll send it off now."

I stood. "Thank you so much. I think you've made the right decision." Not that he cared about my opinion, but whatever.

"Yes, well, we'll know by tomorrow afternoon, won't we." He stood and looked at his watch. "I've got an out-of-office meeting in forty minutes, so I have to run." He escorted me to the door, and I went straight back to my shared office. That had gone better than expected. I smiled. If only I could rush back and tell Patrick, but we'd said goodbye, and I didn't want to go through that again.

No one had come in since I was last here, so I sat and checked my emails. *Oh, look, another story to cover.* A Mrs Winston found moths baked into her bread from the local bakery, Best Breads Bakery. This was going to be riveting. I called Mrs

Winston, and she said I could come right over. *Great. Otherwise, the suspense would've killed me.*

Mrs Winston lived in a neat semi-detached cottage along a laneway about half a mile out of the village. The threatening clouds had managed to keep their moisture to themselves, so the walk was nice enough. All this walking provided me an opportunity to really get to know Manesbury and its surrounds. I still had my sneakers on as I'd forgotten to change into my high heels. Come to think of it, MacPherson hadn't said anything about my footwear. Maybe I could ditch the heels altogether?

Mrs Winston's doorknocker was a silver sparrow, face down. When you lifted it to knock, then brought it down, it was as if it were pecking for food. Ha, cute. I liked her already. Anyone with a sparrow knocker had to be nice.

She answered the door, a smile on her face. "Hello. You must be from the paper."

I smiled. "Yes. I'm Avery."

She scratched her head. "Who?"

I raised my voice. "Avery."

"Oh, yes. Come in, Amy."

I chuckled. This was going to be fun.

She took me down the hallway to the living-cum-dining area. A timber chopping board sat on an oval dining table, upon which reclined the soon-to-be-famous moth-infested loaf. It had been cut in half, each side stained with the grey fluff of deceased moths, their little bodies entombed within the bread. I looked at Mrs Winston. "Do you always cut the loaf in half first?" I always cut it from one end first. This unusual way intrigued me.

"Pardon?"

Someone get this woman a hearing aid. I repeated the question loudly.

"Yes, just in case there are moths. I found a moth in another loaf of bread once, about thirty years ago. It was from the same bakery. I let it go the first time, but this time, I want people to know."

I mashed my lips together so I didn't laugh. She'd obviously been scarred the first time and hadn't forgotten. Talk about holding a grudge. I peered closer at the bread. "Wow, there's about three moths in there."

"What?"

"Nothing!" I might as well just shout everything from now on. "Can you stand next to the loaf with a disappointed look on your face?"

She nodded. "Yes. I would love to."

She did as asked, and I took a few photos and a close-up of the moth-infested bread. At least it hadn't been a rat. I wasn't sure if the bakery deserved being crucified over a few moths. Some would say enjoy the extra protein.

"Will you buy from them again?"

She sighed. "Yes. I can't get to the one in Cramptonbury since my car broke down."

"How long ago did it break down?"

"Five years."

I raised a brow. I wasn't even going to ask. "Ah, okay. Is there anything else you'd like to say about the moths?" If I had to keep yelling, I was going to need a glass of water.

"Yes. It's disgusting. I could've choked on them or been poisoned. Moths carry diseases. I'll be taking this loaf to them and asking for another loaf in return."

I sighed. Should I put that in the article or not? She was so disgusted that she wanted another one. I smiled. "Okay, thanks. Well, that's it." There were only so many questions you could ask about moth-infested bread. "I'm done."

She smiled. "Thank you for coming, Amy. Would you like a cup of tea?"

"No, thanks. I have to keep working. We'll have this in the paper tomorrow."

"We can keep talking if you like, but we can drink tea too."

Oh, Jeebus. "Working, not talking!"

Understanding dawned on her face. "Ah, working. Sorry! I fear that maybe some of those moths got into my ears today." She laughed.

What else could I do but laugh? So we laughed as I backed towards the front door. Using my incredible dexterity, I managed to open her door and step outside backwards without tripping over anything. I waved as I bade her goodbye. She continued waving even after I was off the property. Yes, she was cute, but having to yell at someone to converse was draining.

When I returned to the office, Carina was there, typing away. She looked up from her work. "Hey, Avery. How's it going?"

I smiled as I sat. "Great, thanks. How are you?"

"I'm good t'anks."

My phone rang. I didn't know the number, but at least it wasn't an "unknown number." Normally, I let random numbers go to my messages, but today I felt like living dangerously. "Hello, Avery speaking."

A gravelly male voice said, "You've made a big mistake, Avery Winters. Get ready to meet your maker."

The line went dead.

My brow furrowed. Was that a joke?

"Avery, are you all right, love?"

I looked at Carina. "Um, I'm not sure. Someone just threatened me."

"How so?"

I repeated his side of the conversation, all two sentences of it.

"That's serious. Call the police."

I didn't want to make a big deal out of it, but I'd be stupid not to call the police, so I did, but not the emergency number. I called Sergeant Bellamy. He asked for all the details, which I gave, but there wasn't much to tell. The number could've been a burner phone too. I mean, what idiot would make a threatening call with their normal phone? "We'll check out that number, see if we can get anything from it. I'll also send an officer to check on you later at home. What time do you get home of an evening?"

"I'll definitely be there at seven. That would be great, thanks."

"If he calls again, let me know. When the officer comes, I'll get him to ask you some more questions. Have a think about who might want to threaten you, and have that information ready."

"Okay. Will do. Bye, Sergeant." I put my phone on my desk and filled Carina in.

"So, who do you t'ink would do d'is?"

I had a pretty good idea. "Someone I've never met, but I'm stuffing up his scam." I explained about the land and the article I was working on. "But you can't tell Finnegan. I don't want him stealing my story."

"Oh, right you are. I won't tell him. Not d'at he'd steal your story. He's not like d'at."

"He doesn't cover what you cover though. The last place I worked was ridiculously competitive. I didn't tell my partner what I was doing half the time because he'd steal my ideas."

Her mouth fell open. "No way. What a slug-faced weasel."

"Yes way. Sometimes I think the best thing that came out of me being struck by lightning was him breaking up with me. I didn't think so at the time, of course. But I appreciate it now." I shook my head. The sadness that normally expanded inside my chest, pressing and burning at the thought of Brad and our failed relationship, felt more like a small stone. The weight was there, but it wasn't enough to drag me to the bottom of the ocean and pin me there while I drowned.

"Well, I can guarantee Fin isn't like d'at. You'll see." She smiled but then decided better of it. "Are you going to be okay? I can walk you home tonight."

"No, thanks. I'll be fine. I can probably go home soon. I'll write up the article on the mothy bread; then I'll go home early. I'm sure I'll be safe in daylight." Not that I was a ninja, but my martial arts skills made me feel better too. As long as I saw it coming, I could probably do enough to get away. A king hit on the back of the head would be impossible to avoid, even for a boxing champ, but if I was facing my opponent, I'd have a chance. Being underestimated was also an awesome advantage to have.

She chuckled. "Mot'y bread?"

I laughed. "Yes. See how exciting my life is? I visited Mrs Winston and photographed her mothy bread. It's the article our readers have been waiting for."

Carina snorted. "I can't wait to read it."

"I have no doubt it will be my best work." I grinned, happy for the opportunity to change the subject. Whoever had called me—likely Mr Fairly—wanted me to be scared. He was angry and wanted me to suffer, but I doubted he'd actually attack me. I'd been threatened before, and it had never come to anything.

But maybe he would follow through. He was looking at jail time if the land was contaminated and the police could prove he and his brother made those records disappear. Still, if I let every criminal scare me, I'd never do my job properly. Someone had to stand up to these scumbags. It might as well be me.

I handed in my article—"High-Protein Moth Loaf Bugs Manesbury Local"—then packed up. "I'm heading off while it's still early. I'll see you tomorrow."

"Have you got my number?"

"No."

"Give me yours." She pulled out her phone, and I gave her my number. My phone dinged with a text.

I smiled. "Thanks." I filled in her name, and just like that, I had a new contact.

"Call me when you get home."

"Will do. Thanks. See you tomorrow."

"Bye, Avery."

I was extra watchful on the way home, but nothing happened, and no one followed me, at least not that I could see. There wasn't much traffic in the village, so it would've been fairly obvious. When I got home, I checked the flat. Empty except for the furniture. The back door was locked. Everything was as it should be. I breathed out my relief. See, nothing to worry about. An empty threat. And when all this was over, I'd have the last laugh—I'd have an article-of-the-week winner, and he'd be in jail. Win, win.

I spent the afternoon practicing my hapkido and watching TV. Then I cooked an early dinner so I could have it all tidied up before the police came. When they arrived, it was the young police constable who had turned up the day of the murder, and a young woman pc. They were both friendly and took another statement from me. Since there was only one person I could think of and the reason didn't take that long to explain, they were gone within twenty minutes with reassurances that they'd walk by later to make sure everything was okay. I couldn't ask for more than that.

After they left, I had a glass of wine, which helped relax me enough that I decided to have an early night. Tomorrow was going to be a big day. Meg had agreed to drive me to Fiona's funeral, which was on at one. I'd go into work before that. Because I was taking the afternoon off for the funeral, then for my trip to see Patrick's friend, I wanted to get into work early, make sure I got my article for the day done. "Fiona. Are you around?"

After a moment, she materialised. "Avery, hi."

I'd thought long and hard about this. I didn't want to be seen as crazy, but if there was anything I could pass on to her sister, I had a feeling she'd be open to hearing it. Tomorrow was a day she'd need extra comfort, and I was ready to stop being such a chicken. As long as I didn't hurt anyone, it didn't matter if they thought I was nuts. "Hey. I'm going to your funeral tomorrow. Do you have a message for your sister?"

Grief welled in her eyes. "That's kind of you. Something I didn't anticipate is that I'm grieving too. Alice misses me, but I miss her too. I miss everyone and everything. The emptiness of this place seeps inside. If I don't leave soon, I worry my heart and mind will end up just as desolate. At least Alice has her kids to comfort her." She gave me an apologetic look as tears streamed down her face, and her voice broke. "No offence, but I have no one. You're here, which is somewhat comforting, but I don't really know you, and I can't touch you. I need a hug."

Oh, Jeeze. My chest tightened, and I reached out, but, of course, there was nothing to touch. That just made it worse. "I'm so sorry, Fiona." The words were horribly inadequate, but they were all I had.

She sniffled and waved her hand. "No, it's okay. I know." Her defeated, hopeless gaze broke my heart. "I'm just venting. Thank you for all your help."

"You don't have to thank me. And I haven't given up yet. Simon will end up where he belongs." I made my tone gentle. This wasn't the best conversation to be having, and I didn't want it to be any harder for Fiona than it had to be. "What do you want me to tell Alice?"

Her words poured out with her tears, and when she was done, I was drained and doubly ready for bed. I said goodbye to her, thinking that if tomorrow went well, maybe she'd be able to move on. There was still a chance that faced with arrest, Simon would admit to killing his wife. But then again, pigs might fly. I could still hope.

Just before I got undressed to have my shower, someone knocked on my door. Either the police had returned, or Mrs Crabby wanted something. Maybe she could hear muffled voices and wanted to tell me to be quiet? Not wanting to be stupid, though, I went to the door and asked who it was. "Who is it?"

"Oh, hey, Miss Winters, it's Mr Crowley from Schmidt Estate Agents. Mrs Collins said there was trouble with the plumbing. She wanted me to come and check because she has a leak downstairs."

Hopefully Mr Fairly hadn't said anything to Crowley about what I'd done. I didn't need his judgement on top of everything. I opened the door. The agent stood there holding a monkey wrench. "Hi, Mr Crowley. Come in." Just as I stepped back to open the door, something on his lapel glinted—glittering and shiny, a beacon of death.

Cat's bum.

Fiona's pin proudly sat on Crowley's lapel.

What to do? Did I push the door closed and make a scene, or did I let him in and pretend everything was fine? Or did I let him in, then run down the stairs and call triple nine. What if there was more than one pin, and I looked like an idiot?

My heart raced, caught between being petrified and feeling stupid. Fight, flight, or embarrassment. But how could it be a new pin when no one else had ever had one? I doubted Schmidt had one made and given out just before Fiona's funeral.

My brain had looped. I'd missed my chance as Crowley surged into the room, forcing me backwards. He shut the door and turned to me, his grin unnaturally bright.

Double cat's bum. I had my answer. But so far, even though he looked crazy, he hadn't done anything except barge in. Should I scream anyway and try to alert Mrs Crabby? But if I screamed and he was actually here for the plumbing, I'd look like a right idiot. I stood, feet apart, ready for combat... just in case. My heart raced because even if he wasn't here to hurt me, he was a killer. At least I thought he was. But why? Was he jealous of her success? It didn't make total sense.

The pin glinted in the light again.

Recognition dawned on his face. "You're the woman from the auction house. I remember you."

I swallowed. "Ah, yes. You never called back, and my friend still needs help." Zeus's pyjamas. I crossed my fingers that Fairly hadn't told Schmidt or Crowley who I was.

He smiled. "I'll get their number off you when we're done. How does that sound?"

"Ah, great. Thanks. Um, what plumbing do you need to look at?" Argh, now I had to give him someone's number. Maybe I could give him Carina's? I didn't want to drop Meg in any trouble, and on the off chance he wasn't here for any nefarious reason, he was going to ring that number. Carina would totally go along with the whole thing if I told her.

"The kitchen, under the sink." My shoulders relaxed slightly —maybe I'd misread the situation entirely.

But the pin.

I let him go into the kitchen, but I stayed in the living area. Maybe I should run downstairs and let Mrs Crabby know who was up here... just in case. Better yet, I should text someone. I grabbed my phone off the couch and edged towards the front door while I kept an eye on Crowley. "Why don't we just call a plumber? Surely your office has one on speed dial."

He opened the cupboard under the sink and looked at me. I was sure it wasn't my imagination that his gaze had pinged on the phone in my hand. He smiled. "He's sick, so Mr Schmidt sent me. Can I get your help for a moment?"

*No.* "Ah, what with?"

Without taking his gaze off me, he said, "Can you just turn the tap on and off when I ask?"

Crap. That would mean getting close to him. Although, he could've attacked me when we were in the living room, and he hadn't. I took a deep breath and glanced at the door, calculating the odds of me opening it before he ran me down, if that was even his intention. Maybe I was overreacting? He might be a killer, but why would he want to kill me? I wasn't even sure why he would've killed Fiona since she was happy to give him the sale of the property. Was I on the entirely wrong track?

"What's wrong, Miss Winters? Are you expecting someone?"

"Ah, yes. The police might drop by later. I was threatened earlier today, and they're keeping an eye out."

His expression became one of concern. Fake or real, I couldn't tell. "Oh, that's terrible. No wonder you're edgy. This won't take long. Then I'll get out of your hair. The quicker you help me out, the quicker I can leave."

I swallowed my fear and went into the kitchen as he crouched in front of the open cupboard. I tried to stay as far away from him as possible while still being able to reach the taps. "Tell me when."

He leaned in under the cupboard. Okay, so maybe he *was* here to fix a leak. "Now." I did as asked. "Turn it on max."

"Okay." I turned it until the water was whooshing out.

He lifted his head, and it bumped. "Ow!" He crawled out backwards and stood, rubbing the back of his head with the hand holding the wrench. It hadn't sounded that loud. Maybe he had a sensitive scalp.

Or maybe I was an idiot.

When his eyes fixed on me, I knew.

His gaze darkened until his pupils filled his irises. "You've ruined everything, you interfering trollop." His arm swung down, the wrench reflecting the kitchen light.

Muscle memory took over—the hours, weeks, and years of hapkido training kicked in. I threw my arm up to block his strike and leaned my head to the right, away from the wrench. The blow connected, and pain shot down my forearm. I gasped.

Ignoring the pain, I brought my other hand up to my chest, bending my elbow. I stepped forward with my left foot and simultaneously pivoted my right side towards him, swinging my elbow hard, striking his face while screaming. Hopefully Mrs Crabby would hear me.

My strike connected with his cheek. His head snapped to the side, and he grunted.

*Surprised you, didn't I, slimeball.*

I grabbed his shoulders, pushed so he thought he'd go backwards, and as he braced against me and tried to lean forwards, I used his momentum, pulling his shoulder towards me. I yanked hard, thrust my hips forward, and brought my knee up into his stomach three times. He groaned. I shoved him away. He stumbled backwards and hit the wall. I ran for the front door, screaming all the way.

Shellshocked, and hopefully in pain, it took him a moment to recover—enough time for me to rip the door open and pelt down the stairs to the front door. I threw it open and ran next door, to Finnegan's, my breath sawing in and out, burning my throat. I would've banged on Mrs Crabby's door, but she wouldn't be any help against Crowley. I didn't want her in harm's way either.

I slammed my fist on his door, over and over while looking at Mrs Crabby's front door, waiting for Crowley to exit. What if Finnegan wasn't home? *Oh God, please be home.* I might have surprised Crowley the first time, but he'd be more wary next time, and he had the size and strength advantage over me. You only got the surprise advantage once.

Finally, Finnegan opened his door. "What the hell, Lightning. Hold your horses."

"Help. Call the police. I've been attacked."

His eyes widened. He looked over my shoulder for the attacker. "Where? What happened?"

I looked at Mrs Crabby's. Crowley was nowhere to be seen. Hopefully he hadn't broken into her place too. Damn. I looked back at Finnegan. "Mr Crowley from Fiona's agency. He did it. He killed her, and he came after me."

"How do you know? What, why?"

"He said I ruined everything. I think he killed her because of that land."

"What land?"

"Oh, that's right, you don't know." I jerked my head around. Still no sign. "Can you just call the police?" I'd dropped my phone at some point, maybe in the kitchen, and even if I hadn't, I'd started the adrenaline come down. My hands shook, and my arm ached. There was no way I'd be able to press the right buttons on my phone.

He looked around again, his concerned gaze finally landing on me. "Okay, come inside." He put his arm around my shoulders and ushered me in. When he shut the door, relief washed through me. As soon as he dialled nine, nine, nine, I burst into tears.

What in Hades had just happened?

# CHAPTER 25

After the police arrived, we checked on Mrs Crabby. Crowley had knocked her out but thankfully hadn't killed her. She went off in an ambulance. So I'd done the right thing running to Finnegan's. She'd been in no condition to help or even hear me.

Crowley had done a runner out my back door and down the stairs, but while I'd sat with two police officers and given my statement, another lot had found him in the field behind the house. He'd been trying to run away but had twisted his ankle in an unseen hole in the dark. Sucked in. I hoped his cheek hurt too. My elbow and forearm were sore, but it had been worth it. I'd always wanted to use my hapkido in the wild. I grinned. It had worked out even better than I'd expected.

Of course, after all that stress and drama, I hadn't slept much. Finnegan buzzed on the downstairs security door at ten. The police, at Finnegan's insistence, had made me promise to let him take me to the office just in case Crowley hadn't been working alone. They'd asked if I thought he was the one who'd called me with the threat, but it hadn't been his voice. I was sure of it.

So now I sat at my desk in the office with nothing to do. I had the funeral later—as much as I didn't want to ask for a lift, Meg insisted on taking me, especially after what happened last night. No one wanted me doing anything by myself until the police confirmed whether anyone else was involved. That was going to get old fast.

As I was checking my email for the fifth time, hoping some kind of story needed investigating, Carina walked in. As soon as she saw me, she dropped her stuff on the ground and ran to me. "Stand up and let me give you a hug."

Did I need a hug? No. No I didn't because it was going to make me cry, and if there was anything I hated, it was crying in front of other people, whether I knew them well or not. But because she wanted to do something nice and I didn't want to hurt her feelings, I stood and let her embrace me. "Oh my goodness, lovey. Are you okay?" She stood back and looked at me.

I shrugged, biting my tongue so the burning in my eyes didn't translate into tears. Why did people showing me sympathy have that effect? I took a steadying breath. "I'm fine, thanks. Just a bit of an emotional slash adrenaline hangover, but other than that, I'm fine."

Finnegan, who'd been quietly working away at his desk, looked up and laughed. "You should be calling the jail and asking how Crowley is. She smashed him good."

Carina looked at me with an appraising gaze. "Really? But you're such a petite thing."

I smiled. I wasn't large, but I wasn't tiny. There were muscles hiding under my clothes. "Years of martial arts. I doubt I'd win a fist fight with someone who was ready, but never underestimate technique and surprise." My smile widened into a grin. I was rather proud of myself. "I broke his cheek." Elbows were good weapons apparently.

"Good for you! Do you know why he tried to kill you?"

I looked over at Finnegan. I'd already told him the background story, and he'd promised not to write the article. He'd also looked rather offended when I asked him to promise. Maybe he really wasn't as bad as I thought. In any case, after almost getting killed, this story was going to be way bigger than I thought, maybe even a two-parter. "I uncovered a scam he was going to benefit from. It's looking like Fiona's boss was in on it, too, and maybe the landowner, but I don't know. I'm waiting to hear from Bellamy. They've brought them in for questioning today."

"Wow. I'm just glad you're okay."

"Thanks."

Mr MacPherson burst in the door, his usual, hyperactive self. He stopped abruptly and stared at me. "I just heard. Are you okay, Winters?"

"Yes, thanks." Argh, was this going to be happening all day? I just wanted to forget everything and move on.

"Does this have anything to do with that council, land thing?"

"You're way too observant. Yes, I think so."

"I hear you're waiting on confirmation that you've also helped catch Fiona's killer."

"Ah, yes." How did he get all that news so quickly? It was true what they said about small towns—news travelled way too fast.

"Wow." Carina shook her head slowly. "Not two weeks in d'is place, and you're already making a difference. Way to go, Avery."

I smiled. I guessed she was right, which was way more than I'd expected of myself at this point. "Thanks."

"Are you sure you're okay, Winters?" MacPherson's gaze travelled around my body, but not in a creepy way. He was legit looking for injuries.

I smiled and tamped down the desire to jump up and run out, thereby avoiding the interrogation, as well-intentioned as it was. It took me back to the last time I was hurt—the lightning strike. After the initial concern wore off and annoyance at having to help me set in, my ex had broken up with me, and my parents had treated me like rubbish. I did not need to revisit that. "I'm more than fine. My elbow and forearm are a bit sore, but I'll live." I didn't take my jacket off and expose the huge bruise on my forearm where I'd blocked his strike. It would heal soon enough, and that was definitely drama I didn't need.

MacPherson nodded. "Okay. But if you need some time off, I can spare you for a day. I hear you're going to Fiona's funeral."

Oh my God, did he hear everything? Did I sleep-dial him and tell him my life story? "Ah, yes. I didn't think you'd mind me taking the time off if I was up to date on my articles."

"Of course it's not a problem, Winters. You're representing us at that funeral, so thank you. Maybe take a couple of photos. We can feature it in tomorrow's paper."

"Ah, okay." At least it would give me something to focus on while I was there. The distraction might stop me from crying through the whole thing. I stood—everyone staring at me was doing my head in. "Anyway, I just need to go to the bathroom. I'm totally great, though. So thanks." I smiled and quickly left the room. Only a couple more hours to go, and I could get out of here. I frowned. Hmm, I wasn't exactly going somewhere fun, but at least I could say goodbye to Fiona. I was pretty sure I wasn't going to see her again, but that was a good thing. Right?

⚅⚅

Fiona's funeral was as gut-wrenching as I thought it would be. I stood at the back of the church because all the seats were taken. She was obviously a much-loved woman who had many friends and relatives who cared about her. She would've been happy to know the mistress wasn't here. At least Simon had had that decency... not that it was much.

I'd brought a small pack of tissues and used them all. Thank God for sunglasses to hide the red eyes. After her casket was wheeled off to be cremated, I joined the end of the line to pay my condolences to her mother, sister, brother, and husband.

When I reached the front of the line, anger flared in Simon's eyes. I put my hand up. "I come in peace. I owe you an apology. I thought you had... you know...." I wasn't going to say the words. It was bad enough that I was even suggesting it in church at her funeral. "Anyway, I know you didn't, and I'm sorry. I'm sorry for your loss."

The fight went out of him. His shoulders slumped, and the tightness around his eyes was that of grief rather than fury. "Thank you." He said nothing else, and I took that as my cue to give Alice a hug.

"Avery, thank you so much for coming." She embraced me, and I returned it.

"It's my pleasure. I'm so sorry Fiona's gone."

"Thank you. Sergeant Bellamy called us all this morning and told us you helped find her killer. You've really come through for me... for Fiona. Thank you."

I gave her a sad smile. "I like to keep my promises."

Alice looked over my shoulder. "Sergeant Bellamy."

His expression sombre, he gave her a nod, then looked at each of the family one by one. "Sorry for your loss. I'm actually here because I wanted to talk to you all. I figured you'd want to know as soon as possible."

"I guess that's my cue to leave." I turned to go.

Bellamy looked at me. "No. You need to hear this too."

"Oh. Okay." I looked at Simon, but he didn't tell me to go, so stay it was.

Bellamy cleared his throat. "After some questioning this morning, Crowley admitted to killing Fiona, but he said he did it at the insistence of his boss, Mr Schmidt. When we confronted him, he solicitered up and refused to talk, so we're pretty sure he's in on it." He turned to me. "We traced that threatening phone call back to a burner phone."

I couldn't help but ask, "Oh, so it's a dead end?"

He gave a small smile. "Not exactly. We looked into phone-tower records and found where that phone was at the time you were called. It happened to be at a shopping centre that had security cameras. Who do you think we found on the footage?"

"Mr Fairly?"

"Bingo. We've arrested him. We still have evidence to gather, but we'll be charging them all with Fiona's murder, conspiracy to murder, and attempted murder, plus a couple of fraud charges."

That second-last charge was obviously for me. Bloody hell, that was close. I hadn't had time to digest exactly what I'd escaped. First nature tried to kill me with lightning, now a person had tried. If I didn't know better, I'd say I was a cat. Only seven lives to go. It was more than most got.

Simon looked at me. "It seems as though I owe you an apology too. Thank you for finding Fiona's killer." He looked across at his mother-in-law, then back at me. "I wasn't the best husband to Fiona—she deserved better. I'm just sorry I didn't get to apologise to her as well." Tears shone in his eyes. "I want to thank you for giving this case the attention it deserved. If Fiona were here, she would've thanked you." The tears escaped their confines and slid down his cheeks. My eyes burned as well. I blinked the moisture back, wanting to be strong for the people who really deserved to grieve.

"It was my pleasure. And I'm sure Fiona can hear you, wher-ever she is."

"Thank you."

"I just have a question to ask. I've taken a couple of photos during the service. Is it okay if we put them in the paper tomorrow as part of an article about laying Fiona to rest? I promise it will be only good things."

The family looked at each other, and Alice spoke. "Yes, Avery. Thank you. That would be the closure we all need." She looked at Bellamy. "And thank you for letting us know how the investigation's going."

He gave a nod. "I think I'm done. I'll see you all later."

I said my goodbyes and followed him out. I could email Alice later and send her the message Fiona asked me to. Telling her now might upset everyone else—explaining that I could see ghosts wasn't going to go down well.

When Bellamy and I were out under the grey sky, he stopped and turned to me. "So, you were wrong about the husband."

"Yep, seems I was. I apologised, and I'd like to drop any complaints against him, obviously."

He smiled. "Good. I was going to suggest it. The other thing I wanted to say is thank you for helping us catch the killers. Your investigation into that land deal helped us link everything together." He chuckled. "You have a mean right elbow."

I laughed. "Thanks. It's my secret weapon."

"Seriously, though, have you ever considered a career in law enforcement? We could use someone like you on the force."

I shook my head. "No thanks. I'd rather be uncovering the stories than being part of them. But thanks for the vote of confidence. I do have a question though."

"Shoot."

"Can you extend some special privileges to me... like you do with Finnegan? Sometimes a reporter needs inside info, and I'd be discreet."

He cocked his head to the side. "I'll think about it. Anyway, I must be going. I'll see you next time."

"Next time?" *Please, no more murders.* This was a small town. Surely they weren't due another murder for years.

He gave me a "do you really need to ask" look. "Yes, Avery. Unfortunately, there's always a next time." He turned and walked away.

I took a deep breath. What an emotionally draining day, but we had answers, and I would hopefully sleep well tonight because the excrements who tried to kill me were behind bars. Mrs Crabby had also survived her ordeal and was coming home tomorrow. I rolled my shoulders up and back and took a deep breath. Despite how exhausting the day had been, it wasn't over yet. I still had one more person to visit.

Craig.

# CHAPTER 26

After the funeral, I got a lift home with Meg, then caught the bus and walked. I didn't have the energy to make up a story to explain why I was here... on the front porch of Craig's two-storey house. Across the road, a row of white pebbledash sentinels, forever standing guard over suburbia, were audience enough. My handbag hung at my hip. I clutched it with one hand as elephants stampeded through my stomach. Rolled up in my other hand was today's paper, crushed in the middle by my nervous fingers.

How would he react? Would he throw me off his porch before I had time to explain properly? I hoped for Patrick's sake that he wouldn't. It would break my heart to wander up that hill and see him next to the tree.

I let go of my bag and knocked. There was a car in the driveway, but whether that was his or someone else's, I didn't know. *Please be home.*

The door opened, and I held my breath. A tall young man stood there. One eye hid behind a longish brown fringe. He wore a Ramones T-shirt and jeans. His smile was missing. He looked at me. "Can I help you?"

I kept my smile medium-sized. No need to scare him with overdone joy. It wasn't as if this was a happy occasion. "Hi, Craig. My name's Avery Winters. I'm a journalist from *The Manesbury Daily*. I was wondering if you'd read today's edition of our paper?"

He quirked his lips to the side. "Can't say I have." His deadpan expression did not warm my heart. He was ten seconds away from telling me to leave.

Maybe this wasn't such a great idea. I held up the paper, which was already rolled up so that the page I wanted was facing outwards. I was nothing if not prepared. "We received a letter from someone who claims to be your friend Patrick."

The one eye I could see narrowed. "My dead friend?" His tone skirted the edge of aggressive.

I took a deep breath. "Yes. I know it sounds crazy, but the things he said were rather specific, and I wanted to make sure you read it, just in case. The letter said that you two had promised to write letters via the paper to each other if one of you died."

His lips pressed together as he stared at me. "That's a load of codswallop." As much as he said the words, I was hoping he was curious enough to take the paper and have a read. I held it up to him.

My voice was gentle. "Even if you don't believe me, you should read it. He's sad that you blame yourself. He said it wasn't your fault, and even if it was, he would've forgiven you. He needs you to forgive yourself so he can move on. He also said he's happy for you and Rachel. He said that night you guys ate pizza at the lake, you made a promise to each other. He wants you to keep that promise."

He stared at the paper as if it were covered in spiders, but there was no mistaking the glistening in his eye. *Come on. Please take it.* My stomach clenched in anticipation.

"Patrick needs you to do this, Craig. Please." Tears tingled my nose and stung my eyes. *Damn it, don't cry.*

He looked at me and blinked. He finally tucked his fringe behind his ear, pulling the veil away. His Adam's apple bobbed as he swallowed. He snatched the paper without taking his gaze from mine. "Who are you? How do you know all this?"

Maybe he had the sense that I wasn't just passing on second-hand information. If I stuck to the "someone sending a letter" line, I might lose him. I couldn't let Patrick down, not now. It was like standing on a bridge with a bungee cord tied around my ankles. I would survive the fall; it was just the journey I was dreading. Stuff it. I jumped. "Okay, what I'm going to say is going to sound totally nuts, but this is all true. I met Patrick about a week ago, at the spot he died." It was my turn to swallow. Craig's forehead furrowed, and sorrow flickered through his eyes. "He's stuck between death and where he's supposed to go next. He thinks it's because you're suffering, and he doesn't want that for you. He's alone in a desolate place that looks like here but isn't."

He shook his head. "You're right—that is bonkers. Why would you do that? Come here and bring up the past?"

"Can you just read it? There are things in there that I couldn't possibly know if he didn't tell me. I also know what he said to you as he was dying." I shut my eyes. That hadn't been in the letter because Patrick and I agreed it might be too much, but I needed him to *know*, or he wasn't going to believe me. I opened my eyes. "He asked you to never forget him, to name your first-born after him, even if it was a girl." My smile was sad. Patrick really had been a character. Recognition flared in Craig's eyes. He wanted to believe but wasn't quite there yet. I was sure of it. "He gifted you his collection of teaspoons that was under his bed.

He'd never told anyone but his mum about them because he was embarrassed, but he collected them whenever he went on a trip with his parents, and then with you. There's one in there from when you both went to Ibiza. That was the last one he bought. And I know you haven't shown anyone. Patrick visited you once when you were asleep—it was the dream where you caught a huge carp, and it was so big that Patrick had to help you bring it in. He knows a bit about what you've been going through. He's stuck on that hill, Craig. He forgives you. Please believe me. Set him free." My voice wavered as the tears mounted another attempt at victory. "Please."

He unrolled the paper and read. I bit my lip and moved from foot to foot as I waited. His lips moved silently, forming Patrick's words. My eyes burned, and this time, one tear slipped free.

When he finished, he lowered the paper and slid his gaze to me. His voice was quiet, on the edge of breaking. "It's true. I can't understand how, but it's true." I nodded. If I spoke, I was going to bawl my eyes out. He blinked, tears slipping free. "Thank you, Avery. Thank you. You know that it's his birthday today?"

I let the tears fall. "No, I didn't. You've just given him the best present ever." We stared at each other, our eyes betraying our emotions, our cheeks wet. I stepped closer and opened my arms. He gave a nod, and I hugged him. "I'm sorry for your loss, Craig, but I hope you can move on now."

"Thanks to you, Avery, I can."

We said goodbye. As I turned and walked to Craig's front gate and out, I silently wished Patrick well on his next journey. My heart ached with both sorrow and joy. Endings were hard, but they led to beginnings and hope. I knew this for a fact.

I shook my head. Who would've thought when I boarded that plane from Sydney to London that this was awaiting me? Would I have still gotten on that plane if I'd known?

Hell yes.

A short form appeared in front of me, and I stopped walking. "Hey, Avery. You finally did it. Colour me surprised."

I cocked my head to the side. "Charles. Are you here to check up on me?"

He grinned. "Nah. I was waiting with Patrick. When he went to the light, I came straight here. He wanted me to say another thank you, and that it was the best birthday present ever. You should've seen the joy on his face."

Lips wet with tears, I smiled what I called a rainbow smile— because it was like the sun shining through the rain. "Thank you, Charles. It was kind of you to let me know. So, is this goodbye for us as well?" I hadn't though this far ahead, but now Patrick didn't need my help, I'd probably never see Charles again either.

"Nah, you need me."

"Oh, do I?"

He nodded. "You might never have finished helping Patrick if I didn't push you, and to be honest, you look like you could use all the assistance you can get. You have no idea about ghosts and afterlife things. Frankly, I'm surprised you got this far."

I chuckled. This was why I didn't like kids much—they were way too honest and didn't hold back. "Would it make any differ-ence if I said I didn't want your help?"

He shook his head. "Nope. Just think of me as your new ghost guide."

"New ghost pain in the behind more like it."

He shrugged. "Ye of little faith. We'll have lots of fun. You'll see." He looked up at the sky, then back at me. "Anyway, you better hurry up, or you'll miss the bus. Next one doesn't come for thirty minutes." He grinned and disappeared.

I rolled my eyes. After all the good I did, and now I'm going to be stuck with an annoying sidekick? Funnily enough, I couldn't help smiling. I would never admit it to him, but I could use some help. As I'd discovered, my new ability hadn't come with an instruction manual.

What a day. Thankfully, it was almost over.

I resumed walking and looked at the sky again, elated that Patrick had finally found his way to where he was meant to be. "Bye, Patrick. Good luck in your new home." Like Patrick, this was my new beginning. As scary as it was, I was going to make the most of it because we only got one life, at least here on earth, and I wasn't going to waste another moment.

If you enjoyed this book, you can buy book 2, *A Regrettable Roast*, from November 20th, 2021.

# ALSO BY DIONNE LISTER

**Paranormal Investigation Bureau**

*Witchnapped in Westerham #1*

*Witch Swindled in Westerham #2*

*Witch Undercover in Westerham #3*

*Witchslapped in Westerham #4*

*Witch Silenced in Westerham #5*

*Killer Witch in Westerham #6*

*Witch Haunted in Westerham #7*

*Witch Oracle in Westerham #8*

*Witchbotched in Westerham #9*

*Witch Cursed in Westerham #10*

*Witch Heist in Westerham #11*

*Witch Burglar in Westerham #12*

*Vampire Witch in Westerham #13*

*Witch War in Westerham #14*

*Westerham Witches and a Venetian Vendetta #15*

*Witch Nemesis in Westerham #16*

*Witch Catastrophe in Westerham Book #17*

*Witch Karma In Westerham Book #18*

*Witch Showdown in Westerham Book #19*

*Westerham Witches and an Aussie Misadventure Book #20*

*Book #21 coming July 2023*

*Christmissing in Westerham (Christmas special novella)*

### *Haunting Avery Winters*

(Paranormal Cosy Mystery)

*A Killer Welcome #1*

*A Regrettable Roast #2*

*A Fallow Grave Book #3*

*A Frozen Stiff #4*

*A Deadly Drive-by #5*

*A Caffeine Hit #6*

### *The Circle of Talia*

(YA Epic Fantasy)

*Shadows of the Realm*

*A Time of Darkness*

*Realm of Blood and Fire*

### *The Rose of Nerine*

(Epic Fantasy)

*Tempering the Rose*

*Forging the Rose (Out September 2023)*

# ACKNOWLEDGEMENTS

I have a few people to thank this time. Being the first book in a new series, there was so much for my frazzled brain to worry about—will Avery be very different to my much-beloved Lily (from Paranormal Investigation Bureau) and still likeable and funny? Will the mystery be okay? Will my supporting characters be good? Will people like this one, or will I be only writing three and calling it done? I reached out to one of my lovely readers. Thank you so much, ReBea. Your early feedback gave me the confidence to keep going when I was super unsure. Thank you for taking the time to read and reassure :).

I don't always thank my editor, but, Becky, thank you so much for all your suggestions that made this book and Avery's character stronger. It was important to get it right the first time, and I'm pretty sure we did.

Thanks to my wonderful friend Lisette for proofreading this baby and finding so many irritating errors that avoided previous detection. This is in no way meant to make her look bad if a typo gets through—that's all on me lol.

Lastly, to my readers—old and new—thank you so, so, so much for taking a chance on this book. I hope it gave you hours of enjoyment and escape, and I hope Avery becomes a new much-loved character. I will, of course, still be working on Lily's books too, and there should be a steady stream of both series coming out over the next few years.

Love to you all!

# ABOUT THE AUTHOR

USA Today bestselling author, Dionne Lister is a Sydneysider with a degree in creative writing and two Siamese cats. Daydreaming has always been her passion, so writing was a natural progression from staring out the window in primary school, and being an author was a dream she held since childhood.

Unfortunately, writing was only a hobby while Dionne worked as a property valuer in Sydney, until her mid-thirties when she returned to study and completed her creative writing degree. Since then, she has indulged her passion for writing while raising two children with her husband. Her books have attracted praise from Apple iBooks and have reached #1 on Amazon and iBooks charts worldwide, frequently occupying top 100 lists in fantasy and mystery.

Made in the USA
Middletown, DE
19 September 2024